Waterville Inc. Publishing

Copyright 2011 by Theo Czuk
First printing 2014 / All rights reserved.

ISBN # 978-0-9912872-0-8

Original cover artwork by:
Brian Bloss
www.blaqpanda.net/art.html

Editorial consultant:
Kelly Luce
http://thebookeditor.blogspot.com/

Back cover photograph by:
Kelly Lyon
www.kellylyonphotography.net

Layout and formatting by:
Michael Faris
abouttimepublishing.com

The novel Heart-Scarred is a work of fiction and comes with all of the warranty to the characters and to the locations that a work of fiction would command.

For books and author engagements please contact:
watervilleinc@aol.com

Preambling

Other than the lamp, my bedside table is persistently stacked with a heaping helping of books. Science fiction, mystery novels, horror, classics and, of course, westerns, all hold court on my nightstand. And I might well have used any novel genre for Heart-Scarred. But the western genre seemed to be best suited for the idea of "home" that I wanted to explore. Indeed, I could not imagine a more vivid juxtaposition than the vast emptiness of the western wild and the solitary soul of a boy.

Many are the people that contributed to this effort, both directly and indirectly, and I'm afraid that whatsoever list I gather, I will fail to include some pertinent help. Some of the names that follow, or are omitted, contributed to the shaping of this novel. Some names to the shaping of this man. All deserve a hearty thank you for a piece of this novel; of this man.

With that qualifier in mind, thank you, thank you:

To Dinah Haworth and Della Cowall. Linda Hartmann and Stanford Stewart. Kelly Luce and Susan Zanjani. Saunders Scott and Andy Hirschfield. Bob Donaldson for encouraging my abstract deliberations and Mary Ann Olson for accepting me despite my abstract deliberations.

To Eddie Cowall, a grammar school dropout and a voracious reader who inspired my interest in literature.

To Robert Jones who showed me that home's hearth is not made of brick and stone, but, rather, blood and bone.

And, of course, as always, Karen, my wife, offering fulcrum through my midnight bouts with theoretical notions and conjectural abstractions.

–Theo Czuk

*Home is your history;
Your honor, your sin.
You can't leave your home like you
can't leave your skin."*

Chief Wicasa

Heart-Scarred

by
Theo Czuk

*Manuel,
Enjoy the ride !!*

Theo Czuk

1

PULL ME FROM THE RUBBLE: Part 1

*I'm to my neck
In this emptiness,
So bring along your shovel.
Come on,
Pull me from the rubble.*

J. Bauque

Consciousness ebbed and flowed as Casso chipped at the ice with his Bowie. Three inches of winter ice lay between Rory Casso and water. And food. And life. If he could not traverse these mere inches of frozen liquid, life would be short.

Sucking wind, Casso rolled onto his back to survey his bailiwick. He was in a collection of debris that seasonal floods had tumbled down the gully wash. With the fallen leaves and snowfall that had collected on these jumbled branches, this gully nest formed a winter's womb of snow and ice. The snow pocket was barely large enough for Casso to stretch, and for Rockwell, his saddlebred, to stand. But this cup of a snow-and-branch cavern was a godsend against winter's onslaught, providing enough barriers against the bluster to give Casso and Rockwell a fighting chance at life.

Rockwell was unsaddled, as Rory Casso's escape had demanded a quick retreat. Battered and bruised, he had flung himself on the steed and bolted with slim hope of escape. And though escape from the Thompson gang was managed, there would be no saddlebags of food. There would be no hot coffee against the numbing cold and there would be no axe against the ice.

As the winter tempest rattled the collection of stick and stone of the gully wash shelter, Rory Casso turned his big Bowie once more toward the thick winter's ice until he finally succumbed to the demands of the concussion.

***

The crackling of the small campfire coaxed Casso into consciousness. And on the camp spit, fish. A small hole had been chipped into the ice and gave access to water while the horse, Rockwell, gnawed on the cut winter bunchgrass at its feet.

Snatching his Bowie to his fist, Casso sat bolt upright. But he was alone with Rockwell in this snow sanctuary: this temporal home. Had he, in this trauma-induced concussion, managed to break through the ice, ensnare the fish and set the spit to spark? Casso was alone and he marveled: What can a man do in the frenzy of concussion? What rally is a condemned man capable of? Under what kind of delirium can a broken man function?

Having no memory of chipping the ice hole, catching the fish, or feeding the steed, Casso studied the predicament. His big Bowie yet lay next to the ice hole. The winter's grass that now nourished Rockwell was cut with his blade and the spit fire was built in the Indian manner that he had learned while living amongst the Hunkpapa Indian tribe. This appeared to be every evidence of his handiwork. But memory of this industry was only begun at the cracking and the popping of the spit fire that had wheedled him into consciousness.

Howsoever the fire and the food were managed, Rory Casso understood that this tiny snow cavity, this frozen gully, would need to be his home until he could regain his strength. And he was thankful for the shelter's bounty.

Home? Rory Casso mulled the idea. What is home to a man? Is home but four walls against nature's turbulence? Is

CHAPTER ONE

home the smell of ancestral gravy bubbling in the kettle? Or is home simply the place a man can hang his hat, kick off his boots and rest with some measure of security, knowing that his serrated edges have a sheath and his back has a wall?

This pocket of snow was as much a home to Rory Casso as any home that he had known in his young life. Here would be a good lodge to recover from the bruises to his body and the battering to his brain. But he could not afford to linger in this makeshift home for long. The Thompson gang was yet afield and in their gun sites was Rory's shotgunner partner, Juke Bauque, and the Reynolds Savings and Loan payroll. Too, in the Thompson gang's gun sites, was the salacious covet of Bronwyn Mason.

But these matters would have to defer until the time Rory Casso's body had recovered from the thrashing it had sustained at the hands of the Thompson gang. As Rory Casso considered all of this, unconsciousness reclaimed its subject.

.

2

MOON NOVEMBER

Human scat. It was the smell of human scat that had first alerted Rory Casso to trouble.

Living and learning among the Hunkpapa Indians, Casso had learned to think like the Hunkpapa hunters. To see and to hear and to smell like the Hunkpapa trackers. And, to the best of the Hunkpapa trackers, animal scat is the surest way to track prey.

Setting his saddle, Rory Casso lifted his nose to the late November chill. He could smell the tang of the cottonwood and box elder trees as they spilled the last of their decaying autumn plumage into the crisp air. The sweet fragrance of drying chokecherries along the arroyos and the smell of the browning plains grasses as they bent their golden shafts to the will of the early winter winds. These autumn bouquets of aromas were common smells amongst these foothills and they were to be expected. The human scat scent that imposed itself upon this bouquet was a trumpet to vigilance for the young Rory Casso.

During his time with the Hunkpapa Indians, Rory Casso had learned the many tricks to hunting, to tracking and scouting. He learned the way a ground animal would lay grass as opposed to the way a browsing animal would graze down the grass. He learned how a cougar would lie close to the earth on a stalk, and the way of the grizzly as the bear would backtrack on a hunter, turning the hunter into the prey.

Scat was among the more important lessons that Casso learned, as scat will tell you many valuable things about the quarry. Besides the type of animal that you are tracking, you can discover the animal's age. And you can determine the animal's diet and direction and how long it has been since scat was passed. But a good tracker will also be able to recognize in the scat an animal's proclivities. Whether that animal lies toward the shade, keeping a subtle profile, or pads along the upper ridges in order to better scout. The eaters tend toward the ridges, the eaten tend toward the bush.

Human beings are the vainest in their efforts at scat concealment. Whether out of laziness or just the arrogance of man's self-assessment of his own stench, man is one of the worst at covering his excrement. And because of this, a good tracker, with nose to the ready, will never be surprised by a human crossing his province.

As was their usual custom on these money delivery runs, Casso had dropped back a piece and was following Juke Bauque from behind. Vacillating a half-mile to a mile behind Juke allowed for a better survey of their situation. Although it was Juke that had the Indian blood coursing through his veins, he had never lived among nomadic Indians. Born into money in Florida and educated in Boston privilege, Juke was a foreigner in these foothills. Rory Casso was the better tracker and would be the first to catch the scent of human presence.

The last remnants of a warm autumn breeze pushed gently from the east across Casso's back, bringing with it the smell of human scat and the threat of danger. Casso could not precisely number the human riders in the field but it was close to half a dozen men. This smell of men, coupled with the ever-so-slight scent of pig-fat-tanned leather, meant only one thing. As these Plains Indians used buffalo fat to tan their leather, white men must be afield.

This was not good. The hunting of buffalo and beaver as a profitable enterprise was long ago played out in these knolls, and it was much too late in the season for a wagon train. A collection of white men in these parts at this time of year would either be men, like Juke and Casso, running payroll, or men like the Thompson gang out to relieve the payroll runners of that payroll.

CHAPTER TWO

Night was settling fast and Casso realized that any jack-path trailing that he could do to lose or confuse the payroll hunters would have to wait until the morning. He would camp high tonight with a good fire. The high fire would serve notice to Juke Bauque that their track was ripe and it would be a sign to Juke to lie low and cozy up in a fireless hollow.

Rory Casso set about busying up an obvious camp for himself.

It was getting cold now with November spent and the New Year bearing down. Now was the time for a good-size fire to give the hunting gunners a good track. And if Casso had to flame embers, he would spark a good spit. Coffee, hardtack, and cold jerky was the usual fare on these payroll jumps but, tonight, with the good flame, Casso smoked up some bean stew and sat back easy while the jerky loosened in the bubbling beans. Marking his camp as transparent as a cougar in heat, Casso threw a green branch onto the flame.

The smoky spit served as a two-way signal: first it would signal his partner, Juke, to look wary and keep to cover and, second, it would promote his discovery by the trailing outlaws. That Casso could enjoy a warm fire and a hot meal was gravy.

Rory Casso's consideration ran deep as he sipped at the hot coffee. If this was the Thompson gang, then utmost care would need to be managed. First, the Thompson gang was reputed to be a half-dozen nasty men strong. Men that had rejected society except for the blood they could suck out of it. Secondly, Barrett Thompson himself was reputed to be a gang leader of care and cunning. A businessman outlaw. And a businessman outlaw is the worst kind of outlaw. It would be all business to Thompson.

The plunder that Barrett Thompson would design to pursue would be made as a calculating business decision. The men that Barrett Thompson chose to ride with him would be venerated in their ruthlessness and collected as a business decision. And the killing at the hands of Barrett Thompson would be as cold as a business decision.

If, as reported, this Thompson gang had been responsible

for the takedown of the esteemed Marshal Isham Mason, then this would be one nasty bunch of outlaws to deal with.

Again the drift of human stench imposed itself on Casso's olfactory glands. Whosoever it was trailing these payroll shotgun freighters, Rory Casso and Juke Bauque, they were either clumsy and stupid or confident and arrogant. Casso did well to bet on the latter.

Was it numbers that made them confident and arrogant or was it something else? Rory Casso would need to find out.

After the dinner of hot beans and soft jerky, Casso dusted the flame with more of the green sagebrush. Not enough to be obvious but plenty enough to be found.

Tonight Casso would lump some rocks into his bedroll and slip off into the brush with Rockwell's blanket. He settled himself in a rock escarpment above the camp where he could keep a keen eye on the affairs below. He did not think that an ambush was imminent tonight. Nobody is that stupid. Few are that arrogant. Even so, Casso slept lightly with his shotgun to the ready.

Before the sun would peak the ridge, Casso would set afield and, like the grizzly, turn the hunters into the hunted.

3

HISTORY LAUGHS LAST

The sky was hanging low and the air bone-chilled with the promise of the oncoming winter. It was one of those colds that assumes itself into the folds of your clothes and burrows under your skin. A cold that preambles the gusts of winter.

In the soft light, just before the sun breaks the dawn, Casso threw down some cold coffee and slid into Rockwell's saddle, landing gentle against the creaking cold of the leather. He would have to get far enough ahead of these trailers to provide room for making a wide double-back. Slipping out of camp, he clacked Rockwell to a good pace; leaving an obvious trail would make this job easier.

Small for a mountain man was Rory Casso, just shy of six feet tall, but he was wide and strong in the shoulders and angled tight to the waist. Wavy brown locks cascaded to his shoulders and although his young-looking face was splashed with a wispy mustache, the smooth roundness of his cheeks would give him a baby face well into his golden years. The time he had lived by his wits off of the land had made his body hard and his gait nimble. And now he uncorked his lissome frame to the track.

Rory Casso would follow the ridges. This allowed him not only to make good time up high but also plenty of cover when he dove down to the basins for a double cutback among the brush and the trees of the ravines. As the time to cut back drew nearer, Casso left a less and less obvious track for the followers. To his pursuers, the trail would appear to just peter out. Three hard hours of riding out of camp and it was time to drop for cover.

The good thing about cutting back along the basin is the ground cover. There are plenty of trees and shrubbery along the water cuts of the land offering good cover for concealment. The bad part is if you are discovered. Once you are made down in a shallow, you are trapped. If you are trapped in a ravine by two or more guns from above, your grave is dug. One bullet hole at a time.

***

The ridge that Casso had followed was warmed by the November sun. The ravine that he cut back into was yet in the morning shadows, out of the reach of the low winter sun, and cold. Bitter cold. Casso led Rockwell up the almost-dry creek bed. A late-season trickling of water was most of what remained in this coulee, with occasional pockets of pooled water collecting in wells along the trickle. Rory Casso knew that fish could yet be found in these isolated pools, but now was not the time for the leisure of fishing.

In five months' time, with the melting of the snow and the spring rains, this creek bed would be an impassable torrent. Presently, the bare creek bed rocks cracked hard against Rockwell's hooves and echoed up the coulee. As much as he hated to do it, Casso would have to tether his steed if he did not want to give up his game to the outlaws.

As Casso moccasinned up the dry creek bed, he studied the pools of water that had collected in river bowls. At one particular water bowl the spring floods had tumbled brush and stone to form a natural pocket of refuge large enough to accommodate himself and Rockwell. This envelope of stick and stone provided bunchgrass for the steed to munch and water to drink while Casso scouted the party that was stalking him.

Finding this pocket of good cover for the horse, Casso grabbed the shotgun and sheathed his knives. Extra shotgun rounds in his waist pack and jerky to gnaw for stilling his nerves. His duo of blades, the long moccasin knife and the

CHAPTER THREE

Bowie slung over his shoulder, was the full complement as he slipped into the brush.

Keeping to the dry sand in the creek bed, Casso stalked a mile or so back up the ravine, sighting a goodly amount of ridge that his followers would need to cross on the track that he had lain above. He would have liked to have backtracked further but he wanted to keep Rockwell in a good jogging distance.

Snuggling into the cusp of a tree and biting off a chaw of jerky, Casso settled in for a nice comfortable wait. But the wait never came.

Rory Casso's butt barely nestled the tree's cusp when the first horse appeared on the ridge. He cursed himself for not lying flat to the ground but he could not move now. Movement in the hollow would be like a waving flag to these hombres.

Casso had thought that he would have an hour or more of cold waiting in this ravine but these guns were riding hard. First there was one rider on the ridge. Then two. Four riders in total crested the ridge. This was not good. This was Barrett Thompson's gang.

Rory Casso took stock. What did he know about these boys? Barrett Thompson was reputed to be a cold and calculating businessman. If killing was the path of least resistance, then killing it would be. And the cylinder slinger, Farrot Pierce, and his appetite for killing, was celebrated to be amongst the Thompson's entourage. Kelly Bank? Jim Peterson? Casso rolled the names around on his tongue like a vile taste.

Barrett Thompson had collected an ugly crew of guns, but did he have a tracker in the number? If they had a good tracker that could well read sign, trouble would double.

This was the very same Barrett Thompson gang that had taken down Marshal Isham Mason. And the Marshal had been no greenhorn in the execution of capturing bad men. This would be a wicked collection of hombres to draw leather against.

Working to the good for Rory Casso was that he knew where these boys were, and having run cargo up and down these hills for a few years now, he had the better lay of the land.

Working to the bad was that Barrett Thompson's gang was hunting Casso and they were hungry. And if they were good enough to take down Marshal Mason, they were good enough to take down anybody.

Keeping ever so still in the nook of the tree, Casso watched as they surveyed his tracks. As Casso had marked his tracks wide, they spent little time in study. Spurring on their ponies, they quickened to the chase.

It was good that these boys were riding hard, as Casso would not want to spend much time in that cold ravine, and he hustled back to his steed. It would be a short time before these boys would come upon the crux of where Casso's trail would play out. He did not know how good of a tracker Thompson had but he felt confident in his ability to obscure a track. The only thing better than a good tracker is a good tracker that doesn't want to be tracked.

Even so, Casso had no intention of playing any games with these boys. Now that he knew the foe, Casso would find Juke Bauque and, together, they would hasten their pace to Cheyenne.

That's when Rory Casso heard the cracking of the Winchesters.

Juke Bauque had heard the cracking Winchesters as well. Although it was much easier for Juke to hear the exploding artillery, as the Winchesters' discharge was directed at Juke.

***

They had begun this journey together, Rory Casso and Juke Bauque. Juke had been the more experienced shotgun freighter but they had been running capital—money, furs, gold—together now for better than three years. Up the Platte they would freight the currency to pay for the Western bounty of gold and furs coming from the mountains. Once the payroll was delivered, they would then shuttle that bounty of gold and

CHAPTER THREE

furs back down the Platte.

Weather and temperament permitting, Juke and Rory would make three or four trips a year up and down the Platte. They were as unlikely a pair of shotgun freighters as might be gathered. Juke Bauque, a Boston-educated half-breed of Indian/Black slave, and the young white man, Rory Casso, Western bred and Indian schooled.

Neither of these men were much noted for the slinging of a gun. More of a scholar than a gunfighter, Juke Bauque, the Indian/Black slave half-breed, made up for his gunning deficiencies by manning the huge Remington Rolling Block Buffalo gun; .70 gauge. In most scraps, the sheer size of the Buffalo gun would quell quarrel but, when the situation demanded a hoedown, the big gun would bring the prettiest girl to the dance.

Rory Casso was another matter. Although he sported two scabbards on his pony, one hosting a Winchester for long-range shooting, the other sheathing a shotgun for more intimate engagements, Rory was comfortable with neither gun. Casso, tutored in the warfare of a Hunkpapa warrior, was more at ease with the bow and the arrow. But the bow and the arrow were not practical against an outlaw's gun. The pair of knives that Rory wore, the longer blade cased in his leg moccasin, the Bowie sheathed over his shoulder, he administered as extensions to his own limbs.

They were an odd duo for shotgun freighters but it worked for them. They had never lost a shipment—be it money, gold, or furs—to weather, terrain, or bandit. And now their legend was usually burly enough to sway any would-be desperadoes from attempting to usurp the freight that they transported.

Eight days deep into this final seasonal push up the Platte, Rory Casso and Juke Bauque had settled into their routines like an arrow fits a quiver.

***

When Casso had signaled Juke Bauque to look wary, Juke

had tucked his horse into a quick gallop to put more distance between Casso and himself. Casso would lead the trailers in a southwesterly direction and, as planned, Juke would veer to the north. As the day waned, Juke came upon a good-size culvert to lie low for the night.

It would be a cold night, and there would be the early December frost to greet him in the morning. But in this dark corner of the Western expanse, in veil, such would be the plan.

Before Juke could drop down into this culvert, he caught the first whiff of the camp smoke. Pulling up to the box canyon, he studied the situation. Down below him in the draw was a team of three Conestoga wagons and a hot spit aglow with some kind of rasher toasting the flame. He recognized the wagons and the three teams of mules and he recognized the trail boss, Hickory Dixon. And, appreciating the view, he recognized the women, Bronwyn Mason and Cricket Wynot.

Behind him were some unknown numbered hombres being led astray from his trail by the Hunkpapa tracker, Rory Casso. Below him set a warm fire and food and the company of two beautiful women. In this unruly West, it was very rare to be graced by the company of women. But the company of two women was like finding a gold vein.

The wise path for Juke Bauque would be for this shotgun freighter to find another culvert to crawl into for a cold night of cover. But, oftentimes, a body's brain will be trumped by a body's heart.

Juke took the opportunity to eat a warm meal and cozy up to a warm spit in the company of beautiful women.

***

"Fancy that. Two camps crossing these plains and we chance to junction."

Hickory Dixon, the trail boss, was happy for the male company. And for the extra gun. He pulled on his long emaciated jaw. "Well, I guess, it don't seem so surprisin' to me. We both been pullin' well nigh to the Or-a-gun Trail.

CHAPTER THREE

Seems we'd have to overlap trace somewhere."

The chance for Bronwyn Mason to see Rory Casso again after so many years had stirred memories and prospects. "And Rory's with you?"

Juke Bauque had set down to the fire, warming his hands to the flame, and Cricket had cozied alongside of him. "I 'spect Rory will be spilling down that ridge by morning. Just as soon as he sends that Thompson gang astray."

Now Bronwyn's bearing shifted and a cold seized her chest. "You mean that Barrett Thompson's gang is out there?" This was the band of outlaws that had discharged Bronwyn's father, the Marshal Isham Mason. Absently, Bronwyn Mason's hand fit into the handle of the Colt Pocket .32 that was holstered to her midriff.

Hickory Dixon noticed the movement and directed, "Now don't go getting any ideas in regards to those boys. We ain't got the artillery here for the battle."

But a battle they would have and they would have it before the night played out. Only the battle would not be with the Thompson gang.

***

They came with a rush, and but for the happenstance that they came while Hickory Dixon was relieving himself in the bushes, they would have come undetected. Once discovered, the element of surprise was eliminated from the Indians' repertoire and the assault was turned back in a barrage of slugs and smoke, spitting from the lead shot of Hickory Dixon, Bronwyn and Juke's Rolling Block Buffalo gun.

The marauding Dog Soldiers had turned what should have been a pleasant visit by the campfire in the company of beautiful women into a camp under siege.

***

By the time that Rory Casso had scurried to the top of the ravine, he had long lost the Thompson gang in the lame trail that he had laid for them but, ahead, the rat-a-tat-tat of gunfire was picking up. The fickle rifle reports betrayed to Casso that this was an Indian battle.

Without access to proper gun maintenance, Indian firearm weaponry tends to be a rather hodgepodge affair. Often army discards, the Indians had small occasion to replenish and refurbish their stock. Mostly an odd collection of ancient cavalry musketoons and carbines, Casso had once witnessed the barrel of a '42 U.S. musket sitting atop a '47 cavalry muskatoon. The Indians' ball and powder, in turn, would be just as suspect.

Guardedly Casso tethered Rockwell to a cottonwood and kneed his way to the crest of the ravine to examine the layout.

There were three big Conestogas looped in a tight triangle and held down by the Indian gunfire. The wagons were trapped in a box canyon, held tight against a steep and rocky cliff at the back of the canyon. The gunfire pouring in on them was from the brush at the entrance to this ravine. Half a dozen or so Indians were capping their artillery into the wagons and Casso counted three rifles answering the call. One of the rifles answering the call in the triage of wagons was coming from the boom of a Remington Rolling Block Buffalo gun. Juke Bauque's gun.

***

What the white man had difficulty understanding about the Indian is that the Indian Nations were never a homogeneous group. Indian Nations were as distinct as a German is from a Frenchman and each lived to their own fashion. No Indian Nation assumed to speak for another Nation and, indeed, no tribe within a Nation assumed to speak for another tribe within that same Nation. Each Indian Nation evolved customs, traditions, languages, and histories particular to its proclivities and to its needs.

There were the great warrior tribes like the Blackfoot and the Crow. The Sacs and Foxes with their shaved heads and

CHAPTER THREE

painted faces. The land baron and slave-owning Choctaw, Cherokee and Chickasaw of the Southeast. The Shoshones with their legendary beauty. And the celebrated intellectual leaders of the Nez Pierce, whose greatest leader, Chief Joseph, became a most articulate purveyor of the King's English.

Like warring men of every color and creed, there were those amongst the Indians that could stomach no peace with the white man. White men, their women, and even their children were nothing more than game to be hunted in the field to these Indian renegades. First among these Indian hunters of white men were the Cheyenne Dog Soldiers.

Driven from their ancient hunting grounds where they could traditionally establish their hunting skills against the bear and the bison, the Dog Soldiers now turned these venerable skills onto the invading whites. And they turned these hunting skills onto the invading whites with a bloody vengeance that was matched solely by the bloody toll exacted on their kind by the white men that they hunted. They would match the white raiders raid for raid, rape for rape and scalp for scalp.

This was a time of change in the West. And this change that would come would not come pretty. Somebody would win and somebody would lose and the world would keep revolving.

The box canyon that the trail boss, Hickory Dixon, had chosen to nest within for the night was a solid fort against the raiding Dog Soldiers, and it was the chief reason that the Indian's attack was turned back. But with the security offered with their backs up against the wall of this box canyon came the hitch that they were now trapped.

***

Juke Bauque, Hickory Dixon, and Bronwyn Mason spilled a solid wall of lead up the box canyon and turned the Indians on their heels. With Cricket Wynot doing the reloading honors, the collective's rifles reverberated from the canyon's walls with little relent.

If Juke Bauque had been raised in the Indian warfare of his father's ancestry, he would have been more attuned to the way of the Indian warfare strategy. But he was not. Juke was raised in the privilege of Southern money and, as such, he had not considered the stealth and cunning of these Dog Soldiers. These Dog Soldiers that were, even now, clandestinely descending the steep walls of the box canyon directly behind the Conestoga wagons.

***

Jacque Ulrich Bauque, known as Juke, was a rare half-breed here in the West. His mother, a Black slave woman, was owned by his father, a Choctaw Indian land baron.

After the arrival of the French explorers, the Choctaw Indians of the Southeastern swamplands of the Americas acclimatized quite well to the systems of farming and slavery. It was common for an Indian of the South to reach the status of land baron. And just as common that these land baron Indians would have built their fortunes on the brawn of the Black slave.

For more than a century, Indians of the Southeastern regions were the core of power and prestige. They adapted well to the white man's ways: excelling in government, business, and education. Disciplined and generous—they donated liberally to Ireland during the Great Potato Famine of the late 1840s—the Indians of this region, the Cherokee, the Shawnee, the Seminole, the Choctaw, the Chickasaw, and so many more, were a paradigm of industry and capital.

But this Indian system of land barons and the structure of farming and slavery would change dramatically with the new laws that venturous white men were using to usurp title. Laws that would eventually seize the land and commandeer the power from these tribes and would ultimately send them into exile on the journey of death west on the infamous Trail of Tears.

When Juke Bauque was born, Indian land barons, the

CHAPTER THREE

likes of Jacque Ulrich Bauque's father, were a common feature in the Southeast of the young country.

Born to the land baron Palapa Bauque and his Black slave woman Juniper, who Palapa took as his wife, Juke Bauque grew up in the waning luxury afforded Indians in the province. But Palapa Bauque was a smart businessman and he recognized the Indians' looming misfortune. Long before the whites had set up the laws that would take his land and his assets, Palapa Bauque planned for the prosperity of his son.

To rescue him from the oncoming genocide, Palapa sent his son, Juke, north to be educated in its burgeoning liberal and progressive communities. But even in Boston, where the young Juke landed, some schools would not allow Negros. And some schools would not allow Indians. To his good fortune, Juke Bauque ended up with the most superior of educations, as his father hired the best private tutors that Boston could offer and money could buy.

The young Black Indian, Jacque Ulrich Bauque, Juke, grew up in a world of Boston privilege with chaps on his ankles and a black derby topping his kinky black hair. And his education would be second to none.

Like many of the Eastern cities' elite, Juke Bauque followed the exploits of the conquest of America's Western reaches. Through books and articles, and the occasional paintings trickling east, Juke was awed by the spectacle and the promise that was the West. Through every source available, Juke studied the craft of the mountain man and the Indian. And through these studies he was able to glean a rudimentary knowledge of surviving the wild. And he fancied a time when he might put these book-learned skills to the test.

With the completion of his education in Boston, Juke found himself to be an aberration in the Northern cities. An educated Black Indian stirred to the passion of adventure, Juke felt the wanderlust in the blood of his ancestry. With no home to go back to in the South, Juke set off for the West, where value would be placed on his education more than his pedigree.

***

Had Juke Bauque been more attuned to the wisdom of his forbearers, to the Choctaw Indian blood that coursed through his veins, he might have been aware of the Dog Soldiers that were now scaling down the back walls of the box canyon.

4

TOO MANY TOMORROWS TODAY

Hunting, shooting, and tilling: these are the ingredients of the Western man. The portions of hunting, shooting, and tilling vary in degree from man to man, from situation to situation and from temperament to temperament. But hunting, shooting, and tilling: these are the basic ingredients of the Western man.

The City of Independence was a main port for the mercantile of the Western man. Goods and supplies from the East were proffered for the furs and meats and gold coming down out of the Western reaches. In the confluence of this mercantile, a peculiar assemblage of humanity collected amongst the hustle and the bustle that was the City of Independence.

Mountain men sporting beaver hats and moccasinned feet were rubbing shoulders with the derby-domed and chap-ankled brokers from the East on the muddy streets of this colony. This transitional Western encampment was midway between a wild outpost and a civilized city. A mud-bustling outcropping of two-story timber commerce buildings and complemented by a wide array of clapboard houses and canvas tents. All comers were attended to by an obligatory selection of taverns and churches, rising in tandem, to wrestle over the souls of these Western men.

Bronwyn Mason had come east by stagecoach to Independence from Rawlings with the early snowmelt in the mountains. She had come east to meet a shipment of schoolbooks and school supplies from Chicago that would be used to open the first-ever one-room school in the high mountain plains town of Rawlings in the Dakota Territory.

Marshal Isham Mason, Bronwyn's father, had accompanied Bronwyn east on the stagecoach. From here they would part ways: Bronwyn to return to Rawlings with the school supplies while the Marshal would set off to make his annual summer sweep of the Western territories.

These territorial summer sweeps were a customary affair for Marshal Mason, as he would use the opportunity to commune with local constables, the lawmen and sheriffs of the growing Western communities, and to roost the occasional bad guy from his winter lair.

It was early summer in Independence and the township was in its transitory period between the muddy spring and the dust-choked summer. Getting an early spring start, most of the wagon trains had ambled westward, cutting tracks to the new and green promise that was Oregon.

Marshal Mason sat having coffee with his daughter in the Hotel Sugarfoot lobby. The shoulders of his red plaid shirt were constrained by the limits of the chair back as he relaxed into the leather easy chair. A man with a square jaw that echoed his disposition, Isham Mason cut a hale and hearty figure for a man deep into his forties. The lines that burrowed at his temples bore testament to a man long in the sun and the wind. Folding one long leg over the other, the Marshal set with the calm of a cat in repose, and one could easily overlook the set of big guns, the Smith & Wesson Schofield .45s, anchored to his thighs.

The Marshal studied his daughter with some measure of pride. "You need to make sure you don't get too late of a jump to Rawlings."

Though a woman, it was easy to recognize in a passing glance that Bronwyn Mason was chiseled from the same mold as the Marshal. "I don't want to have to leave without the schoolbooks from Chicago, Pap."

"I understand your yearn but the summer is stretching long already. You can't wait to push those plains too deep into the year."

Like her father, Bronwyn was long and lean, with an

CHAPTER FOUR

easiness in her movement that was betrayed only by the bouquet of wild red hair cascading upon her shoulders. A cascade that no hat or bonnet could readily tame. "Rawlings townsfolk will be mighty disappointed if those schoolbooks don't arrive."

The Marshal's shoulders, squared by brawn, squeezed at the seams of the red plaid shirt as he leaned into a stretch. "Be that so. Your mama can teach out of our kitchen another year with the books she's got now. The new schoolhouse ain't quite built nohow and it won't do the school, nor Rawlings, no good to have you stirring the trail too late."

"I'm hearing you, Pap," and Bronwyn shook her head to change the subject. The flaming red curls danced with every movement and shivered the light. "You'll be out tomorrow?"

The Marshal recognized the way Bronwyn sidled the subject and smiled with the recognition of himself in his daughter. His smile stretched the graying stubble of his squared jaw and he let her have her way. "Yes. Tomorrow. Early."

"Anything special, Pap, aside from making the rounds of the local constables?"

With that question, an ever-so-subtle shadow creased Marshal Mason's brow. "There's a matter or two to deal with."

The subtle shadow that worried Isham Mason's brow would be indecipherable to most, but it did not escape Bronwyn's notice. "What kind of matter, Pap?"

The Marshal considered deflecting the subject. "Just a bad boy or two runnin' amok."

"Is it that Barrett Thompson gang?"

Marshal Mason was not surprised that Bronwyn had heard of Barrett Thompson. His gang had been riding roughshod over the territories since they broke their wintering hideout in the early spring. They left a trail of shot-up banks, stagecoaches, and Indian reservations from Fort Hall to Independence and back again. The young Sherriff Branton of Stillwater was among the dead that the Thompson gang had washed up in its wake.

"Yep. I need to take a look-see at the Thompson brood."

"Alone?"

Isham sipped the remainder of his coffee and unfolded his long legs. "Nope. Got me a young deputy as a kick."

Bronwyn shared the same square jaw as her father and it clenched tight beneath the red curls. "You don't mean that greenhorn Pinto Shaw?"

"The same."

"Why, he's Eastern bred and barely stepped in buffalo dung. What good is that innocent going to do you?"

Marshal Mason smiled at his daughter's accurate estimation of the young Pinto Shaw. "I've ridden with less."

But Bronwyn would not be deferred. "Against a wind as cold as the Thompson gang?"

As he rose, unfurling his long legs and stretching his full six feet four to the rafters, the Marshal smiled again with the recognition of himself in his daughter. "I'll trust you'll come down and send me off sweet-like in the morn," and, with that, the Marshal leaned down and kissed his daughter on the forehead, catching a collection of red curls in his face for the effort.

Although Bronwyn did not know it at the time, this would be a forever farewell kiss.

***

The plan was for Bronwyn to buy three Conestoga wagons, hire a team of wagon pushers, and join a westward-driving wagon train with the school's supplies. By August they would be back in Rawlings. The townsfolk of Rawlings were building the first-ever single-room schoolhouse west of the Mississippi. With the arrival of Bronwyn and the school supplies, autumn would welcome the very first school year at the new one-room schoolhouse for the progeny of the up-and-coming township of Rawlings.

But things had not gone well from the jump. First, news had come to Bronwyn that the school supplies had been delayed in Chicago. This meant that she would not be able to begin

CHAPTER FOUR

the westward journey until August, missing an opportunity to travel in the safety of the numbers of a full wagon train. It also meant that they would have to hire their own trail boss. And the best of the breed of trail bosses were already hired out and well on their trek west.

Then the most devastating of news reached Bronwyn. A full one-third of her family, the Marshal Isham Mason, had been ambushed and killed in the Western frontier by Barrett Thompson's gang.

The details of the ambush on Marshal Mason were sketchy but it would seem that a trap devised by the Marshal and Deputy Pinto Shaw had been inverted and, where the lawmen thought that they had the Thompson gang trapped, it was the Marshal and Deputy that became the ensnared instead.

Besides her own gripping pain, this was hard for Bronwyn to fathom on many levels, for the caution that Marshal Mason employed in hunting criminals was legendary. But the worst part for Bronwyn was the thought of what this news would do to her mother back in Rawlings. Now her return to Rawlings was critical for more than just the school.

For the Mason family, a family that had grown in the security of home and gravy, the loss of the patriarch might be a devastating blow. But Bronwyn Mason was a Western woman. And Western women carried their core a little more vigorously than most. Maybe it was the hard land that gave these women pioneers this disposition. Maybe it was the hardships of dry seasons and grueling winters and the constant threat of an Indian or an outlaw assault. Or maybe it was just the empty Western promise of empty promises ahead. Whatever the cause, the temperament of Western women was as durable as the mustang and as constant as the stars. For their survival, these Western women straddled their horses like men and carried the smell of gunpowder on their fingertips.

It was a great blow to Bronwyn and her mother, Eva, when they received the news of the Marshal's death and the sobs came deep and they came hard. Sobbing of the kind that begins in your throat and ends in too many tomorrows.

But for the likes of the Western women that were Bronwyn and Eva Mason, resolve would only deepen. Rawlings needed, and would have, a school for its future, and Bronwyn would not be defeated and she would not be swayed from her mission.

5

RUNNING WITH THE DOGS

The winds rushing down the gully wash howled with menace, rattling the ice and the sticks and threatening to crumple the cask that molded Casso's refuge. But this drama of winter's first blast would be lost on Casso, vanquished by the fit and fever of his concussion.

Consciousness wrestled with delirium as Rory Casso lay in the culvert chasm's pocket of sanctuary. Tossing in fever from the beating at the hands of the Thompson gang, Casso's dreams leapt from memory to memory with no border of space and no margin of time. His life as a ten-year-old bar swab in Rawlings fused with his life in the Hunkpapa tiyospe. His time spent tracking grizzly intermingled with his life as a payroll shotgunner, which jumbled with memories of red hair ablaze, and half-breeds, and red plaid shirts and Edgar Allan Poe and teeming spittoons. And the fever's swirling hallucinations left no boundary markers between the chronicles.

When perception permitted, Rory Casso could remember leaving Independence with his shotgun partner, Juke Bauque. And he could remember being hunted by the Thompson gang for the Reynolds Savings and Loan payroll. And there was some strong memory of, and feelings for, Bronwyn Mason and the plight of her team of three Conestogas, loaded with schoolbooks and bound for Rawlings.

With his brain diseased from the bruising, Casso's hallucinations returned him time and again to his life with the Hunkpapa. Life with the Indians was the closest thing that he had experienced to a home and, again and again, it was to this haven that his fever-induced trance returned.

***

It was with some amusement that the three Hunkpapa warriors watched Rory Casso's mad attempt to catch fish in the wide river. They had followed the young boy for two days and were now secreted in the brush downstream, and downwind, from Casso.

The sixteen-year-old boy had been two months now on his own, tramping in these foothills of the Rocky Mountains. They were two hard months of bitter lessons since his departure from Rawlings. With no training in these woods, Casso ate what he saw the other animals eat. He copied the diet of the birds and mammals alike. Seeds and leaves and rodents were the staples of Casso's diet. Once, by following the circling turkey vultures on high, he had managed to usurp carrion before the raptors could alight on the fare, but the meat was too rancid for human consumption. On another, more successful exploit, he had managed to chase a coyote from a deer carcass.

The Indians watched in amusement as this raw white boy attempted to liberate fish from the surging river.

When the warriors had first encountered Casso's track, they thought that it might be a wayward trapper. But as the boy's tracks played out, they understood that this was a man who was foreign to life in these wilds. And as they followed his contrary venture, they understood that this novice was a lost boy, and Rory Casso became a curiosity and an entertainment for them. For days they surreptitiously tagged along, following the labored escapades of the young white boy. With some mixture of admiration and sympathy, not unlike the affection one might feel toward a stray dog, the warriors began to secretly root for the success of this boy, lost in these wilds, with only his big Bowie knife for armor.

This feral boy, this unskilled nomad, with no apparent reason to be alive, was defying all odds and was battling the wild's elements on nothing more than boldness. And he was surviving.

CHAPTER FIVE

As Casso flopped about in the river, stabbing madly at the elusive fish, the warriors could control their laughter no longer and, guffawing outright, they exposed their veil. Casso, in surprise and fear, turned the big Bowie toward the warriors in challenge. But this display of defiance by the boy only served to provoke a heartier round of laughter from the warriors.

It was the warrior Owl Song who managed to compose himself enough to attempt communication with the boy. Holding up an empty hand, Owl Song indicated that he held no row with the boy. But the boy, not understanding the empty hand gesture, held firm his ground with the Bowie. The boy's defiant challenge had the effect of sending two of the warriors doubling to their knees in fits of hysterics.

Casso was confused by the jollity of the Indians as Owl Song drew his own knife from its sheath and presented it to Rory. Pointing his blade at Casso's Bowie, Owl Song rolled his knife first with the cutting edge up, then revolving the knife to the sharp edge down. As Casso's attention had narrowed to the Indian's blade, Owl Song used a grand gesture to pitch the blade into the dirt. The Indian's knife stuck tight into the earth, leaving the Indian empty-handed. Again, Owl Song raised his empty palm to Casso, and the boy now understood that they were not here to do him harm. Rory Casso lowered his Bowie and raised an empty palm.

Owl Song was a tall Indian, owing to the ways of his Nez Perce mother, and he moved with the fluidity of water flowing over stone. With one swift and easy movement, Owl Song swung his bow from his shoulder, strung it with an arrow, and fired an arrow over the young man's shoulder. Casso could feel the waft of the shaft as it whizzed by his head. Again Casso lifted his Bowie in defense but, even as he raised the knife, he could hear the fish flopping in the stream behind him.

The fish was shot in mid-stream with the shaft of the arrow clefting the gills.

As Casso watched the fish flailing in the river, he marveled at the skill of the flinging shaft. Appraising the effectiveness of the shot, Casso retrieved the arrow with the fish still twisting on the shank. Owl Song's arrowhead had cut direct center of the trout from a distance bettering thirty paces.

Taking the fish from Casso, Owl Song laid the fish on the ground and indicated to Casso that he should watch. Drawing another arrow, Owl Song pointed the tip of his arrow to the fish and then to his own eye. He then shot the arrow two feet to the side of the flopping fish. When Casso failed to register understanding, Owl Song lifted the now-dead fish and placed it in the river. As he lowered it into the water, Casso noticed that the fish seemed to change position in the water. Light refraction off of the water's surface was causing the image of the fish to move off-center. The deeper the water, the more the refraction would move the image of the fish.

As understanding sparked Casso's eyes, he turned his Bowie to the stream and studied the water. Standing thigh-deep in the current, he analyzed the depth and the light refraction against his own legs. He surveyed the water's drift and how its current played over the rocks on the riverbed. And when a fish fated to his position, Casso let fly his blade. The Bowie caught the fish just below its gill and severed its head.

Now it was the Hunkpapa warriors who marveled. They were no longer laughing at Casso, but, rather, revering the quickness with which Casso appreciated the concept of refraction. And they were awed at the adroit blade-pitching skill of this young knife flinger.

***

Owl Song was a lesser chief in this tiyospe of Hunkpapa Indians. He had earned his name, and reputation, for being of beautiful voice. Owl Song could not only imitate the many birds and animals of the province, but his singing was legendary among the many bands of Lakota and Sioux that traversed the plains. And like his namesake, the owl, Owl Song had learned the voice of the owl and its ability to throw no echo.

With Owl Song's persuasion, the Hunkpapa chiefs decreed

CHAPTER FIVE

that the white boy, Rory Casso, could live among them as family, but it would be Owl Song's responsibility to school him in the ways of the Hunkpapa. In tribute to his vivid blue eyes, Rory Casso would be deemed Boy With Sky In Eyes, and he would be given full privileges in the community.

***

Boy With Sky In Eyes lived with this tiyospe of Hunkpapa for four years. These were good years as Boy With Sky In Eyes learned the Hunkpapa traditions. In this tiyospe of Hunkpapa, Casso learned the skills necessary to nurture life in the wild. To hunt, to track, to trail, and to disappear. He learned what to eat and when to eat it. When to stalk and when to veil. He learned how to hunt the elk, upwind and with your back to the sun, and he learned how a grizzly, the shrewdest of prey, will double back on the hunter and turn the hunter into the hunted.

With the Hunkpapa Indians, Casso learned how to hunt quarry by scent alone: following an animal's musk, a wounded prey's blood, and the narrative smell of scat, on even the feeblest of trails.

Boy With Sky In Eyes excelled under Owl Song's tutelage and, amongst the Hunkpapa, for the first time in Casso's life, he was offered his first taste of the security, and the sanctuary, that is home.

***

The Hunkpapa Indians were a branch of the Lakota Nation, and this was a smaller tiyospe of the nomadic Hunkpapa: numbering thirty-five men, women, and children and governed by two primary elders and two lesser elders. Rory Casso's sponsor, Owl Song, was one of the lesser elders and, though decisions were made by consensus of the four elders, Owl Song carried much weight in the judgment.

Senior-most of the Indian chiefs in this tiyospe was the medicine man, Chief Wicasa. A wise and respected elder,

Wicasa was in the middle stages of old age dementia when Boy With Sky In Eyes joined the band. In the tongue of the Lakota Indian, "Wicasa" meant sage, or wise one. It was Chief Wicasa's wisdom that had guided this tiyospe through the many chapters of war and peace and famine and abundance. Although this was a smaller band of Hunkpapa, it was renowned for its wise leadership in peace and in battle.

But now the ravages of age were playing havoc with Chief Wicasa's cognition. In the earlier stages of Wicasa's dementia, his sporadic crazy talk and senseless actions were attributed to the spirits of nature moving through him. Given to fits of fantasy, it soon became evident that his mind was not sound. Even so, he sat council with the other elders, and his occasional rants were tolerated with all the respect afforded to great leaders.

Because of Wicasa's malady, Rory Casso was adopted into this band of Hunkpapa in the midst of political anxiety. It was Chief Wicasa's son, Cloud Bear, who was endeavoring to take his father's seat of council among the elders. An accomplished hunter and leader of many successful coups against warring Sioux, Cloud Bear felt that his time had come to sit among the decision makers. But Cloud Bear was barely a young man of twenty. Owl Song, and the other elders, though admiring of Cloud Bear's skills as hunter and warrior, were not convinced of the young man's wisdom.

"It will be my birthright to sit amongst council," Cloud Bear often declared.

But Cloud Bear had not yet attained the wisdom that his father, Chief Wicasa, was blessed with, and the elders were united in their decision: "Be patient, young warrior."

If Cloud Bear had sat among council when Rory Casso was presented to the tiyospe elders, Casso would have been turned to the hills. For Cloud Bear hated the young white boy.

When Rory Casso, Boy With Sky In Eyes, joined the Hunkpapa, he was a raw but ready subject. A blank slate that was quick to learn the ways of the Indian, whether tracking or fighting or droning the songs of the Hunkpapa chronicles.

CHAPTER FIVE

A strong and athletic young man, Boy With Sky In Eyes easily dominated the other young Indian warriors in games of wrestling and the sport of the hunt.

The craft of the Hunkpapa hand battle was foreign to Casso but he quickly adopted it to his combat catalog. It was a fighting style that was alien to the brute and bully fisticuffs of the white man. It was a style of fighting that turned the power and the speed and the weight of the adversary back unto the attacker. The aim of the Hunkpapa affray was to usurp the aggressor's power and revisit that power back on its source. When the opponent pushed with their weight, the Hunkpapa fighter pulled at that weight. When the attacker pulled, the Hunkpapa warrior pushed. It was a passive premise that allowed a Hunkpapa fighter, with stealth and with cunning, to turn the foe's advantages into a weapon against the antagonist.

Once Boy With Sky In Eyes understood the fundamentals of this type of battle, he quickly came to dominate the other boys in this band. Even the bigger boys. Even Chief Wicasa's son, Cloud Bear.

Cloud Bear hated the young Boy With Sky In Eyes for the quickness with which he comprehended the idiosyncrasies of tracking and hunting. And Cloud Bear hated him for being a better-skilled wrestler in camp challenges. And he hated Boy With Sky In Eyes for his clear blue eyes that so enchanted the young women of the tiyospe. But most of all, Cloud Bear hated Rory Casso for being a white man.

"Boy With Sky In Eyes has no place among our people," Cloud Bear would argue to the council, "and no place among our spirit."

The wise medicine man, Chief Wicasa, in his yet occasional lucid moments, would remind his son, "He is but a boy. And his spirit has not divided between the red and the white."

But Cloud Bear held firm, "He is white."

Chief Wicasa was a patient man. He smiled at the resolve in his young son, remembering the time in his own young life when life was black or life was white, with no shading allowed for the gray. Impulsive young men who see the world as good or bad, right or wrong, with no variance allotted between the two.

Chief Wicasa coaxed his son, "Boy With Sky In Eyes comes to us with many scars. Deep scars."

Cloud Bear lifted his forearm to present a healed wound to his wrist. "I, too, have scars. And these scars are the scars of the white man."

The haughtiness of youth was upon Cloud Bear but Wicasa tried once again to enlighten his son. "The scars that Boy With Sky In Eyes carries cannot be seen with your eyes. They are scars of the remoteness that one suffers in the isolation of spirit. It is a loneliness that begins at birth and burrows its way into here," and Chief Wicasa gently touched his son on his chest, on his heart. "It is a heart-scar that knows no time, it knows no space, and it knows no color, be it red or be it white."

Through the prism that is the arrogance of youth, Cloud Bear could not see the full color spectrum of Chief Wicasa's reasoning, but he would have to bite his tongue and suffer the presence of this white boy in the Hunkpapa midst. "He should never learn the ways of the Hunkpapa."

"He will stay" was all Chief Wicasa need say.

***

It fell to Boy With Sky In Eyes to oversee the deteriorating Chief Wicasa. As Wicasa's dementia increased, so, too, did the concern that he might do some harm to the tiyospe, or to himself.

As the dementia deepened, Chief Wicasa designed a regimen for his own care. Recognizing his waning lucidity, Wicasa directed that his spirit be released into the mountains. And he chose Boy With Sky In Eyes to carry out this mission.

Physically, the aging medicine man was in good health. He had been a strong warrior and was responsible for many successful hunts and coups and because of this, much respect was accorded his tiyospe from friend and foe alike. And

CHAPTER FIVE

although Wicasa's reasoning was becoming compromised, his body maintained the vigor of a man much younger than himself. It was only his mind that was bowing to age.

What fell to Boy With Sky In Eyes was to exercise Wicasa's body while keeping Wicasa safe and out of the way in the daily affairs of the band. It was Wicasa's foresight and wisdom that had remedied the solution for his own care.

That Boy With Sky In Eyes would be responsible for Cloud Bear's own father was yet another thorn in Cloud Bear's side. And another reason for his hatred of the white boy to deepen.

***

Dogs were common among the Indian camps and Wicasa's tiyospe tallied four dogs in their throng. These dogs were kept as camp pets and as a guard against the grizzly bear, for the scent of canines, packing wolves in particular, is the only scent a grizzly bear will tolerate. During the day, these camp dogs would wander the woods, exploring scents and marking their territory. At night the dogs would return to camp, keeping first alert to grizzlies, cougars, and raiding Indian rivals.

By Chief Wicasa's own command, Boy With Sky In Eyes would tether Wicasa to a dog before the dogs would leave camp to go on their daily wanderings in the woods. This dog would then lead Wicasa on its traipse into the wilderness. With the medicine man, Wicasa, secured to the dog, the daily journey of exploring and marking territory would give Wicasa all of the exercise that his body required while keeping him safe from harm.

Listen close and you'll hear the howl,
Of the pack on their midnight prowl.
When I answer to nature's call,
I'm out running with the dogs.

> *During the day there'll be sticks to shag,*
> *Badgers to chase and bones to beg.*
> *But come moonlight I will bare my jaws,*
> *And be out running with the dogs.*
>
> *I'm no angel, I'm no saint,*
> *There's many good things that I ain't.*
> *Call me the devil just because,*
> *I'm out running with the dogs.*

J. Bauque

So the increasingly demented Wicasa would spend his remaining years in the endeavor of wandering the hills that he so cherished. And it was a great honor among the Hunkpapa to take responsibility for the care of an elder as revered as Chief Wicasa. And Boy With Sky In Eyes gained much esteem in the tiyospe with this task.

This served as just one more motivation for hatred from Chief Wicasa's son, Cloud Bear.

***

There were three Hunkpapa women and maybe a dozen children washing and frolicking at the river's edge. It was a warm, early summer's evening and the living had been easy for this tiyospe of Hunkpapa. Nomadically following the buffalo north in the spring, the hunt was good and the weather had been fair. Play was aplenty and laughter was copious for the children in this time of sun and abundance.

As the warriors were off on the hunt, the women were busying themselves with the production of buffalo and deer products, tanning the skins and sun-jerking the steaks. The Hunkpapa Indian histories were passed from generation to generation by beautiful songs, and the women were sharing these archives with each other while the children played games of kick-stick and corncob dart-ball. This year there would be

CHAPTER FIVE

good buffalo and elk hide for the tents and the blankets and the meats would be bountiful. The low summer sun painted the scene in a warm light and laughter came easy for the children as they frolicked in the cool of the watercourse.

Waiting for the camp dogs to return with Chief Wicasa, who was tethered to the usher dog, the dog that had escorted Wicasa on his daily romp of the wild, Rory Casso sat quietly on a small scarp above the peaceful Indian summer scene playing out below. With the low evening sun warming his back, he relaxed into the vision of these tranquil people enjoying life's abundance. For an outsider looking in, this appeared to be every evidence of what a home must be.

From his overlook, Boy With Sky In Eyes was the first to notice the rustling of the thick brush that followed the cut of the river. The brush was forty feet back from the river's edge and marked the river's perimeter when the snow-melting spring rains pushed the waterway to its fullest. The women were engrossed in the process of tanning hides, the scrapping and washing of the leather, and the children were working hard at their play.

Rory Casso scanned the quaking brush. It would not be the dogs, towing Chief Wicasa, for they would trumpet their arrival into camp with yips and yelps. Turning his attention back to the women and children celebrating life's bounty, Casso did not witness the moment when the big grizzly bear breached the brush, but he heard the bellowing challenge as the grizzly, rising to its hindquarters, shattered the camp's harmony with a bellow that shook the very earth.

The grizzly bear hates man with a zeal that it holds for no other animal. The Hunkpapa believe that this is because man's upright posture is an ongoing challenge to its dominance. When a grizzly challenges a foe, be it man, moose, or another bear, it will rise to its full height, letting the adversary esteem its complete arsenal. It is the erect deportment of man that serves as a constant and viral challenge to the beast. And the beast is always up for the challenge.

It was a flash of fur and fury as the great bear charged

at the childscape below Casso. Valiantly the women tried to position themselves between the bear and the children, but the distance was too great and the bear was in mid-charge. It was the young warrior Cloud Bear that met the charge.

When the warriors left camp on a buffalo hunt, one warrior would be left behind to protect the camp. Today, it had been left to Cloud Bear to guard the tiyospe. Intercepting the grizzly as it charged the band, and standing his ground against the bear's rage, the young warrior took the brunt of the brute's charge.

This would be Cloud Bear's defining moment in the esteem of the tiyospe, and he now stood his ground with spear and knife against the bear's assault. He would defend the camp or he would die. That was the way of the Hunkpapa and that would be Cloud Bear's legacy.

But the grizzly did not understand legacy and it paid no heed to valor. The grizzly began to tear into the warrior's flesh, mauling him with no consideration for Cloud Bear's flailing spear.

When the bear's tantrum on the young brave was cut short, it was not because the warrior had surrendered the struggle. There was yet much flesh and blood to be exacted from the game Indian. No, the cause for the grizzly lifting from the mauling, the cause that froze the women and the children and chilled time itself, was a wailing cry of defiance to the great grizzly. It was a cry that carried grief and pain and loneliness and desolation and it was a primitive bawl that exploded the forests.

The bellowed challenge that disrupted the grizzly's attack came from every wounded heart and vanquished soul of the millennium. A primordial howl, it came from some primitive place that one only knows in the saddest and darkest of hours. It was a cry from a lost and wandering soul that had never known the comfort or security that is home. And the bellow came from deep within Rory Casso's breast.

It was a bawl that stops time and it was the bawl that stopped the big grizzly in its tracks. The women and children

CHAPTER FIVE

froze in marvel at this inhuman bellowing thunder. Slowly the big beast turned to see what kind of challenge this was to its domain. Though limited is a grizzly's eyesight, the beast could make out a solitary figure, much smaller than itself, bellowing the challenge. It was man. Hated man.

Rory Casso stood in defiance of the great bear with the long moccasin saber in his right hand and his father's Bowie in his left. And again Casso thundered his challenge to the big grizzly.

At first confused, the bear reflected on this rash challenge. Dudgeoned, the bear bellowed forth its own roar to the heavens and then charged headlong at the young man threatening its preeminence. And now a ball of teeth and claws and fury was hurling intractably into the challenge that was Rory Casso.

In this instant of dare, a calmness of the moment settled over Rory Casso. In this calmness of moment, there is no fear, only purpose. In calmness of moment there is no past and there is no future. There is only now. When one is in this moment, this now, the moment is empty of weight, time crawls on its knees and space flows like water.

To the women and children on the outside of the moment, they witnessed the enraged behemoth charge Casso like furred lightning.

On the inside of the moment, Casso calmly studied the bear's attack. At forty paces Casso watched as the grizzly threw one paw in front of the other in its charge. The lead paw, the right paw, was thrown forward by the beast and would fold under it as the other three paws galloped forward. Again and again, the right paw was thrown out to the lead only to be tucked under the bear's body while the following three limbs would draw the grizzly forward to the attack.

At twenty paces, Casso's body began to lock in with the rhythm of the bear's bulk as it lunged toward assault. Right paw forward, tuck and draw. Right paw forward, tuck and draw. Right paw forward, tuck and draw. The rhythm was hypnotizing. Right paw forward, tuck and draw. With Casso in the moment, the bear's blitz became less of an assault and more of a dance. A waltz in three-quarter time. One two three, one two three. Right paw forward, tuck and draw.

In the calm that was inside of Casso's moment, the boy recognized that the grizzly's initial staggering blow would come from its leading mitt, the right paw. For the bear, too, was in its own moment and in its own rhythm. It was then that Casso merged himself into the bear's moment and embraced the bear's dance. Stepping into the bear's waltz, Casso partnered to the grizzly's rhythm. One two three, one two three. Right paw forward, tuck and draw.

Boy With Sky In Eyes stepped into the bear's moment; into the bear's dance.

Within four yards of Casso, the bear launched its full weight, pushing off now with both rear legs and, leading with a swat of its big right claw, aimed to crush Casso's skull. But Casso was in the bear's dance now and he was letting the grizzly lead.

As the grizzly swung its big right mitt, Casso tilted his head ever so slightly, letting the big claw swing past his skull. Rory could smell the mustiness of the bear and feel the air rushing over his face as the beast swung past. But dancing to the bear's waltz, Casso had calculated this right paw lead. With his right shoulder braced hard against the blow of the bear's swinging mitt, Casso had set his long moccasin knife at an angle to catch the bear's strike flush on the bear's wrist. And the saber caught.

All of the bear's power and momentum was channeled into the grizzly's lopping swing at the boy's head, and the full force of it slammed the saber square across the bear's wrist. The force of the bear's blow severed the grizzly's mitt through the bone, leaving a knuckled claw dangling from bear skin. Stepping into the bear's moment and into the bear's dance, Boy With Sky In Eyes had let the beast's own momentum, and moment, undo it.

A bloodcurdling shriek of pain and surprise split the spring evening, as the bear tossed back its head and gnashed its teeth to the heavens. But the great bear's cry was halted mid-wail.

CHAPTER FIVE

When the bear had tossed its head to the heavens to bellow its complaint, Casso, yet calm and in the bear's moment, stabbed the big Bowie that was in his left hand deep into the bear's exposed neck, goring the bear's jugular and cutting short its screeching protest to the sky.

When a man's neck artery is breached, that man has about eight seconds of life left. A big grizzly like this, a little more. And in those next few seconds of breath, the bear unleashed a furred fury onto Casso. Pummeling Casso with the left claw and what was left of its bloody and flapping right stump, the bear used its final breath to batter Casso's body.

In the end, the grizzly lay dead atop the mangled, but living, Rory Casso.

With Rory Casso in his moment, this grizzly's assault on the boy played out slowly in a lifetime of decisions and actions, of contemplations and debates and combats and waltzes. To the Hunkpapa women and children watching this event, it was a blur of seconds.

With the killing of the bear, Boy With Sky In Eyes had saved the tiyospe as well as the life of Cloud Bear. This would put Cloud Bear in a life debt to Boy With Sky In Eyes. For now Cloud Bear would owe a life to Rory Casso. For Cloud Bear, this would promote a much richer hatred for Boy With Sky In Eyes.

Cloud Bear had taken the initial rage of the grizzly and had survived. His name would now be Bear Grin, for he wore the mark of the bear's big claws from his ear to his mouth. The wound had slashed across Bear Grin's cheek, giving him a permanent disfigurement. It was a disfigurement that tugged at the corner of Bear Grin's mouth, turning the skin upward into an unnatural smile. A bear's grin.

For Bear Grin, Rory Casso had deprived him of a warrior's death. Boy With Sky In Eyes had usurped Bear Grin's opportunity to be remembered as a brave warrior, with songs passed down through the generations in his honor. Boy With Sky In Eyes should have allowed Bear Grin to either kill the bear or die. In the eyes of this Indian, Casso had stripped him of his destiny. And this left Bear Grin owing two debts to Boy With Sky In Eyes. One debt: for denying Bear Grin a renowned legend. The second debt: for the saving of Bear Grin's life.

Bear Grin's hatred for Boy With Sky In Eyes was deep and it was true.

***

With the Indian wars that were heating up against the white man, the great Hunkpapa leaders, Chiefs Gall and Sitting Bull, were leading raids against the white settlements. And now Chief Wicasa's tiyospe was asked to contribute warriors to the cause. A council was convened to decide what should be done about Boy With Sky In Eyes, for Rory Casso, at twenty years of age, was no longer the cub that these Hunkpapa had adopted.

"He is not of our breed," argued the young warrior Bear Grin, "and he should not be allowed our women." As the first son of Chief Wicasa, Bear Grin held much sway.

When Wicasa was not locked in the dance of disorientation, his medicine yet beamed deep and wise. "Is it your heart speaking now, or is it your hatred?" he queried his son.

> *Two truths, two truths,*
> *Two truths to every spoken word.*
> *One truth that is spoken,*
> *And another one that's heard.*
>
> ***J. Bauque***

Bear Grin had grown into a strong and confident warrior. "Let the wind judge my motives. We are now at war with the white man and we cannot trust this white man to battle his own."

The council gave the matter of Boy With Sky In Eyes full deliberation. They understood that the young braves in this

CHAPTER FIVE

tiyospe were anxious to answer the call of Chiefs Gall and Sitting Bull and to join in the Indian wars against the white man. Boy With Sky In Eyes would not be allowed to answer this calling.

It was time for Boy With Sky In Eyes to go.

Rory Casso was given a pony, dubbed Rockwell by Owl Song, and with the two knives, a long blade that he wore in his long thigh moccasin and his father's Bowie sheathed over his shoulder, he returned to the emptiness of the wandering homeless.

***

The fever that had cursed his sleep and tumbled his nightmares conceded its grasp to consciousness. Rory Casso awoke to the quiet sounds of the small creek gurgling under the ice of his gully wash sanctuary. In a state bordering hallucination, he watched the flames of the Hunkpapa spit fire cast metaphors on the shelter's shield of snow.

6

STREETLY CHILD

The first order of business for Bronwyn Mason was to secure the wagons and the trail boss for the drive from Independence to Rawlings. This late in the season, when the autumn warmth was beginning to show signs of wear, securing wagons and a trail boss would be an inflated task.

The saloons of Independence were the human resources department in the trail-driving market and Bronwyn set to scouring the bars in search of a trail boss.

Bronwyn was of the long and beautiful variety and turned many heads and silenced much conversation when she swung through the saloon doors. A woman wearing pants like a man was a story unto itself, but a beautiful woman sporting a holstered revolver was a complete peculiarity. With locks of red bursting out from under her fedora, and the residual freckles from the long summer glazing her face, Bronwyn quickly became the talk of Independence.

As the daughter of a lawman, Bronwyn was accustomed to guns. She had no compunction in toting her gun and she holstered her Smith & Wesson Pocket .32 on her belt across her midsection so, when she entered a room, the gun led the way. For quicker access, Bronwyn would have preferred holstering her gun to her hip, but a woman's contour does not allow for such slinging.

***

Bronwyn moved from bar to bar in this late summer season on the hunt for a wagon trail outfit. Though late in the season for procurement, the trail boss would need to be the first order of business.

It was Bronwyn's proclivity to swing through a barroom gate and momentarily pause to survey the room. As her father had taught her, she would quickly inspect the room, taking special note of the men and the way they slung their guns. The men who wore their guns slung low and tied down would receive special consideration.

It was with some measure of barroom skipping that Bronwyn finally landed a trail boss, and, when she did, it was not because she liked the man. Hickory Dixon was a skinny and scruffy man with a nervous grin that appeared strained, as it hung awkwardly from one side of his mouth. Nor did she hire him for his reputation, which was challenged by his penchant for alcohol. No, the only reason that Bronwyn hired Hickory Dixon to lead their small contingent of three wagons loaded with schoolbooks and school supplies up the Platte was because, this late in the season, Hickory Dixon was all that was left of the wagon pilots.

When Bronwyn had entered this tavern she had noted half a dozen men littered around the bar. As her father had coached her, Bronwyn closed her eyes momentarily to allow them to adjust to the darkness of the room.

The barkeep was tending a dirty rag to the saloon's plank of wood that set upon three sawhorses and served as the bar counter. The bar back was stocked with two grades of whiskey, or what would pass for whiskey in an outpost such as Independence. A barrel of warm beer concluded the bar's stock. There was a floorboard under the plank-counter bar, but the better part of the saloon's floor was black, hard packed, dirt. Close to the door, to capture whatever breeze the warm August night might offer, sat a contingent of four men deep in the study of their poker game. Their guns were drawn and lying on the table in the manner of men who did not trust their poker mates. An Indian (or was he a Black man?) rested easy against the plank bar, nursing a whiskey: his heavy Remington Rolling Block Buffalo rifle inclined against the plank bar, close to his non-drinking hand. Another solitary

CHAPTER SIX

figure sat at a table in the shadows along the back wall, sipping on a warm beer.

Above and behind the bar a big handwritten sign proffered "Whiskey – five cents. Beer – five cents. Whore – five dollars."

The barkeep was wiping down the bar with the dirty washrag when Bronwyn entered. As the handful of men turned to appraise Bronwyn, the barkeep shared with her an ugly smile and suggested, "Kin I get ya any juice?" The double entendre was not lost on the collection of human vermin at the card table and sordid chortles were exchanged.

With an instructing grimace, Bronwyn suppressed the barkeep's nasty humor. "I am not hunting ugly wit nor ugly men. Please keep your tongue true." It was a commanding scold and the ugly smile leeched off of the barkeep's face.

Chastised and flushing, the barkeep stumbled into an uncomfortable apology. "It's jest we don't git much . . ."

"I'm not placing a social call on your elite establishment." Bronwyn bent the word "elite" into a crooked road to nowhere. "I'm rummaging your tavern for a trail outfit for a jump up Cheyenne way."

Stifling laughter, a poker player at the back table offered, "Unholy shit, lady, a mite deep in the season's spell to be running wagons up ta Cheyenne."

Having been once admonished, the barkeep was completely subdued now. Re-swabbing the plank that he had just wiped, he addressed the men at the poker table. "You hush up your cursin' now and git on wit' your game," and addressing Bronwyn, "Are you serious 'bout running wagons up ta Cheyenne this late on the summer?"

"I am."

The barkeep let his eyes span Bronwyn's frame. He noted the cut of her chin. Her father's chin. And he took special study on the .32 that she wore on her belt. "I 'spect thet you are serious. Then there's your boy over there," and he flicked his greasy bar towel in the direction of the solitary figure nursing a warm beer at the table in the shadows. With that, the barkeep had had enough of this woman. He tossed the greasy rag onto the bar back, rattling the suspect whiskey, and hulked to the rear of the saloon, where he climbed the staircase leading to what must have been the second story of the building.

The man at the table had been contemplating Bronwyn and when she turned to face him, he used a boot to slide out the chair across the table from him. "Have a seat, Missus, 'n we can have a tawk."

Hickory Dixon was a tall, thin, and knotty collection of bones and joints with a face weathered and lined by too many bloodshot mornings. His smile hung from the side of his mouth like it was falling off the edge of his face.

"I 'spect I kin pilot your party up the trail but it is a mite late in the season to be 'temptin' to jump. Is your bizness thet urgent?"

"I believe so."

"How big a party 'n what's the cargo?"

"I'm looking to deliver three wagons of schoolbooks to Rawlings by October."

"Three wagons?" Dixon's smile drew back from the precipice of his face.

"Yep. Three wagons loaded with schoolbooks and school supplies."

Hickory Dixon used his long fingers to take a pull on his sunken cheeks, elongating his face in the process. "Three wagons, you say?"

"That's the plan."

"Ya reknize this be August already?"

"I recognize that this is August already. If we leave within the week we should have three months to make a two-month jump."

Hickory Dixon stretched on his cheek. "Even with jest three wagons we'll need least a couple of trail hands to push the wagons."

"I understand that. I trust you would be able to find the men."

"It's late in the season to find good trail pushers."

CHAPTER SIX

Bronwyn pressed, "I've got no time for you stating the obvious to me. Are you willing to take on the job of wagon pilot or no?"

Hickory Dixon hung his smile on the brink of his jaw. "Miz, you just got yourself a trail boss."

The best of the breed of trail drivers and wagon pushers are always first to be contracted in the spring. The better trail drivers would have a reputation for knowing the best water, the best places to camp, and have a knack for dealing with Indians. In another month or so, after leading the trail west, these already employed trail bosses would be returning to Independence to winter, resting before leading another caravan west come spring. If there is a trail boss hanging around Independence in August it is because he could not hook onto an outgoing train in the spring. Hickory Dixon would be Bronwyn's trail boss by default.

In conversation, it was easy for Bronwyn to estimate Hickory Dixon's competence. He had good experience driving wagon trains, he knew routes and watering holes, and he sipped his beer sparingly. Bronwyn studied Dixon's hand as he lifted the beer to his lips and noted no evidence of the shakes. Hickory Dixon, whiskey, warts and all, would be her wagon pilot.

As Bronwyn was signing, and Hickory Dixon was x'ing, the contract, the saloon suddenly exploded with a girl's shriek as she tumbled down into the bar from the back stairs of the saloon.

Many of these scrubby saloons in these Western towns set aside rooms above the bars for patrons. Sometimes these rooms were used as a hotel to house travelers. Sometimes they were used by the saloon owner's family. And often enough these rooms served as a business to house a collection of the bar's wares. Prostitutes. These brothels would be owned and operated by the saloon owner, who used the women as another source of revenue.

Following close behind the tumbling girl came the barkeep, with fists a-flailing and screaming invective obscenities.

"You'll do who I want you to do and you'll do him gladly," was the general text of what the barkeep was squealing. When he had pitched the girl to the floor, he had ripped open her blouse, putting on display her young breasts.

As the girl toppled to the floor, the barkeep aimed another kick to the fallen woman's ribcage while she attempted to collect her spilling breasts. It was the gunshot tearing up the barroom floor at the barkeep's feet that brought him still. His eyes set aflame with rage, he looked up to see that the progenitor of the floor-splintering shot at his feet was that strange red-maned woman in man's clothes, standing at the ready, with her gun aimed willfully at his stomach.

Bronwyn was comfortably posed with her legs spread slightly to absorb kickback. A gunfighter's stance.

Seething, the barkeep spit, "Who the hell makes this your fight?"

For the moment Bronwyn said nothing, studying first the battered girl on the floor and then the heavy-booted barkeep, and so the barkeep continued, "This here is my whore. I own 'er."

The contingent of poker players held in silent alert while Hickory Dixon drew back his chair, freeing his gun hand from the angle of the table. All eyes were now on this strange woman with a Smith & Wesson Pocket .32 aimed decisively at the barkeep's gut. This woman was of a family of lawmen and her demeanor betrayed her beauty.

After a long moment, Bronwyn responded, "Ain't saying that I'm in this fight . . ." as the girl on the floor collected her breasts into her blouse, ". . . yet."

The barkeep took this as indecision and once again moved menacingly toward the girl. "I own this whore and . . ." Bronwyn's second shot took the heel right out from under the barkeep's boot, knocking his foot out from under him and sending him sprawling to the floor.

A Smith & Wesson Pocket .32 hammers a slight report, but in the tight quarters of the bar, it went off like a cannon. And the .32's second outburst brought all four guns at the

CHAPTER SIX

poker table quickly into the fists of the players. As these guns were angled to the right and behind Bronwyn, it left her at a severe disadvantage.

The poker players' guns were now inclined in the general direction of Bronwyn. The barkeep, still sitting on the floor but recognizing Bronwyn's predicament of having four guns now trained on her backside, shared a wicked smile with her. "Meybe you'd like to take this whore's place?"

Hickory Dixon was now on his feet with his Colt out and leveled against the poker table, but his singular .45 appeared meager facing down the artillery of the four poker players. An earsplitting silence settled on the room and charged the air like a heat storm, tingling neck hairs while waiting on the next lightning jolt.

The next jolt came in a deep and warm voice that, if calm could be severe, would have shaken the rafters with its tranquility.

"I've worked in a warehouse of broken-down dreams,
With row after row of what might have been,
But I never lost touch, I never lost faith.
'Cause I have been in flood and I have been in the flame."

It was a serene voice that shook the rafters with its quietness. Vibrant, vibrato, and verbose, the calmness of the voice and the rhythm of the words set spell to the room. The voice was smooth, assured and commanding, and it was the voice of the Black Indian resting against the bar.

The strange Indian/Black man had rested his big Buffalo gun easy on his hip and had leveled it in the direction of the poker table. Save for the barkeep's attention, as the barkeep would not divert his vision from the barrel of Bronwyn's gun, all eyes turned to the strange bard at the bar.

With Bronwyn's .32 commanding his full attention, the barkeep did not turn to look at the stranger at the bar, but talking out of the side of his mouth, he demanded, "Who'n the hell's recitin' Shakespeare?"

With some humor and deep in the vibrato, the voice answered, "You flatter me, sir. And you shame Shakespeare.

Alas, those words were homegrown."

Cricket Wynot, still sitting on the floor but now with her breasts fully covered, allowed herself a smile. A pretty girl with a smile sweetened by a slight overbite that promised paradise. "You wrote that poem?"

In ill humor and not an aristocratic patron of the arts, the barkeep scoffed, "Ya fancy yourself a poet, do ya?"

The warm baritone riposted, "Sometimes, in my musings, I fancy myself a poet. Sometimes I fancy myself just a purveyor of too much noise. Right now I fancy myself the purveyor of a Remington Rolling Block Buffalo gun with a .70 caliber chamber."

While this brought a smile to Bronwyn's face, it brought a look of consternation to the face of the barkeep, and he could not help but look away from the Pocket .32 to the stranger at the bar. He saw the Buffalo gun now and demanded, "Who the hell are you, Mister, and what makes this your bizness?"

Still holding his rifle on the guns at the card table, the dark stranger at the bar turned his head toward the barkeep. "I go by the name of Bauque. Friends call me Juke. You can call me Mister Bauque."

Phlegm sneering the words, "Well, Mister Bauque, who the hell are you and what makes this your bizness?"

With a nod of the Buffalo gun, Juke Bauque steered the barkeep's attention to the card table. "Supposin' we get your friends here to set aside their iron and we can chat about it."

The barkeep demanded of the poker players, "Don't set 'em down, boys, you've got four guns to his one."

"This is very true, boys, I've only got one gun. But it's a big gun," smiled the dark stranger with the warm voice, "and loaded with buckshot. I do believe that I have enough scatter to cover the full table."

Livid now, the barkeep spit, "Nobody loads scatter in a Buffalo gun."

This dusted the corners of the Bauque's full lips into a smile. "I know one man that does," and then he waved the gun ever so gently at the poker players. "What do you say,

CHAPTER SIX

men, want to find out if nobody loads their Buffalo gun with buckshot?" As if in one moving part, the poker players eased their guns back down onto the table. "And it's okay if you want to ease back from the table now," and the one moving part that was the poker players stepped away from the table.

Again the barkeep demanded, "What makes this your fight?"

But the dark stranger ignored the barkeep and spoke to the girl on the floor. "Get up, girl, and then go stand by that redhead lady there."

There are a plethora of reasons why a woman might be drawn to a particular man. Some women might be drawn to the cut of a man's chin. Some women find the attraction in a man's carriage. Others, his eyes. Or maybe just a man's way of thinking. There are many means of a man that might resonate for a woman.

When Cricket Wynot heard the low rumbling that was Juke Bauque's voice, it stirred a province in Cricket that had hitherto gone unexplored. As a prostitute, Cricket was knowledgeable in the ways of the flesh, but this new sensation tugged at a hunger that she had never surveyed. The rich reverberations that were Juke's voice echoed deep within the girl and the timbre timbered her core.

Bronwyn's gun had never wavered from the barkeep, and now it was centered on his belly. "Now suppose that you explain to me why a big man like you has got to be beating on a little girl like that?"

Though it did not quell his anger, the barkeep duly noted where Bronwyn's .32 was directed. "Who the hell are you that I gotta answer myself to?"

"Fair enough question," and Bronwyn let the gun barrel angle ever so slightly down, "and my answer will be that I am the one directing lead at your manhood."

The barkeep well noted the situation and the redirection of the .32 and, with distaste, answered, "My whore here refused to service a client."

Keeping the gun trained on the barkeep, Bronwyn turned

her questions to the girl on the floor. "That so, hon? You refuse to work?"

In the Western towns like Independence, ladies of the evening were not the scourge of society that they were in the more refined climes of the Eastern cities. Prostitutes were thought of, and treated as, working women. Honest working women. Much like the ditch digger who hires out the brawn part of his body to an employer, the demimondaine would hire out the comparable commodity she could proffer. Prostitution was simply business.

The girl, maybe twenty but looking less, nodded her head in affirmation.

Bronwyn pursed her lips. "Why do you refuse to work, girl?"

The barkeep opened his mouth to intervene but Bronwyn silenced him with a glare and a nod of the .32. "Go ahead, girl, you can speak."

The girl, less shaken by the barkeep's blow than by the stirrings that Juke Bauque's voice had inspired, answered with hesitancy in her voice, "He's had me working the night long. I'm raw and I'm bleeding and now he's got three men lined up in the corridor for me." The room was silent with the girl's confession.

Bronwyn nodded at the girl and turned to the barkeep. "Seems like a fair assessment of her property."

"That's my property. Not hers. And I'll be the judge of my property."

Bronwyn considered this. Then, again to the girl, "You got a name, girl?"

"My name's Debra Wynot but most folks just call me Cricket." The girl was a tiny affair with a soft, chirpy voice, and there was no mystery from where her nickname was drawn.

Turning back to the barkeep, Bronwyn inquired, "You got papers on Debra Wynot but most folks call her Cricket?"

"Nought papers. Don't need 'em. I'm the one what saved the girl from the gutters when her folks were killed 'most two years past."

Bronwyn smiled at that statement of salvation. "Saved her?"

"I call it saved. And I been feeding and boarding her since."

"But you got no papers on her?"

"Nope. Like I said, she works for me."

Deliberately Bronwyn considered this. "I don't think that she works for you anymore if she doesn't want to work for you anymore."

Rage reddened the barkeep's ears and set his jaw to clenching while he thought this through. But the Pocket .32 kept his butt on the floor. "She ain't got no home and she ain't got no job if she ain't working for me," and he thumbed his chest in ownership.

Again Bronwyn considered this. "Is that right, girl? You ain't got no home if you ain't got no job?"

Cricket spoke to Bronwyn but her eyes were transfixed on the big half-breed at the bar with the Buffalo rifle and the voice of a Sunday service rapture. "Yes, Ma'am, my folks deceased four years past now. We were waiting on a train east but an accident took them from me. Mr. Sledge here took me in, I was sixteen then, and he put me to work straightaway."

Bronwyn assessed the situation. The barkeep had pulled himself to his feet and, with the one heel blown off of his shoe, stood there in a silly and lopsided manner. The prostitute girl, too, had collected herself and, though still on the floor, had pulled her knees up to her chest.

Looking now directly into the girl's eyes, Bronwyn said, "Look at me, girl. Can you read?"

Reluctantly, and with some effort, Cricket turned her eyes from Juke Bauque and raised them to Bronwyn. She did not understand the query. "What?"

"Can you read and write, Cricket Wynot?"

"Yes, Ma'am, I can read and write."

Bronwyn smiled and looked directly into the barkeep's eyes. "Looks to me like this young girl has a new job."

Surprised and confused, "Whaaaa . . . ?"

"Debra Wynot, sometimes known as Cricket, is now a teacher in my employment."

"But you can't . . ."

"I can. And I just did." While still keeping her gun trained on the barkeep, she now spoke to the stranger at the bar. "What do you think Shakespeare would say to that, Mister?"

"Shakespeare always did fancy education, Bronwyn."

With the mention of her name, Bronwyn's brow furrowed, and, keeping the .32 leveled on Mr. Sledge, she now turned her head to look directly at the stranger. "Do I know you, Mister?"

There was humor in the warm and deep voice of the stranger. It was a voice that snoozed by a lazy river on a summer's eve with a fishing string tied to its toe. "Yep. Reckon we met a time or two."

"I can't rightly seem to place you."

"Even so."

This stranger knowing her did not sit comfortably with Bronwyn, but for the moment, and in these circumstances, she would need to leave it lie.

Seething now, the barkeep burst in, "Hate to break up your family reunion, but we need to settle up on my property here."

Bronwyn turned her attention back to the barkeep, her disposition souring now. "I explained to you, Mr. Sledge, you have got no more claim on this girl." And then, to the girl, "Come on, Cricket. Me, you, and this Mister Dixon here have got a lot of preparing to do for our jaunt up to Rawlings."

"Rawlings, Ma'am?"

"Yep. Rawlings. Out in the Dakota Territory. Cricket, you have just been demoted from prostitute to schoolteacher."

This coaxed a chuckling tug on the fishing line in the river that was Juke Bauque's baritone, but the barkeep failed to grasp the humor.

And just like that, Hickory Dixon now had two women to go with the school's contingent of books and supplies to

CHAPTER SIX

deliver across the Western plains. And only three months before winter's wrath to deliver them.

***

They had backed out of the saloon with guns drawn against Mr. Sledge and the bar's patrons. First Bronwyn and Cricket, then Hickory Dixon, and, finally, Juke Bauque, with his Remington Rolling Block Buffalo gun covering the hostelry.

Juke Bauque shared his deep and calming baritone with the tavern before he swung through the gate. "Mr. Sledge, I left my tab over yonder on that bar, there's enough there to buy a round for the house and a tip for your good services," and he waved the gun once around the room. "And I bid you all a very nice day, gentlemen." And with that, like a long iron tail, the Buffalo gun's barrel followed Juke out through the bar's swinging gates.

7

WOODEN NICKELS

Outside, under the overhang of the porch's ramada, Bronwyn did not holster her gun, but she had lowered it to her side. Turning square to Juke, she queried, "Now, Mister ...?"

Juke Bauque shared a smile. "Jacques Ulrick Bauque, Ma'am, but I prefer Juke."

"Okay, Juke, maybe you would share with me just exactly how I know you?"

"As I said, Bronwyn, if it's okay to call you Bronwyn? Your father recommended me for my present position. I'm employed as a shotgun freighter with the Pinkerton Detective Agency."

Some strange and foreign stirrings were roused in Cricket Wynot as she interjected, "A shotgun freighter? What's a shotgun freighter?"

Bronwyn answered Cricket Wynot's question. "A shotgun freighter runs payroll and goods, pelts and gold and such, up and down the mountains." And then, turning to Bauque, "And...?"

"I guess I met you once or twice in your child days. In your pap's office. You were just a knee duster so I suppose I didn't make much notice then. I know your pap well enough, though."

"You work with my pap?"

"Kinda. I guess you could say that. I was fresh from the East, then, a new Pinkerton shotgun freighter, your pap was good enough to take me on my first few runs up to Cheyenne and Rawlings way. He counseled me well on both the territories and on gun slinging."

Now Bronwyn laughed, and when she did her green eyes flickered and her red locks set to dancing. "Pap taught you to use that?" indicating the big gun slung on Juke's shoulder.

The Remington Rolling Block Buffalo gun was a long-barreled and cumbersome affair. At .70 caliber it was as close to a cannon as a shoulder iron could come. This gun was many things but one thing it would never be mistaken for is subtle.

And Juke joined in the humor. "Nope. Can't say your pap ever encouraged this thing. But try as he might, he never could get me comfortable with the subtleties of a handgun or Winchester. I figured that this cannon could overcome a lot of my gunning shortcomings."

With her hands knotted behind her back, Cricket could not quite look directly into Juke Bauque's eyes. "You talk too sweet for a gunslinger, Mister Bauque. Even poetry."

"I suppose that is due to the best Boston education money could buy."

"You were educated in Boston?"

"Privately tutored and socially cultured."

***

The first half of the nineteenth century were exhilarating years to be a scholar in Boston. Ideas of politics and principles and philosophies swirled in the air. It was a new country, this United States of America, a bold new experiment for humankind. The energy of America's youth was ubiquitous and exuberance for the future was intoxicating. Everywhere was talk of what America, and Americans, could be, should be, and would be.

And Juke's first love, literature, too, was turning to a new and uncharted province. Boston was becoming a hub for experimenting, and literature would not be denied its place in these experiments. With a diverse collection of notable scholars and writers, Boston was welcoming all

CHAPTER SEVEN

comers of thought and script.

Just up the road, in the hamlet of Concord, Ralph Waldo Emerson, and the abolitionist ideas he propounded, had the young Juke Bauque soaring with possibilities. Juke, the half Indian, half Black slave, was the walking embodiment of America's potential.

Boston, too, can be credited for bestowing upon this new petri dish of ideas the first authentic American writer, Edgar Allan Poe. Born to Boston in 1809, Poe established a genuine voice in American-speak of literature; casting off the traditional shackles of the Elizabethan dialect, Poe wrote in the voice of these new territories and these new peoples. And Juke Bauque was determined to become part of this new articulation.

But it was Henry David Thoreau that would have the greatest influence upon Bauque, mapping the landscape of Juke's life, with the publication of Walden in 1854. When Juke read the words: "I went to the woods because I wished to live deliberately, to front only the essential facts of life, and see if I could not learn what it had to teach, and not, when I came to die, discover that I had not lived," his course was set to the uncharted territories of the West.

When opportunity presented itself in a Boston newspaper in the form of a payroll escort for the Pinkerton Detective Agency, Juke was quick to the test.

***

This peculiar, well-educated Black Indian set Cricket's spine to tingling. "And now you run beaver skins?"

"Yes'm."

Bronwyn pressed, "But, with all your education, why shuffle goods for Pinkerton?"

With the warm baritone that reached deep into his African ancestry, Juke rolled the answer on his tongue. "Well, Ma'am, I guess I needed to learn something about myself. Seemed to me the surest way to learn it."

"What is it you needed to learn?"

Considering, Juke Bauque set the butt of his Buffalo gun in the dirt and leaned on its long barrel. "Not exactly sure, Miss, but I believe that if I keep putting one foot in front of the next, eventually, I will be lucky enough to trip over it."

"Careful you don't fall flat on your face."

As the shapeliness of Bronwyn's hips required, she wore her holster to the front, and, sheathing the .32, she added, "I know a shotgun freighter. Name of Casso."

"Rory Casso?"

Surprised, not unpleasantly, at hearing Rory's name, "The same. You know him?"

"'Spect I do. He's my partner."

Bronwyn flushed under her freckles. "Rory Casso is here?"

"Nope. Sorry to say but he won't be in town for a month or more. He'll be joining me for a late payroll run up Cheyenne way. We won't be leavin' Independence till October at the earliest."

With good fortune, Bronwyn's wagon train of books would be deep in the trail by then. "I guess I'll miss him, then. It'd been nice to catch up."

"I'll let him know that you thought of him. And let me express my condolences about your pap."

"My pap? What about my pap?"

"Oh, no. You don't know?" This was not how Juke Bauque would have preferred that Bronwyn be informed of her father's demise. "I'm sorry, Bronwyn. You haven't heard? Your pap was ambushed."

Bronwyn's shoulders began to fold inward on her chest, and tears made their first appearance in the corner of her eyes. "What do you mean? Ambushed! How . . . ?"

Cricket moved to Bronwyn and reached an arm around her waist. Juke Bauque touched his tongue to his lips like he had some bitter taste in his mouth that he needed to spit out. "I'm sorry. Word reached Independence a few days ago. I assumed you knew."

CHAPTER SEVEN

Bronwyn was wounded deep now. "How...how did he..." and she had trouble finding the words.

"My understanding is that it was that Barrett Thompson gang. He was on their trail. They got the drop on him and..."

With her fists set hard at her side, "Nobody ever got the drop on Pap. Nobody!" The first stage of loss is denial.

8

LORD, PLUG THIS HOLE

It was an ambitious idea: taking a three-wagon train of Conestogas across the plains this late in the season. The plan was to push the wagons to Cheyenne, where they would lie for the winter and then finish the jump in early spring to arrive in Rawlings in time for the spring school semester.

But now, with the news of the demise of her father, Bronwyn set her chin to the wind. It would be time now for her to get back to her mother, Eva, and their homestead, and her track would take her directly to Rawlings.

***

Eva Mason. How empty the house must be. Isham and Eva were thirty years together. Raising a child and building a home. Building a life. Together, Isham and Eva Mason saw Rawlings grow from a dusty trapper outpost to a city of commerce and industry. With these thoughts, Bronwyn now cried for her mother's pain as her mother suffered through the loudest of silences.

> *I've been so lonely,*
> *When the only*
> *Comfort I could get*
> *Is the solace of*
> *A gravedigger's pick.*

J. Bauque

The silence was deafening as Mrs. Isham Mason, Eva,

moved from room to room. It was a big house for Rawlings, built as a thank-you to the Masons for the Marshal's liberating the town from the grasp of the outlaw element. Eva wandered as an apparition in the domicile, forgetting her purpose as quickly as she had decided the objective. Holding fast to one of Isham's red plaid shirts, his signature red plaid shirt in these territories, Eva roamed the empty house meaninglessly.

Death will do that to a body. Death will leave a body wondering about what it is all for: the pain, the toil, the hardships and the grief. Is life one step forward or two steps back?

And the death of a husband, a lover, and a friend, such was the death that Eva now found herself trading in.

Thirty-plus years earlier, Isham, the trapper and hunter, had arrived in Rawlings from the wild Western reaches with a dozen beaver skins and two fists full of guns. A mountain man, big and strong in physique, honest and true in spirit, he had come to town when Rawlings was in the throes of outlaws, scoundrels, and a crooked sheriff. Isham Mason esteemed the situation in Rawlings and designed to do something about it. One by one, with fist and gun and guts he took them all down, in their time. It was a long and bloody negotiation but, in the end, it was the young man from the Western mountains that had prevailed.

Isham Mason was rewarded for his efforts by being delegated the first Territorial Marshal of these Western reaches. The good folk of Rawlings built this big home in the midst of their growing community and deigned that he live among them. But Marshal Mason was quick to declare that his real reward for his labor was the winning of Eva as his wife.

Now Eva, ghost-like, ambled about the big house, lost in the pain and the fog of bereavement. In her hands was one of Isham's rumpled red plaid shirts, scented to his musk and stained to his powder. How it got there, she knew not. Its purpose there, too, obscure.

It wasn't supposed to be like this. This was to be the

CHAPTER EIGHT

Marshal's final summer patrol of the territories. His farewell tour of the West and then off to the province of retirement.

After delivering their daughter, Bronwyn, to Independence to retrieve the school appurtenances, the Marshal was to cycle the territories. He would sweep south, then north and west, communing with local constables and sheriffs. Mason was then to come home and settle into retirement. It was to be a quick sweep and Isham was to be home in time for the raising of the new schoolhouse. It would be Rawlings' first, one-room, schoolhouse and it would sit adjacent to the Masons' homestead. Eva and Bronwyn were to teach in the new school and Isham, retiring from the life of the gun, would try his hand at farming: plowing under the big muddy outback of their spread.

But now that life of retirement for Marshal Isham Mason was closed by an outlaw's gun and Eva was lost in the muddle of bereavement.

Every cup that Isham had held to his lips held a memory for Eva. Every floorboard's creak held fast to Isham's step and every view from every window in the big home was viewed through Isham's gaze. The nights for Eva were long and tumbled affairs blotched with sweaty fits and nightmares that left her bolt upright and haggard.

I've been so long in the wind,
I can't feel my own skin,
Lord, plug this hole
And start all over
Again.

J. Bauque

But Eva Mason was a Western woman, toned to the hardships of these Western privations, and, in due course, she would manage to future her affairs. For their daughter, Bronwyn, for the township of Rawlings, and for the progeny of the strong women to follow, Eva Mason would rise above the grief and, in time, once again stretch at the seams of these Western chronicles.

But tonight, like last night and tomorrow and for many nights to follow, Eva Mason would crawl into bed holding fast to the harbor of the red plaid shirt, its scent of powder and musk a refuge against the emptiness of the big house.

***

Now Bronwyn would need to hasten her way home. The tough Western seasons can wear on one's dwelling with a vicious tenacity and, if not tended to, days will age like years. And, too, the business of setting up the school, indeed, the entire reason for coming east was to do good by the young folk of Rawlings, and neither late delivery of the books from the East, a late start on the trek home, nor even the loss of her father would keep Bronwyn from her track. Such was the mindset of these Western women.

9

DAMNED IF I DO

Damned if I do,
Damned if I don't.
I'll be damned if I give a damn,
And I'll be damned if I won't.

J. Bauque

Now the women were numbered two in the company. Cricket Wynot became keen to the idea of teaching in the Western school, in a town that would offer her a new start, far away from the livelihood of prostitution that wore on her body and sucked at her soul. Though fully realized as a woman in body, there was much childhood that Cricket had missed.

There were wagons and staples to secure and trail hands to hire for this journey. The women shared much concern and consternation over settling on Hickory Dixon as wagon pilot but choices were meager this late in the season and time was scant.

It would be Dixon's job to secure the Conestoga wagons and to hire the trail help that would push this trail throng west. This much can be said: Hickory Dixon did a fine job of finding true and sturdy wagons and a well-bred team of horses worth their weight. But the trail hands, this deep in the summer, were problematic. It was not so much Hickory Dixon's fault as it was the lateness of the season that the two trail hands that Hickory managed to secure were of the unsavory variety.

Hickory Dixon, following a trail of ". . . did ya try the saloon across from the livery?" and ". . . I hear tell there might be a couple of boys up ta McMaster's saloon." Hickory finally caught up with Jack Bettle and Kipper Dunn tipping a bottle in a plank bar on the outer reaches of Independence.

These plank bars were slapped-up affairs of stick and canvas with a big wood plank functioning as the bar counter. They were located on the edges of a town, serving forty-rod whiskey to the swarthiest of men.

"Yer crazy," offered Jack Bettle.

"Damn fool," seconded Kipper Dunn.

"Lookit 'ere, boys. This 'ere's good tender wages, the wagons are sturdy and the horses are true. It should be an easy push if we leave quick enough."

Jack Bettle scratched at the stubble that imbued his pock-ravaged cheek. "But winterin' 'ere with potation and harlots sounds a mite more comfortable than trying to outrun winter to Cheyenne." A big brooding bully with a flat nose and a chin that retreated to his neck, Jack Bettle was accustomed to getting his way by bluster, intimidation, and fist.

Hickory Dixon had few cards to play. "Should be easy on the trail. All of the spring and summer trains that pushed the trail already will have hard-packed the track, making it a quick sail west."

Jack Bettle turned to Kipper Dunn. "What ya think, Kip, think we join this old drunk and his schoolbooks in a drive up Cheyenne way?"

Small and fat with grease-stained buckskin and tobacco-rotting teeth, Kipper Dunn looked like a walking spittoon. "I 'spect not. Don't need the plunder 'n I druther fort up here warm like for the winter."

Bettle was done. "There you have it, Dixon, it's a no go."

Hickory Dixon knocked back the warm beer that he had been nursing. "Sorry to hear thet, boys. The women will be disappointed."

The mention of women brought Jack Bettle and Kipper Dunn to full attention. "Whoa there, now, Hickory, you got

CHAPTER NINE

women on board?" asked Bettle.

And Dunn took up the call. "Say, Dixon, you ain't pushin' that train what's bein' pulled together with thet Mason girl, is you?"

"That be the train."

"And thet Cricket whore from up the Sugarfoot saloon?"

"Yep. But thet girl, she quit the whoring. She's gonna be a schoolteach up Rawlings way now."

Sordid memories squeezed a smile into the pockmarks on Jack Bettle's face. "She sure is a sweet little whore. Jes' the thought makes me want ta pay her 'nother visit."

Dixon was firm. "Like I said, Cricket Wynot don't whore no more."

Gears turn slowly on the face when a slow man like Kipper Dunn is thinking. When he finally grasped the implication of Jack Bettle's suggestion, Kip's pudgy little pork face broke wide with a smile. "Why, surely, that's one thing to consider."

Some men keep their ugliness inside, fooling the world to their deviousness. Some men are ugly just through and through with no accounting for deception. Jack Bettle and Kipper Dunn were of the latter variety.

"Like I said, Cricket Wynot don't whore no more."

"Sure, sure, and beavers don't build dams no more. I heard tell thet Bronwyn Mason is mighty fine stock, too." Kipper Dunn rolled his tongue over his rotting teeth.

Hickory Dixon could feel his skin crawl. "Sorry to bother you boys, I 'spect I'll move on ta the next watering hole an' leave you to your drinks."

Jack Bettle was calculating now. "Now don't rush off so hissy like, Dixon, we's only playin' 'round. We might be 'vailable for your push up ta Cheyenne way."

"I'm not confident that you boys understand the parameters of this job."

Jack Bettle slowly eased the smile from his pocks. "Sure, Dixon, we git it. You need some trail hands that will act in a gentlemanly manner wit' the ladies. I think thet we kin do thet."

"Why sure, we kin be mighty gentlemanly when we set a mind to," added Dunn.

Hickory Dixon was not sold on the idea of these two unsavory characters joining himself, Bronwyn, and Cricket in the push to Cheyenne but, with August being quickly spent, options were slight.

Dixon was going to nip it quick. "These women, they ain't like that and they won't be no vile antics on this trek."

"Why sho 'nuff, Dixon ol' pard, we wouldn't a thunk of nothin' untoward like to these proper ladies." Kipper Dunn smiled.

"Course not," seconded Bettle, and with the pockmarks squeezing tight at the acne of his grin he deflected the thought. "Now what'd ya say the tender you is payin'?"

The hair on Hickory Dixon's neck tingled. He did not like the cut of these boys at all, and but for the scarcity of trail help, he would have not even sat at the same table with them. But today he set with them and drank with them and x'ed a contract with them. Jack Bettle and Kipper Dunn were contracted to jump the plains with this Conestoga contingent. But Dixon did not care for this choice by default.

With the covenant inked, Dixon made a promise to himself that this trip would be different. The promise that he would stay sober the entire expanse of the journey and that he would deliver the women and full complement of cargo to Cheyenne safe and secure.

So it would be. Hickory Dixon would lead the small contingent of three Conestogas full of books and school materials to set up the first school ever in the Western reaches of Rawlings. This, with the two young women, Bronwyn Mason and the former child prostitute Cricket Wynot, would be his responsibility. And along with this brood would ride the hired wagon pushers Jack Bettle and Kipper Dunn.

These wagon pushers who would prove to be the weak nut on the wheel.

10

PULL ME FROM THE RUBBLE: Part 2

*There's no blame,
And there's no shame,
Don't even take the trouble.
Come on,
Pull me from the rubble.*

J. Bauque

Lucidity came slowly as Rory Casso's consciousness played a game of tug-of-war with the comatose. Coherency ebbed and flowed on a tide, lapping at the shores of time between the be, the used to be, and the maybe.

Snow had fallen during the night and the little shelter of sticks and stones that had tumbled down this gully wash was proving to be a warm and cozy cote.

With the new snow providing good insulation, Rory Casso's and Rockwell's body heat alone would provide enough warmth to sustain life, but somehow, it seems, Casso, in his delirium, had managed to once again stoke a small spit fire. It was a testament to how deep Casso's delirium must have been that he did not remember busying the fire, nor, for that matter, collecting the wood that fueled the flames.

The gunshot that had ripped through Rory Casso's leg had closed tight, but the head wound he'd suffered in the fall from Rockwell was tender to the touch and he nurtured it gingerly. The head gash would take time to heal but that was time that Casso did not have.

While using his Bowie to stick the fish sizzling on the spit fire, Rory Casso worked at the edges of his memory, coaxing, little by little, recall to the fore.

As the fog of the fever eased, Casso gnawed on smoked fish and attempted to reconstruct his predicament. He remembered that he had suffered the head wound as a result of his fall from Rockwell. A fall that was precipitated on the stalk of elk. And the hunt for the elk had been a consequence of his and Juke's engagement with Bronwyn and Cricket and the Conestoga wagon train. Soon, the entire chronicle of the Thompson gang and the Reynolds Savings and Loan payroll lay clear to Rory Casso. These were not happy thoughts. There would be hard decisions to be made and consequences would be harsh.

But for now, Rory Casso needed to rest, and he tried to squeeze these unsavory decisions to the periphery of thought. Like a horse returning to its barn stall, its home, at the crack of thunder, Casso returned to the thoughts of Bronwyn Mason. Ruminating on the fated encounter with Bronwyn in these outer reaches of the wild, Casso stroked the memories of him and Bronwyn as children playing in the dust and dirt that were the streets of Rawlings.

***

The freckled little redhead bouncing about Rawlings, quick to scold Rory for not coming to school, slow to leave his company. Mischievous cohorts of Rawlings playing games of hock-a-stick and sham-sham and stealing the sweet summer tomatoes from Mrs. Pennybody's garden. The guilt-free laughter as the pilfered tomatoes' syrupy juices dribbled down their shirts in the hot summer shade. Hell and damnation never tasted so sweet.

In the carefree innocence of youth, Bronwyn would promise, threaten?, to marry Rory one fine day, while Rory wrestled in that conflicted age of hating girls, even as the first yearnings of manhood were agitating his sleep.

"Pap thinks that you don't want schooling. Mama just

feels sorry for you."

Rory Casso was four years older than Bronwyn and he had been the caretaker of his father's drunken digressions for the better part of his thirteen years. It was Rory that would rescue his father from his morning stupors off of the plank-board sidewalks of Rawlings. It fell to Casso to secure their lodging, be it a loft in the livery or a room at the back of a saloon. The young Rory Casso had been dealt the role of custodian for an alcoholic father. Deuce's wild.

> *The way the cards will fall,*
> *You wonder if you trust the deal.*
> *But if you fold and never call,*
> *You'll never know if it's for real.*

J. Bauque

"I don't need nobody feeling sorry for me. My pap and me do alright by us."

It seems to be part of the terrain of being a woman, and, by extension, a girl, to have an inbred way of recognizing when they are treading on the thin ice of a person's fortitude. Bronwyn Mason witnessed Rory's defensiveness and sidestepped lightly.

"Do you want me to bring you another book?" Bronwyn had been bringing Rory books for the better part of two years and she coached his study as best as she could. With the meager help that Bronwyn was able to provide, and the many nights Rory spent in solitude while his father was out badgering his liver, Rory was able to learn to read.

"Surely another book would be fine, that is, if'n it's okay with your'n mama. I've spent Shakespeare now four times, least. Although I could probably read that there bard more'n a dozen times more and not understand the damn thing. They sure got some funny ideas over there in that England country. And they talk so's a body can't always understand what they're trying to say."

Bronwyn enjoyed discussing books with Rory. The boy's blue eyes would sparkle when he discussed prose, and even reclining on the ground with one leg lazily draped over the other, Casso seemed to be sitting on the edge of his seat. "Mama says that they talk like that because language to them is like exploring and the words are just the ships that they use to sail on their voyage."

This coaxed a smile to Rory's face, to his eyes. "Ships on the sea, eh? Words on a voyage? I reckon I can see that. Words floatin' in a boat on the sea of ideas. I just think that sometimes that Shakespeare fellow has some water leaking in his craft."

Bronwyn was tickled with the image of words leaking out of Shakespeare's craft. "Mama likes that you are learning to read. She says that if you came to school, why, you would be the smartest boy in the entire territory."

"Thet's awfully nice of your mama to say but I don't feel so smart as all that."

"She just worries 'cause you 'n your pap ain't got no home."

This was a thought that Rory Casso was not eager to linger over, and with some finality, "I've got more'n I need."

But somewhere deep within the boy this tweaked the lesion of his spirit. Envious, though never jealous, Rory admired the way that Bronwyn would set in the lap of her pap on the jailhouse porch. Hours lingered as Marshal Mason and the befreckled little girl whiled away the hours together, chatting, laughing, or, often, just setting together in silence. From afar, the Marshal's lap looked about as good a home as one could hope to erect.

"You best run off to your school now. Your mama will be waiting."

Bronwyn was an astute enough child to recognize the pain she had touched in Rory at the mention of home, and she yearned to ease his loneliness. "Okay, but I'll bring you something new to read tomorrow."

"That would be swell."

"It's a new American writer."

CHAPTER TEN

"An American writer?"

"Yep. Mama says that he is a Romantic writer but there ain't nothing romantic about his writing. Pap says he is the first true American writer because he don't worry none about how they speak in England, he just writes in the way that Americans would speak."

"That so? He writes like you 'n me would talk? None of that floatin' shipwreck talk?"

"Yep. But his stories can be pretty scary. Name's Poe. Edgar Allan Poe."

"An' he writes like people talk? Like Americans talk?"

"Uh-huh."

"Well, thet sure would be a craft I'd like to set to sail, then."

***

These were the good memories to Rory Casso. These were glimpses of belonging. Of bonding. Of being a part of something that was outside of the walls of his own skin.

But even as these good memories played to Rory's ease, the thoughts of the wagon train, and the trouble it now faced, intruded into Rory's deliberations.

Casso finished his meal of smoked fish and drank a little of the cold water that had been accessed in the chipped ice. He felt comfortable here in this cozy cave of snow and when he lay back, unconsciousness quickly and quietly consumed his ruminations.

11

DOWN TO THE BONE

    The trail across the plains can become a monotonous affair. Minutes dragging into hours dragging into days dragging into weeks dragging into months. On the summer wagon trains that cross these shadeless plains, a body might wish for a good summer rain's soaking if for no other reason than to break the boredom of the sun-baked trail west. And if a summer storm does by happenstance unload, the bogging muddy wallows make a body yearn for the tedium of the shadeless terrain once again.

    Although these autumnal months do not hold the heat and mud extremes of the summer drives, the monotony is the ever-present beast on the trail. Sitting the buckboard of a Conestoga, bumps and humps and lumps churn in an ever-spinning eddy of grass and stone. To save the team of wagon breeds, and one's own backside, walking in the dust and dirt along the trail is a sad escape for spelling the trail's tedium.

    The good thing about driving train this late in the season was that the trail was well worn and hard packed between the watering holes and the campsites. The bad thing about leaving so late was that the trail was gritty and the watering holes were stale as they would not be flushed and refreshed until the rains of spring.

    Hickory Dixon was front-scouting the trail while the train of three Conestogas endlessly bumped along the North Platte. While a dry, windy-warm waft reddened cheeks and desiccated lips, parching away the inner juices, Bronwyn Mason and Cricket Wynot set the reins of the first Conestoga. Jack Bettle and Kipper Dunn were driving the two trailing wagons.

The initial seven weeks out of Independence were smooth and steady. The weather was fair and the buffalo grazing in a southerly winter migration provided plenty of fresh provisions. Bronwyn, reining the wagon, and Cricket, sitting beside her, had become attuned to the rhythm of the lurch and sway of the wagon. The spring and summer sojourners before them on this trail west had packed the wheel grooves rock-hard into a solid highway.

Except for the occasional off-color and suggestive asides from Jack Bettle or Kipper Dunn, the trail was a drone of clackety carts and squeaking leather, punctuated by the occasional slap of a whip.

Spelling monotony, conversation pulsed easily between the women as they harmonized their rhythm to the cadence of the trail.

"Your eyes, they kinda sparkle when you speak of that Juke Bauque."

"Is it really that obvious?" Cricket answered as her eyes lit to a sparkle. Although her body had known hundreds of men, her heart had been untapped, and Cricket Wynot blushed with the innocence of a schoolgirl. "I just never figured a man could be like that."

"Big and strong?"

"Sure, there's that, 'course. But the way he speaks. I do believe he's the smartest man I ever did know. His voice, why, it's like molasses and the words are like butter."

"He does have a way of knotting a couplet."

The wagon was in a rhythm of the well-worn ruts of the trail and Cricket was musing, "Kinda funny about those boys, Juke and Rory."

"Funny how?"

"You know, funny about how that Rory boy's pap was a writer, even had his own newspaper, and he turns out to be an Indian scout. And then that Juke Bauque's pap is an Indian and he turns out to be a poet."

Bronwyn mulled on this. "I see what you mean. I know

what my pap would say to that."

"What would your pap say?"

"Only in America."

"Ha! Guess that's about right. Think we might meet up with them up Rawlings way? The way he talked, it sounds like he and that Rory Casso fellow might be pulling into Rawlings about the same time as us."

"Seems likely, if we don't get stalled over in Cheyenne for the winter."

"You knew that Rory Casso fellow as a boy, right?"

Bronwyn Mason's thoughts lingered for a long moment in the haven of her and Casso's childhood. "Yep. I sure did know Rory Casso as a boy."

Cricket caught the ephemeral coo in Bronwyn's reply. "Now who's got the sparkle?"

Bronwyn Mason turned in seriousness to address Cricket's accusing eyes. A moment of defensive challenge was exchanged between the women. Then the two women burst with laughter.

When the laughter subsided, Cricket probed, "You've known that Rory Casso deep, huh?"

"Yes. Deep. Not like how you're thinking, I imagine. Rory and me were children together, playing through the infancy that was our Rawlings."

"You both had homes in Rawlings?"

The memory triggered crow's-feet to the corner of Bronwyn's eye. "Well, I sure enough had a home. Me 'n Pap and Mama. But that Rory boy, he never really had no place where he could hang his hat permanent like."

***

Her red curls flopped about her shoulders when she jumped onto the Marshal's lap. It was a long and hard lap, hardened by the years in a tough country and cold saddles, but Bronwyn had learned to navigate the hard as she rode sidesaddle across his legs.

Marshal Isham Mason brushed the curls from Bronwyn's face, exposing the girl's wrinkled forehead and the creased brow. Gently smoothing her brow with his thumb, he said, "What's got my cowgirl's brow so rutted?"

"Just thinkin', is all."

Mason knew what was concerning Bronwyn. It was the same issue that she had voiced unease with on many occasions, but he kissed her forehead and gave her rein. "Uh-huh. Thinkin' about what?"

Bronwyn wiggled uncomfortably on Mason's lap. She was eight years old and she had been worrying this problem now for a good three years. "It's that boy."

Smiling sadly at the thought of Rory Casso, Mason enveloped the girl into his chest and softly rested his chin on top of her head. "You mean that boy Rory?"

The freckles on the girl's button nose crinkled as she scrunched her nose, searching for words.

The Marshal was with the town's doctor/veterinarian/mayor at the instant that Rory was discharged into the world. That was the same moment that Rory's mother was taken from the world. A moment that, to Rory's father, William Casso, would endure as the defining moment of William Casso's life. The moment when William Casso lost the war with life; when he lost his will to live. And Marshal Mason was there in the ensuing years as William Casso degenerated from Rawlings newspaper publisher to the town drunk. From respected writer of script and prose to the notorious village slot.

The death of William Casso's wife, at the convergence of Rory Casso's birth, left the elder Casso a shattered man. By the time that the young Rory was old enough to know his father, William Casso had been subjugated to the role of bar swabber.

"Why's that boy always got to be working, Pap? He don't never come out to Mama's school."

"Well, honey, that boy's got a heap of accounting for a boy that age. His daddy's got a sickness and it's fallen to Rory to man-up things."

CHAPTER ELEVEN

Bronwyn scrunched her nose and the freckles danced in the soft morning light. She pressed those freckles into her father's red plaid shirt. "I seen Mr. Casso about, looking sick all right, but what kind of sickness does he have?"

"He's got the bottle sickness, honey."

"But how do you get the bottle sickness, Pap?"

Mason took his time to find the right way to explain this to Bronwyn. Taking a deep breath, he held Bronwyn in the warm envelope that was his red plaid shirt. "Well, baby, different men get bottle sickness in different ways. Some men get bottle sickness because it helps them to remember something that they may have lost. And some men get bottle sickness because it helps them to forget things that they may have found. And some men are just born with an inclination to the bottle sickness."

"But what about Mr. Casso, pap, where did Mr. Casso get into the bottle sickness?"

Remembering the defining moment that Mrs. Casso had passed away and Rory Casso had been born, Marshal Mason searched for the words. "Well, baby, Mr. Casso fell into the bottle sickness when Mrs. Casso died. I think that he might be trying to remember something he lost. The sad thing is that it's making Mr. Casso forget something that he might have found."

The girl considered this as she hollowed into the plaid shirt. She was comfortable there, in her father's sinewy arms, wrapped tight in the red plaid, at ease in the aroma of horse and powder and the oils from well-kept guns. "How long has Mr. Casso been in the sickness, Pap?"

"Well, how old do you reckon Rory Casso is now?"

Silently counting on her fingers, she declared at last, "He's four years older than me so that must make him twelve years old."

"Then I 'spect that Mr. Casso's been in the bottle sickness for the better part of those twelve years."

***

Rawlings was a town in transition. The community's texture was evolving from the false-fronted and weather-beaten structures that had sprung from the dirt to a township of secured fortifications. Trappers and hunters were being usurped by farmers and family men and churches were rivaling the number of saloons. Commerce was settling along the boardwalks of Rawlings, and family homes, with whitewashed fences and trimmed garden beds, were pushing out at the edges of the settlement.

This evolution was turning Rawlings from a frontier roughneck out-village to a community of purpose and future. The haphazard collection of clapboard houses that catered to the transient miners and hunters was now giving way to more permanent lodgings and enduring peoples. Mercantiles and barber shops, a bank and a telegraph office had taken root on Main Street. Liveries and smithies, and someday soon the town would build its first-ever one-room schoolhouse. And the schoolhouse would be the definitive sign of a civilization taken root.

Rawlings was becoming a community of consciousness of itself and of the future. A future built on the labor of the plow and the gift of the harvest.

***

"But does Mr. Casso blame Rory for Mrs. Casso's death, Pap?"

Imperceptibly Mason squeezed Bronwyn to his chest a little tighter. "Maybe he did at first, baby. But I don't think that he does anymore. It's just that once a man slips down the neck of the bottle, it's a hard climb back out."

"It just seems a thorny way to go for that Rory boy, don't it?"

Now the Marshal considered the young Rory Casso. He had watched the boy from the spit. A good and honest boy saddled with a father that never could get past the pain and the angst of losing his wife. "You're right, baby, it is a thorny

CHAPTER ELEVEN

way to go. But some folks, well, thorny is all they get."

Mason did not like it any more than Bronwyn and, over the years, he had tried to do right by the boy. But the boy had a pile of pride and the Marshal needed to tread lightly with his aid as the proud young Rory Casso would resist anything that resembled charity.

"But why'n'ya think God gives people the thorns, Pap? Why'n God give Rory the thorns?"

Isham Mason deliberated on this apiece. He began slowly, while trying to make sense of it for himself, "Well, baby, I guess I can't speak for God none but I can maybe guess that God gives some folks the thorns because he kinda wants to test their mettle. The roses smell a lot bit sweeter if'n you stick a few thorns along the way."

Clasping tight to the security of her father's red shirt, her freckles designed a pout. "Don't seem fair, is all."

"That sure enough is right." And, as was the Marshal's way, he deflected Bronwyn's excavation of Rory and God and thorns and roses. "But you best get yourself down to home for your schoolin' or your mama's gonna thorn a stem for me."

"Awww, when is this town gonna get a school? I hate schoolin' in my own home."

"Someday, baby, someday. But you best git along now." And he bounced her off of his lap and gave her the familiar cuff to the seat of her pants, dusting her down the busy street of Rawlings.

***

From the jailhouse stoop the Marshal watched Bronwyn's cherry locks bouncing up the dirt main street of Rawlings. Once home, she would be joining the three or four other children that constituted the student body. In Rawlings, school teaching defaulted to the Marshal's wife, Eva, only because she was the most able reader. At one time that responsibility would have fallen to William Casso, the town's newspaper publisher, but that was long before he took up a permanent habitation in the bottle.

    Discussions were rife around Rawlings about building a one-room schoolhouse. The population was growing rapidly and the township's progeny was erupting at an escalating rate.

    A cavalry man turned buffalo hunter, Isham Mason had come to Rawlings in early settlement, as the buffalo were playing out. He had been Rawlings' first and only marshal for the better part of fifteen years and he breathed deep with pride at his role in detaching Rawlings from its wild beginnings. And he took much pride in Bronwyn as well, as she took to books with a knack and a fancy. She was a smart girl and she, too, would be a part of the future that was germinating in Rawlings.

    Mason's eyes drifted up and down the storefronts. He stood on the stoop of the square, gray-brick jailhouse and overviewed the vibrant community of Rawlings. The livery stable was new and sported the first coal-fired furnace west of the Mississippi. The Maltins were putting up a bigger building for their dry goods mercantile right next to Rawlings' first church, Saints of Peace. And now Saints of Peace was joined by two additional churches in Rawlings, contesting with the five Rawlings saloons for the souls of the community.

    It was a warm spring morning, and as Mason stood there mulling the future of Rawlings, the Smoke Stack Tavern's door kicked wide and Rory Casso splashed a bucket of dirty water into the street. The boy was making his morning rounds of the town's taverns, bar swabbing and spittoon scrubbing. At twelve years old this boy should be sitting up at Mason's place twisting words and ideas with his wife and daughter and the other students of Rawlings. But Rory's pap could be found passing the early day deep in a drunken snore, waking only in time to find his way to another barstool. And so it fell to the boy, Rory, to keep the Casso family flush.

    Rory Casso was a good boy, true of spirit and strong of body, and Marshal Isham Mason worried after the lad. Swabbing bars and flushing outhouse stools was no way for Rory Casso to grow. A young man with no sense of a home

CHAPTER ELEVEN

would deliver a man with no sense of roots. And a man with no sense of roots would be a soul out of sync.

Many a townsfolk shared the sentiment about how it was a shame about Rory's plight. Some well-intentioned church ladies even took up a fund for the boy, but it only managed to heap a measure of embarrassment on top of Rory's shame. The boy would have to find his own path and, as much as one might want to intervene, one could only watch and hope for the best.

Marshal Isham Mason ruminated on what Rory's future might hold and how he would fit into the future that was Rawlings. But the vision was vague and rutted.

***

"Didn't that boy Rory have no folks?" Cricket pressed Bronwyn.

"No mother. And not a father to speak of. At one time Rory's pap was the tip of the town. He published Rawlings' first newspaper and was highly regarded by friend and foe alike."

Cricket's chirpy voice was quieter now. "What happened then?"

"Well, I wasn't there, but it seems that Rory's mother died giving him breath. His father never did recover from the loss and spent his remaining years traipsing from bottle to bottle."

The spell of quiet thought was interrupted by Bronwyn snickering in memory. "I do remember promising my pap that I would be marrying that boy."

Cricket warmed to the thought. "You thought you would marry him?"

"That's what I told my pap."

Laughing now, Cricket said, "It sure is some kind of world a child can design."

"Sure is."

"Ha! Just imagine, marrying your childhood sweetheart."

Bronwyn let the memory hang there like a favorite jacket

with patches on the elbows and a missing button.

***

For the early part of the drive, from Independence to the westernmost prairies, the trek went smoothly enough. The trail was wide and tramped hard from the long summer of earlier wagon trains that had packed wide tracks, and the weather had yielded to a warm Indian summer.

Three Conestogas, a wagon pilot, two wagon pushers, two women, and eleven weeks out of Independence is when the trouble began.

From the jump, Jack Bettle and Kipper Dunn had played to their lower side with crass comments and sideways glances aimed at the ladies in the train, reserving a special vulgarity for the ex-prostitute, Cricket Wynot. They bestowed disdain on the now often-inebriated trail boss, Hickory Dixon, and, at every crossing, as the trail wore on, became more belligerent and loutish. And as the train began to climb from the flat plains up into the long and rolling foothills of the Rockies, Jack Bettle and Kipper Dunn became more and more vile.

As the days shortened their stride toward the approaching solstice, Hickory Dixon began to spend more and more time in the company of his whiskey.

12

STRONG ENOUGH TO RUN

The change from the long grass country of the plains to the sub-alpine terrain had been sudden and dramatic. The topography was rising and falling with high meadows and toppling flumes, as prairie grasses gave way to strands of ponderosa pines along the eastern walls of the mountains.

Driving a wagon train west is a tough business, and as the team dug deeper into the west, Bronwyn Mason and Cricket Wynot found themselves reining the wagons more often than not.

The original plan was for Dixon, Jack Bettle, and Kipper Dunn to be the primary wagon pushers, with the women occasioning the reins to allow one of the men to scout the trail ahead or to hunt up game. This worked fine at first, with Dixon, Bettle, and Dunn splitting the scouting and hunting. When Bettle and Dunn began to scout out together, leaving the three wagons to be driven by a half-drunk Hickory Dixon and the two women, the track began to slacken. With little discipline proffered by the wagon pilot, the pace of the caravan had slowed to a crawl.

More and more time was being spent by Bettle and Dunn scouting and hunting. And hunting had become nothing more than an excuse to target-shoot the late southern migration of buffalo. Following the drifting buffalo, the train was getting plenty of meat, but not much headway was being made toward Cheyenne.

Lost in the bottle, Hickory Dixon was now becoming more of a liability than an asset, and Bronwyn resigned herself to making some changes.

In the spring and throughout the early summer this trail was teeming with wagon trains heading to California, Oregon, and the sacred sanctuary of the great salt flats. Sometimes as many as two hundred trains at a pull, each wagon packed tight with the promises of tomorrow, would fill these wagon-wheel grooves. It was not uncommon for one train to be setting up a night camp in the very spot where the preceding train had broken camp early that morning. Sometimes it seemed like an unbroken column of wagons stretched from Independence to the Snake River.

Not so as the Mason party made its journey westward. Except for the occasional passing of a wagon or two returning east after surrendering to the hardships of the worst that the West had to offer, no human contact was made. These eastward-traveling wagons came complete with the defeated men and women who had relinquished their dreams of the mythical West of geese and gravy.

It was not many weeks deep into the drive that Hickory Dixon reverted to his bottle. At first he would have a solitary nip before retiring at night. Soon he added a snort when camp broke in the morning. Too many leagues into the drive to change course, Hickory Dixon was reining the wagon with his bottle setting in the seat next to him. With the loss of a sober trail boss came the loss of protocol. And with the loss of protocol, Jack Bettle and Kipper Dunn became more and more variable as well.

Late one morning, as the wagon train traveled abreast of a herd numbering forty or so buffalo, Bettle and Dunn swept into the saddle to lay waste to the trove. Bronwyn had had enough of these trail pushers and their killing games and leapt on her own steed to follow the boys out to the killing field.

This land of rolling knolls, foothills to the Rockies, obscured the path that Jack Bettle and Kipper Dunn had taken, but the pop-pop-popping of their Winchesters made for an easy track for Bronwyn to follow.

Bettle and Dunn had already dismounted and were

CHAPTER TWELVE

spending lead on the buffalo herd when Bronwyn drew up to the men. Preoccupied with the target shoot, the men failed to notice Bronwyn's approach.

Swinging down from the saddle and whipping off her hat in one fluid motion, Bronwyn cuffed Kipper Dunn across the back of his head, drilling his rotting teeth face-first into the hard late November dirt. Bronwyn had not meant to deliver such an ample blow—it was the momentum from swinging down from her mount that gave the blow such force—but it did not break her heart, either.

Jack Bettle reeled at the commotion, his Winchester yet warmed by the buffalo poach, and the barrel swung toward Bronwyn's midriff. But recognition came quick to Bettle and he raised the gun to a rest against his shoulder. Slowly a smile squeezed against his pocked cheeks.

Kipper Dunn came up cursing and spitting dirt.

But Bettle was now in full humor. "Wahl, wahl, if it ain't our own little missy wil'cat, Bronwyn Mason," he suggested lecherously.

Spewing invectives and Rocky Mountain foothills from his rotting teeth, Dunn was not amused, and confronted Bronwyn with fists tight. "Jes' who da 'ell ya think ya is, ya coyote bitch?"

With her crown of strawberry curls waving in the early winter breeze, Bronwyn right away smacked Dunn's face. "I'm the coyote bitch that is paying for that lead you're chucking."

The smacking of Kipper Dunn caused Bettle to explode in a guffaw; he was having fun now. "Awww, did da little gurl hurt the big cowboy's mush?" he mocked.

Kipper Dunn was not used to being manhandled by a woman, and he seethed, "You shore like to play wit' fire..." Dunn bettered Bronwyn by a hundred pounds and, clenching tight his fists, he loomed over her. "You may be payin' for thet lead out of a good whoopin' of your ass."

But Jack Bettle was getting other ideas. "Now jes' hold on a minute there, Kip, meybe there be another way thet she might want ta pay for the liberties she taking on you." And then Bettle lowered the Winchester from his shoulder and again into the general direction of Bronwyn's torso.

Rage, then confusion, and finally realization rolled over Kipper Dunn's face. When the understanding of Jack Bettle's innuendo finally reached Dunn, a wicked smile that shared the full breath of Kipper Dunn's rotting mouth furrowed his face.

In a frozen, quiet moment, Jack Bettle, Kipper Dunn, and Bronwyn Mason understood that a line had been crossed.

Jack Bettle stepped a barrel-length away from Bronwyn and teased the buttons on her shirt with the rifle's muzzle. "Meybe her collateral is 'ere?"

Kipper Dunn was now full in the party and he stepped to her, but before he had a chance to reach out for her, she smacked his face again. Surprise and then rage burst out of Dunn and he let Bronwyn have the full measure of it. A heavy right fist to her face, a hard left to her midsection, and a full roundhouse right to her face again sent Bronwyn sprawling face-first to the ground.

Again Bettle guffawed, but Dunn had tasted blood. "Get up, ya little piss, ya been a-beggin' a mite whoopin' right out of Independence an' now I'm gonna deliver." But Bettle licked his thin lips with a more sinister arousal.

Kipper Dunn had understood Bettle's suggestion, but he was not ready to let go of the beating that he had planned for Bronwyn. Kicking her boots as she lay face-first in the dirt, he demanded, "Git up, girl, I'm fixin' to kick your cougar into a pussy."

Bronwyn lay flat-faced on the ground. A lesser woman, or man, would be cowering in fear with this threatening status, but Bronwyn, face to the earth, was calmly estimating the situation. Kipper Dunn was towering over her with clenched rage and Jack Bettle was hovering with ardent loins and a warm Winchester.

With his right hand still training the gun on Bronwyn,

CHAPTER TWELVE

Bettle began to unbuckle his belt. "Now, hang a minute there, bud, maybe we 'ave a little fun wi' the kitty before ya mess up its pretty puss."

Having spent some of the rage with the three punches, especially the full roundhouse right he'd delivered to Bronwyn's face, Kipper Dunn began to warm to the idea of another kind of scuffle. As anger gave way to the warming in his nether reaches, a lecherous and rotting smile creased his face. "Why, shore, maybe we let the irons smolder on the coals 'fore we brand our heifer."

Jack Bettle and Kipper Dunn were flushed with excitement and expectation. Their voices warmed into a husky intoxication. "Never much cottoned ta women prancin' round in trail jeans." Bettle's voice was throaty, bull-in-heat throaty. "May be best ta just slip 'er dungarees off'n."

Lying face in the dirt, Bronwyn could taste blood in the corner of her mouth. The blow that Dunn had delivered to her midsection had spilled her wind and the right that he had delivered to her jaw had stunned her. But now she was collecting herself. And she was calculating.

Dunn and Bettle were enjoying their amusement and their hegemony as they tightened the circle over Bronwyn. Jack Bettle had his belt in his hand for the beating he had promised Bronwyn, and Kipper Dunn had already let his pants drop to his ankles, exposing his rigid manhood to the warm December sun.

Reaching down, with anxious mitts, Kipper Dunn grabbed the ankles of Bronwyn's boots and flipped her on to her back; his eyes were glazing with the expectation of animal gratification. "Let's jes' get a little kitty . . ."

But he never got the chance.

When Dunn had grabbed Bronwyn Mason's boots and flipped her over, Bronwyn had used the revolving spin of her body to draw her Pocket .32, and she came up blazing.

The first shot spit warm air past Jack Bettle's pocked cheeks and the second shot sent Kipper Dunn's hat flipping into the December sky. Two more reports splintered the gunstock of Bettle's Winchester and spun Kipper Dunn, with his pants wrapping up his ankles, toppling butt-naked to the turf. Stunned, Jack Bettle stumbled backward, and Bronwyn used the moment of surprise to scramble to her feet.

Kipper Dunn, sitting bare-assed in the high plains dirt, jostled to free his .45, which had twisted in a knot in the pants that bound his ankles. The final blast from Bronwyn's revolver separated Dunn's right ear from his skull and sent the ear chasing his hat as they tumbled westward to the Rockies.

As Bronwyn turned to cover Bettle, Kipper Dunn clutched the bloody hole where his ear had been, cursing and screaming in agony.

When Jack Bettle had removed his belt for the whooping he had planned for Bronwyn, he had laid his revolver on the ground. Now, bending to reach for the iron, he looked into a close-up view of the barrel of the Pocket .32 just inches from his nose. For his part, Kipper Dunn was trying to stem the flow from his bloody ear as he set with his bare nuggets against the cold earth.

With Dunn whimpering in the dirt, Bronwyn smiled now at Bettle's predicament. "It's okay with me if you want to try my patience."

Carefully, Jack Bettle eased his hand away from his gun and stepped back as his face contorted between anger and alarm.

Cupping his bloody ear with one hand, Kipper Dunn began to push himself up from the dirt with his free hand, but Bronwyn waved the pistol in his direction. "Suppose we just let you sit there like that for the moment while I figure out what I'm gonna do with you little bad boys." Adding, as she waved her revolver at the seething Bettle, "He sure does bleed pretty."

With Bronwyn's gun trained on his manhood and the deep huskiness of expectation gone from Jack Bettle's throat, he negotiated. "Lookit here, Miz Bronwyn, we

CHAPTER TWELVE

warn't meaning ta..."

"Shut up," Bronwyn commanded, and Bettle obliged. "I just can't reason an idea why I shouldn't leave you two boys here to feed the butte."

Kipper Dunn, cupping a pool of flesh and blood in his hand, whined from the dirt, "Thet be murder."

"Yup" was all Bronwyn could manage.

Save for the sound of the buffalo grazing on their slow march south, all was still as Bronwyn mulled her options. Somewhere on high, a sparrow hawk's shrill call: "Killy-killy-killy-killy-killy."

"Lookit 'ere, Miz Mason," Bettle tried again, and Bronwyn raised the gun barrel level to Bettle's nose.

Sweetly she mocked him, "Yes?"

Yet stemming the blood flowing from his ear, Kipper Dunn was feeling the humiliation of sitting exposed, pants wrapped around his ankles and his testicles chilling in the dirt. "Suppose I pull up my drawers while we talk."

"I don't think so." Bronwyn waved her pistol in the general direction of Dunn's gonads and added, "That twig you're displaying kinda reminds me of a pocket mouse. Except yours is a wee bit smaller."

Kipper Dunn kept his hands to his ear, his pants to his ankles, and his butt to the ground. In embarrassment and pain he whined, "My ear, you shot my goddamn ear off you goddamn bitch."

Jack Bettle had a better grasp of the situation and yelled at Dunn to shut up.

"Listen to your pard, Dunn, 'cause I can just as easily shoot your mouth off."

The dirt under Dunn was wet with his blood. He had pulled off his bandana and pressed it tight to the wound to stem the flow.

With his hands raised and palm open, Jack Bettle offered, "Let me he'p him wit' thet ear."

Considering for a moment first, Bronwyn gestured with her .32. "Kick your gun here, first."

Bettle turned to help Kipper Dunn, but Bronwyn froze him by whistling a shot that kicked up the dirt at his boots. "The gun first."

Squinting in anger, Jack Bettle kicked his Colt toward Bronwyn and sidled over to Dunn.

Bronwyn offered, "In case you weren't counting, I have only two rounds left in this gun. I can't afford to waste them on any more management shots so they are now reserved for your vests, if you want them."

Kipper Dunn was not deterred from his pain. "You shot off my goddamned ear."

Bronwyn smiled sweetly. "I truly am sorry for that, Dunn. In haste, I was forced to hurry my aim. I was endeavoring to rift your eyes." This time Kipper Dunn shut up.

Holding the scarf tight to Dunn's ear hole, Jack Bettle demanded, "Okay, now, what's your play?"

Gliding on the winter's current high overhead, the sparrow hawk screeched its advice: "Killy-killy-killy-killy-killy."

Bronwyn was contemplative. "Well, I guess I was fool enough for engaging you hombres from the jump, that's my fault. But I'll be damned if you'll mosey on further with us."

"Ya ain't thinkin' about driving wagons 'cross these hills with two women and an old drunk, is ya?"

Bronwyn ignored that. "I'm thinking maybe it's time that we part our company. You two can just mount your ponies and shag some plains."

Jack Bettle began to say something, then, considering the Pocket .32, kept it to himself. Reaching down, Bettle hauled Kipper Dunn to his feet and pulled Dunn's pants to his waist, buckling his belt. After assisting Dunn to step into the saddle's leather, Bettle turned to retrieve their guns.

"You can just leave those laying right there."

"You ain't thinkin' of turnin' us loose on these ranges wit'out iron?"

"I ain't thinking of turning you loose at all," is all Bronwyn replied.

CHAPTER TWELVE

Dunn, clasping the bloody bandana to his ear, began a moaning protest. "But ya can't . . ."

"Can. Will. And now, done." Bronwyn offered the barrel of her gun. "Those ponies you're sitting are mine as well, but I'm just gonna write them off as a loss to my bad management. Now git."

There would be no movement in this woman and the boys understood this. Jack Bettle picked up Dunn's hat, dust-slapped it on his thigh, and set it askew on Dunn's head, slanted across the good ear.

Climbing onto his own steed, Jack Bettle turned to meet Bronwyn eye to eye, glare for glare. No words were exchanged but the meaning was clear. This humiliation would not go unrewarded.

Gunless, Jack Bettle and Kipper Dunn turned their horses to the trail.

The sparrow hawk's counsel, "Killy-killy-killy-killy-killy," went unheeded, and, in time, regretted, by Bronwyn.

***

Bronwyn took her time walking her horse back to the wagons. This would be a major development with this wagon train, as the train really did not have the manpower reserve. It would have been a tough enough push with Bettle and Dunn along, but now that they had been escorted out of the party, hard track loomed ahead.

Pondering Jack Bettle and Kipper Dunn led Bronwyn down the road of pondering men in general. The desires of men. The needs of men. Eventually, as the pondering of men often did, it led her to thoughts of Rory Casso. As her horse clopped to the stone, Bronwyn Mason remembered the boy without a home.

These circular ruminations of men, the desires of men, and Rory Casso inspired the memory of a conversation she had once held with her pap.

***

"The Bible got it right, baby, they just got the spelling wrong," said the Marshal.

Bronwyn was of the age, then, of crossing that great divide between girlhood and womanhood. Maturity was waving hello from across the passageway. Her shirts were beginning to present the twin pinnacles of puberty and her jeans, for she yet insisted on wearing the denim, were stretching to the contours of her ever-rounding hips.

With her fishing line fastened to her big toe and the twig bobber playing on the rivulet's current, Bronwyn was confused. "What'a ya mean, Pap, and what's the Bible got to do with that Rory boy?"

"Well, like you say, that boy's got a heap of gone in him."

"But what's he running from, Pap?" Bronwyn was mulling as she absentmindedly watched the fishing line bobber dance to the river's song.

Isham Mason thought on this question for a moment. The river had been good to them this day. They had a grassy piece of shade to while the hours and a string of pan-ready fish dangling in the water.

"I'm not convinced that Rory Casso is running from anything. Seems he might be just trying to find his place on God's globe. A boy like Rory, growing without a real home, always seems to have a tougher time getting his feet under him."

"You mean shiftless, Pap?"

"No, honey, not shiftless. More like he's uneasy with his stride. The boy's got a pretty good sense of himself, he just doesn't quite know how he fits in the bigger picture."

Light reflecting off of the stream set Bronwyn's eyes to sparkle but her furrowed forehead betrayed her discomfort. "But he could always of come to live with us, couldn't he, Pap?"

Isham pulled more string from the breast pocket on his red plaid shirt and drew a longer lead on his fishing line. "Yep. He coulda always come and stayed with us. Made us his family. Your mama would have liked that. And Rory

CHAPTER TWELVE

knew that, too. I guess the boy just always felt that he needed to find his own what, wheres, and why-fors."

Contemplation silenced Bronwyn as she considered the struggles within the boy that must be wearying Rory. She had always known the love of a mother and the love of a father. She had always had the security of knowing she was not alone. Bronwyn Mason had always had a home and she just could not fathom grappling with the solitary quest that Rory pursued.

Finally Bronwyn breached the silence. "But what do you mean that the Bible got it right, Pap, but the Bible spelled it wrong?"

Marshal Isham Mason smiled at his young daughter, so eager to learn. So eager to help. So eager to be a grown woman. And so eager to love.

"Well, the Bible got it right to where all the roads lead."

"You mean about all the roads leading to Rome."

"Yep. But, for Casso, they got the wrong spelling of it. For that lost young man trying to find his comfortable place in the world, I 'spect that all his roads lead to roam."

Bronwyn crinkled up the freckles on her nose in chagrin. "Awww, Pap, roam? All roads lead to roam?"

Isham Mason enjoyed provoking his daughter. "Even so, that boy Casso is bound to be roaming. Roam is where all of that boy's roads will lead."

Bronwyn ignored the tugging tell of her fishing line as the bobber bounced on the water. "But won't Rory ever settle down, Pap? Won't he ever find some kind of home? It's got to be awful lonesome out there by hisself."

"First ways," corrected the Marshal, "being alone and being lonely are two different animals. Why, a body can be in the middle of a raucous crowd and be as lonely as a moaning loon."

Bronwyn thought about this for a moment while her fishing line bobber skipped with urgency.

"You got a bite, baby."

"Uh-huh." Bronwyn yet ignored the fishing line. "It

seems like that boy is touring a lot of pain to get where he is going."

"Maybe not as much pain as from where he's been."

"Maybe not," the girl agreed.

And Bronwyn Mason's fishing line snapped.

***

As Bronwyn drew rein at the train, Cricket and Dixon were spelling the horses.

Hickory Dixon was the one to speak. "Where'er the boys?"

"I kicked them to the trail."

"You fired Bettle and Dunn?" Dixon was aghast.

"They were getting a mite too shaggy and they needed a good trimming."

Deep furrows busied Dixon's brow and he pulled at his long chin with his hand. "Sorry to say this, Miss, but we're in a heap of woe if'n it's just the three of us pushing these buggies. You shouldn't a oughtn' fired them boys."

"And you shouldn't have oughtn' hired them boys." And she spun on her heels and strode away.

For a long moment Hickory Dixon stared at her backside as she walked away. Bronwyn's hips strolled with the sway of a woman. But Bronwyn Mason rumbled like a man. Turning his attention to the direction of the Western reaches, Dixon gave a long, wistful gaze at the oncoming winter.

13

LONG WAY HOME

The fever wracked Casso's sleep with a violence for the ages. The jumble of sticks and stones that constituted the gully wash shelter held fast against the early winter blast that scoured the coulee and, as the winter broiled outside, Casso's fever broiled within.

Bathed in sweat and trembling with the shakes, his dreams were a muddled affair of ethereal images. Clouds became bears, bears became people, and people became wraiths. And then the wraiths returned to the clouds to complete the circle and begin again.

At some point Rory Casso was returned to the nightmare of his youth. The time in his adolescence when he was taught the hard lesson of what he was and what he was not. Mostly what he was not. And what he did not possess.

***

They meant well, these churchwomen folk. It was a somber collection of the women of the First Tabernacle Church of Our Lord and, in their desire to serve the Lord, they would define the parameters of God's work. This is common among the Evangelists: To be God's arbiter. But these churchwomen had meant well.

There were many moral kinks to be worked out in a young township like Rawlings, a wild frontier town transforming itself into a civilized borough. A city government needed to be established, businesses developed, banks and jails and schools begat. It was a town passing from adolescence into adulthood, and the seams of its wardrobe would need to be let out to accommodate the wider shoulders.

And it was a town ripe for the saving of the soul. Churches had sprung from the dirt to trumpet salvation, complete with fiery brimstone ministers to minister the fallen. And the good churchwomen of the young Rawlings would not be denied their opportunity to make their mark on the lost souls at this junction.

As the town's drunk, William Casso would have seemed the obvious target for the women brigade's wrath of redemption. But William Casso, it was deemed, was too far gone for salvation and so the churchwomen set their sights on the younger Casso, Rory.

Salvation began innocently enough, as most good intentions do. Having recognized the depth of what they perceived to be the young Rory's dearth, the churchwomen went about trying to right this wrong. And if they had just limited their attempt at reformation, to the occasional hand-me-down clothes or the hot meal on the holidays, it might not have been such a bad thing. But such is the arrogance of the Evangelists that their belief in their own righteousness necessitates that they busy themselves in the calmest of waters.

"It just ain't right that that boy should be swabbing bar floors like that," preached Mrs. Pennybody. Mrs. Pennybody was the best-intentioned of the well-intentioned and she spoke with the conviction of God's representative.

Encouraged over the ladies' chorus of "amens," Mrs. Pennybody continued, "We need to save that child of William or that boy will end up just like his pap, laying in the gutters of Rawlings with a bottle in one hand and the devil in the other."

"Amen amen amen to that, sister, but what can we do to save this young wretched soul?"

The cause was upon Mrs. Pennybody now. "What can we do? My sisters in charity and light, it is not what can we do, it is what we must do." Mrs. Pennybody was now at the most grandiose of her advocacy. And this is when an Evangelist becomes her most dangerous. These moments of grandiose advocacy are the moments when the Evangelist's belief in her own correctness trumps any consideration of what is right and what is wrong.

"What we can do, sisters, nay, what we must do," and Mrs. Pennybody was in full deliverance now, "we must usurp that poor child from his father. We must make room for Rory in our own homes, in our own hearts. And we must teach that boy the meaning of a real life. A real home. A home in the salvation and love that is the Lord." The Evangelist is resolute to sanctify the opinions of the Lord.

"But to take the boy from his own father?"

"It is true. We must be judicious. We must be kind. But as God's disciple, I have given this matter full consideration." The Evangelist's greatest confidence comes from knowing that she speaks for God. "And as God guides my deliberation, I can assure you that our best course would be to partition this boy's soul from that septic environment."

"But can we legally take that boy from his father?"

"Our vocation is above any laws proclaimed by men. We must answer to the laws of God." Hammering her right fist into her left palm, Mrs. Pennybody would not be denied her rectitude. "We will speak to Marshal Mason and we will make him understand that it is in the best interest of this unsullied soul to be separated from that world of vim and vermin."

"The boy does play with the Marshal's daughter," heartened one of the choir.

"And maybe Bronwyn can hold some sway with her father, she seems like such a reasonable child," offered another.

"But the Marshal will not be easily swayed. When we tried to get him to make Bronwyn wear dresses he only shrugged and suggested, with what he must have thought to be humor, that maybe she would grow out of her pants," cautioned one of the choir.

"And the way that the Marshal is teaching that girl to shoot a gun! Shoot a gun! Disgraceful! And she is not even ten years old!" added another.

But Mrs. Pennybody would not be deterred in her

conviction. "Then we will go to the mayor. For these are minor annoyances. We will save that boy from his father's scourge and deliver him unto the lap of our Lord."

"But who amongst us will take the boy in? Who will Rory Casso live with?"

With a heavy sigh deep in her breast and filled with the torment of the righteous, Mrs. Pennybody concluded, "We will all share in the burden."

This arrangement suited the Evangelist women well, for now they would all have the voice of the Lord at their disposal.

And so it was settled, through some small manipulation of Marshal Mason, his daughter Bronwyn, and the hell and damnation suffered upon the newly elected mayor of Rawlings, the church women were able to successfully wrest control of Rory from his father.

It was in Rory's eleventh year that the experiment of shuttling him from holy household to holy household in the upstart community of Rawlings was endeavored. From churchwoman to churchwoman he was dealt about like a holiday fruitcake. With nuts.

Often he would run away, back to his father, and just as often he was apprehended by the do-gooders and resentenced to the churchwomen's idea of home.

But in the end, the boy could not be smothered to the hustle of the Lord. And the only lesson that Rory was able to glean in this year of zealous appropriation is that he did not have a home.

It had never occurred to Rory before that he was so poor. Or that he was homeless. He had never given the idea of home much thought. Before this time of Evangelist home hopping, life was just what it was. Now he was confronted with the full weight of what he did not have. He did not have a home. And now he knew it.

***

The blustering winter winds were slamming Rory Casso's

fortress of ice, bearing a bone-chilling wind, stealing between the branches and the stone. It was a kind of cold that scoops up your bones in the dice cup, rattles them around, and spills them onto the crap table. 4, 6, 8, 10: the hard way.

The fever's circular nightmares of clouds becoming bears and bears becoming people and people becoming wraiths and wraiths becoming clouds held little horror compared to the recognition that Rory was a creature set alone. With no direction home.

14

LET ME EASE THOSE TIRED SHOULDERS

For a long time Rory Casso lay above the box canyon watching as the Indian siege on the three Conestoga wagons played out. He numbered at least a half-dozen Indians holding down the wagons with gunfire, blocking the only exit to the canyon. Whosoever had escorted this train into this canyon had done a darn fool job of escorting. He could not have secured a better trap for the wagons had he mapped it out.

Studying the steep ridge that the contingent of wagons were up against, it did not take Casso long to spot the three Indians descending the rocks. Classic Indian warfare. The Indian guns blocking escape of the box canyon were holding the wagon party tight with steady gunfire, but it would be the Indians rappelling the wall behind the wagons that would do the real damage. And those Indians would be amongst the wagons in short order.

Casso overviewed his options and he didn't like the vista. He had four rough riders, the Thompson gang, dogging his trail out of Independence for the payroll that he and Juke Bauque were freighting. He had just given the gang the tumble and now he could ill afford to capitulate his position to them if they, too, were somewhere on this ridge, watching the story below unfold. And why wouldn't they be? By now they had played out his cloaked trail, and fireworks would be as good a way as any for the gang to sniff him out again.

Casso was rolling these equations around his head when he heard the boom of the big gun. It was the boom of a Remington Rolling Block Buffalo gun and it was Juke Bauque's gun. Whether he wanted a piece of this fight or not,

Casso was now obliged to come to the defense of the wagons.

Studying the situation with more urgency now, Rory Casso overviewed the quandary. There were eight Indians holding down the box canyon's entrance, with three more Indians descending the steep wall behind the wagons. This deep in the winter season would find most Indians now either wintering on reservations or encamped tight at their winter camps, their provisions stocked full for the winter. Too late for the hunt; these were not a stray hunting party of Indians. These would be warriors. Warriors of the first order. The Indians laying siege to the Conestogas below would be a collection of Cheyenne Dog Soldiers out to plunder and pillage.

Rory Casso removed his buckskin coat and rolled it on the earth in front of him to steady his gun. As Casso had left his Winchester in the care of Juke Bauque, his selection for this ambush was limited to his Colt .45 or his shotgun. Neither weapon was designed for this type of long-range discharge. He would use the shotgun, though, because its report would command more respect.

Setting his sights on the Dog Soldiers rappelling behind the Conestogas, Casso was less concerned with a kill than he was with the warning. By casting lead at the descending Indians he would serve notice twofold. First, he would let the Dog Soldiers rappelling behind the wagons know that they were discovered and that their element of surprise was compromised, and second, he would be sending a message to the rest of the attacking band to let them know that they, too, were being ambushed by some unknown adversary.

Dog Soldiers are no fools, and these messages would not need translation.

The low December sun was throwing shadows across the ravine, refracting the light. Although the closest Indian was almost upon the wagon, Casso set sights on the trailing Indian, further up the coulee's face, accommodating the shifting shadows. At this distance, with the shotgun for a weapon, Casso had no chance of hitting his mark, nor did he want to. If any shotgun pellets did reach this warrior, it would

CHAPTER FOURTEEN

wound him at best. And this was preferred, for if Casso were to kill a Dog Soldier, vengeance would then be a blood bond between the Conestogas and the Indians.

Many things need to be considered with a long shot like this. The distance, of course. Gravity. The play of the wind. And, too, whether Casso had packed the shells with enough gunpowder to power the flight of the discharge at this great a distance. These were considerations that would run swiftly through the mind of a marksman. Once considered, Rory laughed at the thought. Laughing because none of these equations matter when attack is imminent. Steadying his aim against the buckskin jacket prop, Casso let the buckshot fly.

Even as the shotgun pellets spattered dirt into the face of the trailing Dog Soldier, Rory Casso pumped the second barrel at the Indian that was closer to the wagons, missing him by a dozen feet.

When Casso's shotgun roared on the ridge overlooking the box canyon and spit dirt into the face of the advancing Dog Soldiers on the coulee wall, the Indian raid came to a quick halt. From his perch, Casso watched as the Indians on the ridge above the encampment scrambled a retreat and the Indians entrapping the box canyon below quickly melted back into the bunchgrass.

When Juke Bauque had come upon this party, he was looking for a low place to hide from the Thompson gang. And that he found. Unfortunately, a band of Dog Soldiers followed him into the coulee and right into the laps of the Mason party.

Normally, the Indians would just hold down the encampment until provisions for the train ran low and the entrapped would either surrender or starve to death. But now it was deep in the season and the Dog Soldiers were on their last hurrah in this early winter, and time was at a premium. This would be the time for the last of these Indian renegades to be in the field. And now that the Dog Soldiers were uncovered, they would be off to their wintering quarters. If Indian habit held true, this would be the last that they would see of these Dog Soldiers.

In the wagons down below Rory Casso's perch, Bronwyn, Cricket, and Hickory Dixon squinted to the ridge as they tried to determine the identity of their liberator. Juke Bauque already knew the redeemer.

But Rory Casso's shotgun reports, the reports that sent the Dog Soldiers off to their winter encampments, did not go unperceived by only the participants in this row below. Barrett Thompson's gang was now apprised of the game.

15

I'VE BEEN IN THE FLAME

These were the transformative years in the West. The time between the rule of the gun and the rule of the plow, when outposts were becoming towns and towns were on the verge of burgeoning into cities. Laws and the lawmen that enforced these laws were becoming an important equation in this transition.

Communities were evolving into more than just the keeper of the horse, the gun, and the plow. Trading posts for trappers became dry-goods stores for farmers. Bars and churches, in a constant dance for the souls of men, were being planted on opposite sides of Main Street. And schools for learning, the crowning achievement of any society, were beginning to furrow the turf.

These were the years for the final big hurrahs of the Indian Nations. These Platte River Indians were of many tribes and many temperaments, and each left its particular brand upon the expanse.

But for the outlaw, for there will forever be outlaws, the West was just another opportunity to play wild. To lay waste. And to suck at the blood-trough of the civilized man.

***

Barrett Thompson led his gang of slingers and thugs like a businessman. What outpost to lay waste, what stagecoach to assault, what Indian encampment to siege upon, these were business decisions. Killing, too, was a matter of business.

A stocky and rotund man incongruously light on his feet, Barrett Thompson viewed his gang as his business. Guns were merely inventory capital. And horses were capital. And the outlaws that Barrett Thompson surrounded himself with were also capital, to be traded in his commerce. Like a banker reviewing resumes, Thompson assembled an unsavory collection of employees to further his enterprise. Barrett Thompson was accustomed to taking what he wanted from smaller men, stealing what he wanted from smarter men, and running when he was bettered by bigger and smarter men.

Marshal Isham Mason was a bigger and smarter man, and he was now on the trail of Barrett Thompson and his band of desperados. It would be only a matter of time before Marshal Mason and his deputy, Pinto Shaw, delivered Barrett Thompson to justice. Dead or alive.

Marshal Mason, in his late forties now, was a weathered lawman with a lined and windswept face that he wore as a testament to the years he'd spent in the field and on the trail of outlaws and renegades. He would be retiring from the life of the lawman in short order and had already laid stake to a small farm outside of Rawlings where he and his wife could retire. He would become a subsistence farmer while his wife and daughter opened the first-ever school for the children of Rawlings. Mason had been an intrinsic part of civilizing this corner of the West, and he was now looking forward to being an intrinsic part of educating the next generation of Westerners.

As a lifelong tracker of men, Mason was confident

CHAPTER FIFTEEN

in his ability in capturing, or, if need be, killing Barrett Thompson. It was just a matter of will. That being said, Marshal Isham Mason was a man of caution. He understood the game afield and when he tucked into the track of Barrett Thompson's gang, it was not without some care and cunning.

Deputy Pinto Shaw was an opposite cut of Marshal Isham Mason. An enthusiastic young man, fresh of the East, come to stake his personal claim on the adventure that was the West. He was studied on a quick draw that he held great hopes of exhibiting. Pinto Shaw looked and smelled of the East. He especially smelled of the East. His clothes were store-cut and crisp. His artillery yet had the sheen of fresh oil and his livery was untested to these rocks. Pinto Shaw was the type of a young man that seeks adventure at all costs. And costing all is the usual result.

Mason's employment of Pinto Shaw was more for expedience than for experience, as rare was the man that desired any part of Barrett Thompson's legend. For Pinto Shaw, this was the type of legend that he came west to address. And Pinto Shaw was the type of green that could be trouble.

Marshal Mason and Deputy Shaw had tucked into a warm Thompson track three days running and were following it through the rolling foothills in the eastern shadows of the Rockies.

The Thompson gang, numbering a dozen men, was leaving a wide track for Mason and Pinto Shaw. This excited Deputy Shaw, as he was eager to try his mettle against the Thompson gang. But the Marshal was unnerved. This was a wide and clear-cut track that was being laid to be followed. This was the track of a businessman with a plan.

As the trail warmed, Pinto Shaw double-checked the chambers of his gun and lashed his holster tight to his thigh in excited anticipation.

In piqued wariness, Marshal Isham Mason slowed the stalk.

***

Marshal Mason had reason to know most of the men riding with Barrett Thompson. Mason was not a man that wanted to kill another man but he knew that Thompson's men held no such scruple. Save for the slinger, Farrot Pierce, he doubted that the men of the Thompson gang liked to kill, but they would kill. And they would kill with no regrets.

The men who rode with Thompson were an ugly collection of desperados and crooks held together by the wits and cunning of Barrett Thompson and the Colts of the gunslinger, Farrot Pierce. They were dirt-hardened and gun-savvy. And they were hungry.

Where Barrett Thompson was a calculating businessman, Farrot Piece was the intangible wild card. Quick to draw leather, Pierce had gained the reputation of a hothead throwing hot lead. And if Pierce were the type of slinger to notch his gun handle for every man he killed, he'd be down to a stub for a handle. Although he was quick on the draw, he was quicker to the kill. For Farrot Pierce was not averse to shooting a man in the back.

Marshal Mason had noted the collection of scoundrels that rounded out the Thompson gang. Hideous men with ugly reputations. Men like Kelly Bank, built like a bull ox with a disposition of a wolverine, had scars up and down his arms from setting blaze to a settler's homestead on a

CHAPTER FIFTEEN

dare. Jim Patterson, whose sharp, angular face gave no quarter to humor and whose hard and high cheekbones could cut glass. Billy Hager and Tanner Croft and Swill Durago collected among the other lesser-reputed hombres under the organization of Barrett Thompson. Lesser hombres, but the lead is lead no matter whose gun is spitting it.

The Thompson gang knew that Marshal Isham Mason was on their trail, and they knew his reputation. They were none too keen to confront this hunter.

"I'm jes' suggestin' that we might fare a mite better'n if we split this 'ere pack up," Billy Hager challenged Thompson.

Ever since they had discovered that Marshal Mason was on their trail, Billy Hager had been pushing to split up the Thompson gang, and Barrett Thompson was getting tired of hearing about it.

Thompson rolled his cigar butt from one end of his fat jowls to the other. "And I'm jes' suggestin' thet I don' care what the hell you think. My idear is thet there is safety in numbers and my idear is how it will be played."

Billy Hager opened his mouth to offer the umpteenth objection when Thompson finally got tired of the banter. Drawing his rotund figure into Hager, Thompson stuck his face into the smaller Hager's chin. "You'll be shut of thet idear or I'll be shut of you."

By way of habit, as Thompson leaned into him, Billy Hager slid his hand over his holstered Colt .45. The movement and meaning were not lost on the men.

First wonder, then anger, and finally humor rolled over Barrett Thompson's big face. Stepping back, he looked up and down; first to Hager's gun hand and then up to Hager's face. Finally Thompson settled his glare into Billy's eyes.

Pulling the cigar from his mouth, Thompson shared a sickly smile with Billy Hager. "Ha, thet there's a good one. Ya think ya got the nuggets to throw some lead with me?"

A quiet settled on the outlaws' camp. Somewhere the low, plaintive song of a Say's Phoebe moaned, "Phee-uer, phee-uer," and Farrot Pierce eased himself from the crux of the tree in which he was leaning, freeing his gun hand.

Billy Hager was in a bind now and he knew it. Quickly he diverted eye contact with the portly man. Flitting his eyes about the camp, Billy Hager tried to grasp an eye connection with the other men that were now bunched and witnessing this exchange. But there were no eyes that accepted his appeal. Even if others might agree, Billy Hager was standing alone, and he knew it.

Wanting no part in this dance, Billy Hager shrugged his shoulders only slightly so that his movement would not be mistaken for a play on his gun. "Now. Now, hold on a minute, boss, I ain' a sayin' thet . . ."

Now in full and ugly humor, Thompson's wicked sneer cut him off. "What are you sayin', exactly?"

In full retreat, Hager absentmindedly held up empty hands. "I guess I'm tryin' ta agree wit' however you want to play it, is all."

Barrett Thompson let this triumph of intimidation hang in the air. Again working the cigar around his mouth, he studied Billy Hager.

Billy Hager had been a sore spot with Thompson's outlaw collection for some time now. Behind cold eyes, Barrett Thompson weighed the loss of a gunner in his gang's artillery against the need to assert authority. Thompson considered how Billy Hager could best serve Thompson's business plan. Looking into Hager's face,

CHAPTER FIFTEEN

Thompson spoke out of the opposite side of his mouth that housed his cigar. But he was speaking to Farrot Pierce. "What'a ya think, Pierce? Think this hombre should hang wit' the gang or should we cut him loose to the trail?"

Having slid clear of the tree, Farrot Pierce relaxed, his legs splayed comfortably. A slinger's stance.

"No, no no," Hager quickly protested, waving his hands in front of him for emphasis. He was happy for a reason to take his hands away from his guns. "Yer the boss. I'm behind yer call."

Barrett Thompson was enjoying the little man's squirming and milked his response. "Wahl then, I guess we kin call ourselves square, then."

This brought obvious relief to Billy Hager, and with a nervous laugh he emptied his lungs in deep breath. "'N thet's jes' fine, boss, 'cause I never meant no offense," and he stretched out his skinny little hand.

Ignoring the hand at first, Thompson continued, "Even so, I 'spect it might be time fer you to move on."

Nobody walked away from a Barrett Thompson camp, and Billy Hager knew this.

Thompson looked at the hopeful hand that Hager had extended, and then he looked into the face of the frightened little man. Again, a sick sneer broke halfway across Thompson's face, pushing the cigar to the edge as he took the little man's hand. "Why sure, pard, I guess we are all squared up now. Thet said, it's time you pack your plunder and clack your horse to the trail."

Billy Hager's nervous smile dissolved from his face. "Sure. Sure, boss. I'll git. I'll collect my wages . . ."

"Wages? You want your wages?"

This was the end of the line for Billy Hager and Billy Hager knew it. A gray acceptance shadowed his face, and his eyes glazed as he looked over Barrett Thompson's shoulder into the rolling hills beyond. If Billy's life was flashing before his eyes it was an uncomely vista, for Hager's face registered a resigned angst.

And Farrot Pierce shot Billy Hager in the back.

***

Forming a posse is easy; holding one together is another matter.

For the most part, a posse is made up of local townsfolk. Farmers and shop owners and blacksmiths and barkeeps that eventually need to return to their place in society. Sometimes the lawman can get a stipend for the squad, sometimes not. It all depends on how badly the government wants the outlaw. But even if a stipend or reward is available, it doesn't account for the crops or the business that is lost in the time that the farmers and shop owners are on the trail.

What started out as a posse of ten men strong pursuing the Thompson gang had dwindled down to eight. Then to four. Now, two weeks deep into Thompson's trail, it was left to Marshal Isham Mason and Deputy Pinto Shaw to bring home the quarry.

Young and brash, Deputy Pinto Shaw was a shining example of the glorified legends of lawmen that he had read about in the newspapers and books back in the civilized world of the East. Manicured in the style and the study of a gunslinger, Pinto Shaw had practiced the slickness of his gun draw habitually, collecting "oohs" and "ahs" from the folks back east. And sideways ridicule from the Western man.

Just having the two of them, the Marshal and the Deputy, on the hunt gave some pause to Marshal Mason,

CHAPTER FIFTEEN

but he was not one to let a trail run cold, no matter the odds.

Mason and Shaw had discovered the Thompson gang's tracks a full week before the Marshal designed their strike. The summer was hot and dry and the trail had lain clean, but the lawmen were outnumbered a dozen men to two and Marshal Mason would need to plan carefully if he and the deputy were to make a successful roundup. It was a long week of study for Deputy Shaw, as he was most anxious to test his hardware on the desperados.

The lawmen had been surreptitiously studying the general direction of the band's campaign and had set their mark on intercepting the Thompson gang at the wall of a rock outcropping that Mason had scouted. It was a crux of stone where cover would be light for the Thompson gang, and the two well-directed guns of Mason and Shaw could readily cage them in. This conceived ambush would mean either surrender for the band of outlaws or easy pickings for lawmen. Either end game would be satisfactory for Marshal Isham Mason.

The trap was designed to ensnare the Thompson gang in a compromised position in the lawmen's crossfire. To intercept the gang, Mason positioned Deputy Shaw high up the rock wall, opposite Thompson's squad, with a panoramic view of the outlaws' assemblage. With Pinto Shaw's Winchester rifle above, this turret would provide Shaw with ample overview, keeping the gang held tight to barely a few yards of dirt and stone. Chagrined at not being allowed the opportunity to sling his .45s, Pinto Shaw dug into the stronghold.

With Pinto Shaw holding the Thompson gang tight to the rocks, Marshal Mason would make his way below the bevy to either negotiate their surrender or, if need be, gun-smoke them out. Mason's position offered a much more precarious perspective than Shaw's. Where Shaw could pick off the gang members one by one as they showed their heads, Mason did not enjoy the overview's advantage and, without Deputy Shaw holding the gang tight to the rocks, would be easy pickings for the gang. But this was a tried and true method for the Marshal, and he felt comfortable in knowing that, eventually, the Thompson gang would recognize the futility of their predicament. Or die trying to refute it.

That was the plan, simple enough, except for the one contingency that Mason had not accounted for.

Mason positioned himself to put the Thompson gang into his and Deputy Shaw's crossfire. Once the trap was set, the Marshal fired off a warning round and called out the terms of Barrett Thompson's surrender.

"You can chuck your guns or die with them in your fists. Makes no matter to me."

The Marshal's offer was met with a hail of gunfire, to which Mason rejoined. The problem was that there was no overlapping gunfire from Pinto's overview. Because of this, Mason found himself under a withering hail of artillery assault from the dozen guns in Thompson's party. The rock Mason was employing for cover was being blistered with munitions, slashing his face with rock shards.

Even as Mason brooded on Pinto's whereabouts, Pinto Shaw was crawling, knee over hand, hand over knee, down to the Marshal's placement below the Thompson gang.

Mason watched Pinto Shaw in bewilderment, and then disgust, as he crawled up to join the Marshal in this compromised position. "What in the hell are you doing here?"

CHAPTER FIFTEEN

The young and eager Shaw was all smiles. "This seemed to be where the action was, 'n I thought I'd get me a fair piece of thet Thompson gang."

There's green, and then there's stupid. Marshal Mason cursed himself for not recognizing just how green, and stupid, Deputy Pinto Shaw was. This omission would be his final blunder.

With no interning fire to confine the Thompson gang's guns, it was short order before the Thompson boys were able to outflank the lawmen, beating them back with a wall of gunfire. Even so, the trapped Mason, fighting like a caged animal, managed to more than halve the number of the Thompson company before the Marshal and Deputy Shaw were driven over the edge of a cliff, permanently silencing Marshal Isham Mason's guns.

When Barrett Thompson, Farrot Pierce, Kelly Bank, and Jim Patterson reached the site of Mason's last stand, these four outlaws were all that remained of a gang that had once numbered a dozen.

Eighty feet below the cliff where the outlaws now stood lay the body of a bloody and broken man in a red plaid shirt. Marshal Isham Mason.

With the taste of blood of the fight yet on the outlaws' tongues, Pierce, Bank, and Patterson poured lead into the crumpled, lifeless red plaid shirt.

16

STOKIN' THE FIRE

Casso lay quiet on the ridge. The Conestogas below were still and the Indians had retreated. The Dog Soldiers, being outflanked, were of little concern now, for they would have been looking for an easy mark this late in the season. And this party of wagons and women had proven itself to be anything but easy.

But the outlaws sniffing the trail of the Reynolds Savings and Loan payroll were another matter.

Knowing that the Thompson gang was in the field and hunting up the payroll that Juke and he were freighting was a bear for thought. Not only had Juke, apparently in the wagons below, given up his position with the booming Buffalo gun, Casso had likewise divulged his own post.

It was warm and restful as Rory Casso lay in the late November sun. The cottonwoods and box elders in the box canyon below him were just about bare of their leaves, leaving just their naked arms to reach up in worship to the heavens above. From this perch Casso could discern the entire layout of the Conestogas' compromised position.

Movement below betrayed three, maybe four people in the wagon collective. A small contingent to push three wagons across this Western wildness. As he analyzed the cluster below, flashing red flit among the outfit. Long and wild red hair? Rory Casso had known a girl in Rawlings with long and wild red hair. Could it be? His heart stilled as his study focused on the red mane waving amongst the Conestogas. But what could bring Bronwyn Mason to these innermost reaches of these territories?

The wagons were trapped tight against the back wall of the box canyon. The cut of the canyon was deep and narrow and the back wall would not allow a wagon's ascension. Two guns at the mouth of this ravine would easily be able to block any exit, and a gun on each overlooking wall would make life miserable for the quarry trapped below. Four guns would be all that was needed to tie down this contingent. And the Thompson gang offered just that complement.

The gun battle that had just transpired between this train and the Indians would have alerted the Thompson gang to their position. If the train had any chance to clear this box canyon's trap, they would need to move swiftly. Rory Casso pushed himself up from his comfortable lookout and swung into Rockwell's leather. Now would not be the time for these Conestogas to dally in this entrapment.

Whosoever had led these Conestogas to fort up in this placement had done this wagon train no favors.

***

After Bronwyn Mason tossed Jack Bettle and Kipper Dunn from the drive, the numbers of the wagon train were down to three. Bronwyn Mason, Cricket Wynot, and the trail boss, Hickory Dixon, were the remaining contingent. And it soon became apparent that two women and a besotted old man would not be enough to drive three big Conestogas across this Western expanse.

Hickory Dixon may have been a little free with tipping the bottle, but he was not a stupid man. It was decided that he and the women would have to let the Conestogas winter alone while they saddled up the wagon breeds and pushed on to Cheyenne. It was just getting too late in the season for any hope of driving this train through to Rawlings by way of Cheyenne. They would deposit the Conestogas into this box canyon and tie them down for the winter, securing the school's cargo as best they could until a late spring rescue.

Having tied down the wagons side by side, and stretching

CHAPTER SIXTEEN

tight the canvas to cover them, they would let the wagons winter in this coulee. The next order of business would be to assemble the stock, food, and ammunition, and strap it tight to the saddles of the wagon ponies. And then to scurry on to Cheyenne.

***

Steering Rockwell down the edge of the ravine, Casso took inventory of the layout. Three wagons and four guns spitting fire out of the encampment at the Indians, and one of the guns was Juke's Rolling Block Buffalo gun.

Coming out to meet Casso's horse now was Juke Bauque and a woman. The woman was tall and redheaded and she was wearing men's trousers. She wore her Smith & Wesson Pocket .32 in a holster across her abdomen and held a Winchester in the crux of her arm. This was Bronwyn Mason.

As Rory Casso swung down from his horse, Bronwyn ran to clasp him like the old friends that they were. Her face flushed as she looked into his face, and Casso matched her flush for flush. Their embrace began in their arms and extended into tomorrow. In the enthusiasm of the embrace, Rory kissed Bronwyn on her lips. This was the first-ever kiss for Bronwyn Mason and Rory Casso, and Juke and Cricket bore witness to it. This kiss surprised Bronwyn and Rory, as they had never broached these feelings before. But it felt natural. And it felt right.

It had been years since Rory Casso and Bronwyn Mason had last met. And Bronwyn marveled at how, in the intervening years, Rory Casso's body had hardened into that of a man. When Rory had dropped from Rockwell, Bronwyn had noted the strong and sturdy man in buckskin leather, wide in the shoulders and angled slender to the hip. And as she embraced Rory, she could feel the hard and muscular man that he had become. She noted that Rory Casso's scent, too, was different. It was yet the same sweet sweat that Rory carried as a child, playing their silly childhood games in the dirt of Rawlings, but now Rory bore the husky musk of a man. Holding Rory, after lo these many years, Bronwyn felt a surging in the lower reaches of her body. It was a bubbling surge like a river in a full spring torrent. And it was not an unpleasant surge.

There were many ways that Bronwyn could have recognized Rory Casso as he rode into camp that day. She could have recognized him by his long and wavy hair slapping at the air. Or she could have recognized him by his piercing blue eyes. Even the way that he set astride Rockwell, Rory Casso was of singular stature. But Bronwyn recognized Rory like she had always recognized Rory: by the peculiar hunger she got deep within her breast whenever he was around. It was a woman's hunger that she'd felt even as they were children splashing the muddy streets of Rawlings. It was a hunger that transcended their young age. A hunger that transcended time. And now, as Rory dropped down from his perch on the ravine's ridge and into camp, Bronwyn felt this hunger again.

Stepping back from their embrace, Rory Casso let his eyes take in the full stature of Bronwyn, and he was not unimpressed. "My, my, you are not the skinny little ragamuffin that I remember. You seem to have given new meaning to the design of the dungaree."

Bronwyn brought her sun-glazed freckles to the fore with a blush from underneath. Slapping his shoulder in mock chide, she admonished, "My designing dungarees are my business, Mister," as they shared an awkward laugh.

They may have stood there the afternoon long, in that status of new appreciation, if not for the warm baritone breaking the spell. "My sense is that you two might know each other," Juke Bauque ventured with a smile.

With the resonance of Juke's voice, the outside world intruded into their moment, and they flushed as they relaxed their squeeze. This candid clinch was the first acknowledgement to each other, and to the world at large, of

CHAPTER SIXTEEN

their newly discovered feelings for one another. Keeping an arm around each other's waist, they opened their embrace, as one, to the world.

Following Juke and Bronwyn out from the wagons, Hickory Dixon and Cricket Wynot joined the reunion. It was Cricket that spoke first. "I suppose that this is that Rory Casso boy that you've been telling of."

Blushing, Bronwyn commenced with the introductions. "Yes. This is Rory Casso. Rory, this is Cricket Wynot, she's going to be the new schoolteacher in Rawlings."

"How do, Miss."

"And this is Hickory Dixon. He's our wagon pilot." Rory Casso gave a quick study of Hickory Dixon, up and down. And Casso was not enchanted with the vista.

The glow of Rory and Bronwyn's reunion was waning as the thought of the trapped wagons jumped to the forefront of Rory's mind. "You led these wagons into this snare?"

"Tain't all his fault, Rory. We had some bad boys pushing these wagons with us and I needed to kick them to the trail," Bronwyn intercepted.

With the Thompson gang foremost in his thoughts, Rory urged, "We need to collect these wagons and be quit of this basin in the quick."

Juke Bauque assured him, "The wagons are strapped down for the winter. This party'll be running on horses for the rest of the jump to Rawlings."

Rory Casso digested this information quickly. "Then run they must. And they must run now."

Hickory Dixon, sliding his mouth to the corner of his face, queried, "But we got shut of the Indians. I don't 'spect they'll be back."

"It's not the Indians that are the issue now. It's the Thompson gang."

The mention of Barrett Thompson and his band of renegades sobered Rory and Bronwyn's reunion. Now thoughts of Bronwyn's father, Isham Mason, came to the fore.

Rory had caught the flinch in Bronwyn's face at the memory of her father. "I sure was sorry to hear about your pap, Bronwyn. He was a good marshal and he was a better man."

The memory of Marshal Mason's demise stained Bronwyn's face, and she held on to Rory's waist a little tighter. "I do thank you for that. You know my pap held great esteem for you."

"And I for him. After my own pap passed, he was 'bout the best compass a boy could have to set his bearing to. Don't 'spect anybody will ever match him stride for stride."

In the manner of her father, Bronwyn set her jaw to the future. "I expect not. But now I worry about Mama. I need to get back to Rawlings and the homestead."

The mention of the Thompson gang furrowed Hickory Dixon's brow and brought his mouth back from the edge of his face and into a tight grimace. "Barrett Thompson's gang? You think thet Thompson's gang is somewhere on our tail?"

Rory Casso again turned his study on the trail boss, Hickory Dixon, still not appreciating the depiction. "Thompson's out there somewhere, to be sure. And time is stunted."

***

It was chilled in the box canyon in this early December as the sun rose late over its eastern wall and set early over its western wall. But the cottonwood deadfall in the chasm provided plenty of tinder and, as they were already discovered, they could enjoy as hearty a flame as they hankered. Except for meat, they were gravy with provisions, as the wagon train was packed for a three-month journey and they were barely two months down the road. And munitions, too, were copious with ball and powder. The box canyon itself was a good fort up as the walls would be hard to traverse, and the sole way in, the canyon's mouth, could be comfortably covered by the Winchesters.

CHAPTER SIXTEEN 129

But Rory Casso knew that as solid a fort as this box canyon provided, eventually, when provisions ran low, it would be just as solid a trap.

There were five of them now, sitting around the warm fire with hot coffee. Casually, Juke Bauque sat facing the coulee's aperture, with his big Buffalo gun resting easy on the log beside him. Rory Casso was analyzing the box canyon's back wall. The wall was steep, with minimum cover. A moccasinned Indian could scale this barrier, but could a man with steed?

Cricket had positioned herself next to Juke and her glow betrayed her arousal. Filling Juke Bauque's cup, "How does a Black Indian come about with such a deep education?"

Juke nodded a thanks for the refilled cup. "Luck of the draw, is all, I guess. My pap, a smart Choctaw, knew he would lose his land when the Choctaw Nation ceded their farms in the Treaty of Dancing Rabbits. So he sold out first, becoming rich in the process. Sent me north to Boston where my color didn't always dictate my station."

"What happened to your pap?"

Pain crinkled the corners of Juke Bauque's eyes. "He died fighting for the Confederates."

"He died fighting for slavery?"

Smiling at the incongruity, "Yep. Like most of the Choctaw tribe, he believed in slavery. He had a mite bit of turmoil inside, trying to reconcile it with his slave wife and his half-breed son."

Though experienced in the way of a woman's body, Cricket was young in the ways of the heart. And young hearts are quick to reach out and grasp when they have been tugged. Cricket's infatuation with Juke Bauque was wearing her smile out. "And now you're a shotgun freighter poet?"

Juke Bauque's warm laughter echoed deep in the well of his black ancestry. "Well, I never thought of it much like that, hon." Juke Bauque used the word "hon" as a familial salutation: Cricket took it to heart. "Kind of hard to wrap myself around the notion of me being a shotgun freighter. Or a poet for that matter."

"But you're pushing that payroll. And your poetry is so beautiful."

Ever since Juke and Cricket's first encounter, when Cricket had lain bare-breasted on the saloon floor in Independence and Juke had come to her rescue, she had held a steaming regard for him. And his voice. And his poetry. When happenstance had landed him in her camp in these outer reaches of wilderness, her inner world turned the tumult of a young lady coming of age. New and strange emotions were stirring deep within the young woman, and misting regions in her that heretofore had only been used and abused. In the thirty-six hours that Juke Bauque had been in the box canyon's camp, Cricket had pestered him to share his poetry with her. For Cricket, Juke's sonorous voice and clever smithing of words resonated from the walls of this ravine and filled an emptiness within her breast that she was not even aware she held. She would be willing to be ensnared in this winter's confine with Juke only for forever.

Happy for the audience, Juke Bauque accommodated the pretty girl. "Well, I guess I do push payroll, so there is that, and I do thank you for the kindly words about my poetry. I'm touched that you enjoy it."

***

It was cold but it was clear: the sky fetching tall and billowing clouds, slowly shape-shifting for the amusement of dreamers. It was the kind of sky that invited fantasy and fancies. Rory Casso watched as the clouds drifted and he envisioned walls of sanctuary and towers of security. The mouth of this box canyon was flat and fertile and the canyon's spring water ran clear and true. His imagination conjured a cabin, a home, at the canyon's mouth, with crops in the valley and grazing cattle on the bench above. This little cut of earth would give every stroke of homeland.

Home? Is a home in the brick and in mortar? Is a home

CHAPTER SIXTEEN

in the people that surround a body? As a child, Rory Casso did not know a home of brick and mortar, and the only home of people was the company of a drunken father and the pity of the townsfolk.

Was his time with the Hunkpapa tiyospe home? Yes. And no. He could move and speak and eat and hunt with the Hunkpapa, but everywhere was the reminder that he was of a different breed. An outsider seeking asylum. The Hunkpapa were good to him, but they would never be family. Time with the Hunkpapa was voyeuristic and, as it would be, as it should be, it was limited to the margins of the tribe.

As the towering clouds rolled above, offering new vistas and new dreams with every tuck and turn, Casso shook himself away from the netherworld of the cumulus and refocused his attentions on the task at hand. For Rory Casso, home was a blissful vision in the clouds, but in this winter chasm lay the trap of life or death. With some melancholy, Casso shook loose from the clouds' fantasy of a home and turned his attention to this present predicament.

Squatting on his haunches at the base of the box canyon's wall, Rory Casso turned his study to the coulee's barrier. He scrutinized the box canyon's cut and the way the ridges would play along the crag's face. He had witnessed the Dog Soldiers sliding down the wall, and he'd witnessed them scurrying up the wall when he threw lead at them. But moccasinned Indians scaling this precipitous wall was one thing. Five fugitives on horseback clambering up the impasse was another matter.

As he crouched there surveying the trace, Bronwyn drew up with a cup of hot coffee. "Coffee's not good, but there's plenty of it."

Rory Casso accepted the coffee, glad for the company. Glad for Bronwyn's company. "You never could make much of a cup of coffee, nohow."

There was much that was familiar in their relationship. It was a familiarity, and a comfortableness, that began in their fused childhood, playing the dusty streets of Rawlings like a game. They had read great works of literature together, shuddering over campfires at the horrors of an Edgar Allan Poe series while anxiously waiting for the next newspaper, bearing Poe's next installment. They had skinny-dipped together in the cold summer rivers of the high deserts, attired in the innocence of the young and bare bodies of childhood, before the fuzz of puberty had come between them. Bronwyn knew the dysfunction of Rory Casso's father and the scars it had wrought on the young man. And even deeper than that bond, Rory Casso knew that she knew of his scars and she accepted him as he was, blemishes and all.

The childhood they shared was wider than any miles that could come between them.

"It's a good idear about the school you and your mama will be settin' up in Rawlings. You're pap would be happy."

With the mention of her father, the slightest sadness tugged at Bronwyn's temple. Rory Casso caught the sadness of Bronwyn's ache and he encouraged her, "I sure was saddened to hear about your pap."

Bronwyn had needed someone to talk to about her loss. Someone that would understand. And she did not miss her opportunity. The pain, the anger, the denial of her loss all came flooding to the fore, and her eyes spilled with the pent-up grief. Rory wrapped his arms around her, pulling her deep into him, and let her have at it. Bronwyn cried and she cried and she cried. Deep and terrible sobs. Torrential sobs of sorrow's loss. Rory Casso held her fast as she spilled her heartache.

When Bronwyn's deep sobbing finally subsided, Casso offered, "Sometimes death is like a gift."

"A gift?"

Ever so gently, Rory touched Bronwyn's breast, over her heart. "Sometimes you don't know how deeply you can feel about something until you lose it. When you lose that something, it cuts deep. The deeper the cut, the more your love. Your pap's loss may be just about the deepest cut you will ever know."

"Maybe."

"And maybe that's the last gift he gives you. Now you know just how deeply you can love."

"It's a pretty deep cut all right."

"Yes."

Silence now engulfed Rory and Bronwyn and they set like that, folded together in each other's arms, tight against the world.

***

"Sad that these books and supplies won't be making it to Rawlings," and she indicated the tied-down wagons.

"Never you mind that. They're tied down tight and they'll be there for a spring rescue." And indicating the rock face before them, "Right now, that piece of stone there is our snag."

The two of them, Bronwyn Mason and Rory Casso, squatted in quiet contemplation at the ravine's wall, sipping on the bad coffee. Rory appraising the box canyon's steep barrier. And Bronwyn appraising the stalwart man that Rory Casso had become.

Finally, Bronwyn broke the meditation. "Do you think that we can saddle back up that wall?"

Rory Casso had not only this study of the wall; he had also reviewed the buttress when the Dog Soldiers were negotiating its precipices. "I think there is a way, but I'll need closer study. There're two problems. The wall, of course, and then there's knowing that it will need to be surmounted in the cover of darkness. That'll make a shaky scramble for the horses."

Bronwyn now turned her attention from the man and overlooked the coulee's enclosure. "Can't be jumped in the daylight?"

"Not likely. Not enough cover. We'd be easy pickins for Barrett Thompson's party."

There is a rhythm of voice when a mother speaks to a

child. And there is another rhythm in the cadence when a friend speaks to a friend. Another in the challenge of enemy to enemy. Somewhere along their history, Bronwyn Mason and Rory Casso had begun speaking to the rhythm of lovers.

"I'm more easy now that you will be accompanying us," offered Bronwyn, and she rested her hand on Rory's thigh as they squatted before the precipice before them.

And Rory Casso covered Bronwyn's hand with his own. "Big wall before us."

"But a big wall behind us, I think."

These are the moments when commitments are made. When promises are promised and contracts are signed. And nuptials are exchanged, not in the script of legalese, but, rather, at the convergence of a specific point in time and space and spirit. In the way of a man, Rory Casso knew this, and, in the way of a woman, Bronwyn Mason felt this. But as the couple communed in this prospect of a future as one, a rifle blast splintered the tree's branch over their heads and sent the limbs and leaves bouncing to the rocks at their feet.

A hoarfrost voice now called from the coulee's breach, "We'll take the money and the women. No negotiatin'." It was Barrett Thompson.

17

WOMB TO TOMB

Rory Casso's backtracking and trail obfuscation had left Barrett Thompson's gang lost and confused. The collection of banditos had spent the better part of a day scouting a wider and wider circle in hopes of baring Casso's track. To no avail.

The Thompson brood had resigned itself to losing the track of Rory Casso somewhere to the stone when they chanced to cross the fresh tracks of a pair of riders. Believing that they might be the tracks of Rory Casso connecting up with Juke Bauque, and the Reynolds Savings and Loan payroll, they tucked in to that trail. And it did not take the Thompson gang long to overcome the two riders that were leaving the trace.

Jack Bettle and Kipper Dunn were of ill humor when they rendezvoused with Barrett Thompson and his band of outlaws. They were cold, they were hungry, and they were bereft of their armaments. Kipper Dunn was, furthermore, bereft of an ear.

Slapping the thigh of his horse-bowed legs, Kelly Bank was in full humor. "So, thet Bronwyn girl jes' kicked ya to the trail...

"Warn't like thet, she kinda got the drop on us is all." Jack Bettle was defensive and shamed, and his pockmarks seemed to deepen in the shadows of a blush.

"And without yer iron, ta boot." Jimmy Patterson had joined in on the fun.

Kipper Dunn, gingerly touching the remnants of his ear, "Hoot if you will, now, but thet filly's got some measure of account to tally. Lend me yer gun and I'll show you the reckonin'."

"Don't know if we kin afford to let thet girl take one of our guns from you." This brought a rowdy round of rolling guffaws from the outlaws.

The deeper in contemplation, the more Barrett Thompson's cigar would rotate from one corner of his mouth to the other. And right now the cigar was rolling like a log on a snowmelt river. Being a humorless businessman, Barrett Thompson wanted only the details of the Mason party and their plunder. He wanted merely to assess the value of the wagon train and the upside and the downside to the enterprise of commandeering it. As Bettle and Dunn laid out the train's capital, Thompson was little impressed. What good would a trainload of schoolbooks be to an outlaw?

But Jack Bettle was in the disposition of revenge. He wanted to find the Mason train, and Bronwyn in particular, and exact an ugly revenge for his and Kipper Dunn's humiliation.

"Don't 'spect it'd be worth a bother for the little pickins we could tweak outta thet train," Thompson measured. Even the act of thinking made the fat businessman sweat, and Thompson wiped the beads from his brow. Just as quickly, Thompson's forehead trickled sweat again.

Jack Bettle pressed his case. "The women alone are of a mite heap of capital out 'ere. Ya got yer professional kitty in thet Cricket gal an' if you like yer meat fresh, thet Bronwyn is ripe fer the market."

Droplets of sweat were playing at the tips of Thompson's eyebrows. But Thompson was not convinced. "The payout is a tad suspect ta start pushing the slave trade."

"And Bronwyn is a Mason woman," Bettle pressed.

This brought Barrett Thompson's cigar to a standstill and coaxed more sweat to his brow.

"Ya hear thet, boss?" Kelly Bank was now in this argument. "Thet girl's of the Mason brood what took out more'n half of this 'ere gang."

CHAPTER SEVENTEEN

Calculating quickly, "Revenge don' pay no bills." Barrett Thompson was a businessman and appropriation was a business decision. If the gain didn't reckon the loss, it wasn't a gain worth pursuing. "If'n we are scoutin' fer anything, it will be scoutin' fer those shotgun freighters and thet Reynolds payroll."

With Bettle and Dunn joining the brood, Thompson's gang now numbered half a dozen men. Men that took the bounty of a woman on these desolate plains at a premium, and with Bettle and Dunn's portrayal of the women, loins had been stirred amongst the gang. Even so, Barrett Thompson's decision was the finish in this band, and he was not convinced that the booty of the Mason train was booty enough. And he had Farrot Pierce's gun to back him.

But this debate and this decision were squelched tight when they heard the gunfire. It was gunfire from some distance north and there was plenty of it.

All attention now turned to the direction of the shootout. Every head tilted first this way and then that way in an effort to identify the exact location of the sound of the gunfire. All heads tilted, that is, except for the head with the singular ear of Kipper Dunn.

It was apparent that many rifles were now dueling it out in a fierce firefight. Many of the rifles popped with the clutter of second-rate gunpowder. Indians. But some of the rifles had the clean pop of top-shelf Winchesters. White men. As the Thompson gang sat there trying to read the story in the artillery, a distinct and big boom roared from a Buffalo gun. A Remington Rolling Block Buffalo gun.

Farrot Pierce was the first to put the word to the thought. "I 'spect we might wanna check this'n out."

Calculating, calculating, calculating, "I 'spect we might," was all Barrett Thompson needed to add.

***

The box canyon was proving to be a solid fort but this

entrapment would not hold forever. A play would have to be made.

"Seems to me we've got two options here," Juke offered. "We can saddle up the wagon horses and make a run at the gang with guns a-blazin'. Maybe if'n we get lucky we bust our way through."

But Rory Casso rejoined, "Don't like that. With us bouncing on our horses and them sitting cozy like in the rocks, why, they jest pick us off like a fowl on a fence."

Cricket put in, "We could try to run the breach with one of the wagons for cover."

"Thet would only last as long as it took to drop the lead horse, and then that pen would be tighter than this here wall."

"Yep," and Juke turned his attention to the steep wall at the back of the ravine that they were held tight against. "Then I suppose all's we got left is this crag 'ere, an' it don't look none too inviting."

The rock face appeared insurmountable, with abrupt edges, precipitous angles, and little cover. With the winter stripping the foliage of its color, the crag took on the look of a gray prison wall.

"Of course, there is one more option we need ta consider." This was the first time that Hickory Dixon had spoken since his liquor had run out the day before. Already his shaking hands were showing the signs of his withdrawal. "We kin always try to parley with Thompson."

Bronwyn spit her reply. "You heard Thompson, no negotiating, no deals."

"I understand thet's what he said, but, you must admit, options be a bit limited right now." Dixon was trying to hold steady through the withdrawal tremors.

Bronwyn's hand unconsciously rested on the Pocket .32 holstered on her belt. "That just ain't an option."

Even in his alcohol withdrawal, the placement of Bronwyn's gun hand did not go undetected by Dixon. Nor anybody else.

CHAPTER SEVENTEEN

Rory Casso stepped between them. "Nope, Dixon, there ain't no bargaining with thet Barrett Thompson. They want the Reynolds Savings and Loan payroll and they want the women. And neither is up for barter." And then Casso turned his attention back to the precipice that loomed over the party. "But there might be some negotiating with thet stone," and Casso squinted in his study of the rock face.

Juke Bauque studied the crest with Casso. "Do you really think there is a way of clambering up that wall?"

In distracted absorption, Casso answered, "Got to be. It's all we got." As he scrutinized the barrier, "And tonight I'll bear it out."

The Mason party was running short on patience and the weather was threatening a turn for the worse.

"Tonight I'll track my way up the wall."

Juke was not especially confident. "It'll be a dark night pickin' along those stones with the cloud cover a-buildin'."

"I'druther be stumblin' through the dark than a fixed target for the Thompson gang's amusement."

***

When Rory Casso took to the escarpment blocking the Mason party's retreat, it was a cold and late night, with little light from the clouded sky. As is the bent of the sun in these deep canyons, the sun set early over the high western ridge and the dark had settled fast.

Not quite able to lift her eyes to look into Rory's, Bronwyn advised, "Take care your step. I don't want to have to catch you tumbling back on us."

Rory smiled at that. "I could think of a heap worse things than falling into your arms." And this brought a smile to both of their eyes.

Turning to Juke, he said, "You set wary of the coulee's mouth. I don't 'spect that Thompson will make a play, he knows that he's got this canyon hemmed tight, but there's no account of how eager he might be to close this snare."

Juke Bauque was looking past Rory and onto the wall that he would be challenging. "What's your play when you breech thet wall?"

"First ways, I'll need to scout out Thompson's camp. I won't be able to avoid them if I don't know where they lay. Then I'll hunt up some fresh meat for our party."

"You think we got time for you to go a-huntin'?"

"There won't be no time for huntin' once we begin our scramble to Cheyenne. 'Sides, I won't be able to crawl back down thet wall till dark settles tomorrow. Huntin' up some winterkill will temper my mood while I wait for the nightfall."

"It'll be just as rough comin' down thet wall as it will be climbin' it."

"Rightly so. But I'll cut good sign going up so's the path back will be legible."

With that, Rory Casso turned his attention to Bronwyn Mason. If they had only moments together, then they would make those moments count. And the counting would wear out an abacus. Hand in hand, they left the light of the campfire to have a quiet moment together before Casso challenged the wall.

Silence overtook the encampment as the campfire scolded the cold canyon shadows with flickering fingers of flame.

***

The going was slow as Casso led Rockwell up the crevasse stone by stone. As he went, Casso cut sign, a slash of bark here, a stack of stones there, so he would be able to trace his return down into the chasm. Hours passed on tippy-toes as Casso tread lightly on the edge of the darkness. A misstep here, a false toehold there, and too quickly, Casso would find himself once again at the base of this wall, much worse for the wear. Every step became a hurdle and every stone became a mountain. It was deep into the night when Casso finally peaked the canyon's crown.

CHAPTER SEVENTEEN

Cresting the coulee's summit, Casso set about the first order of business. He needed to identify the encampment of the Thompson gang, for he would not be able to avoid the gang if he did not know where they were hunkering down. Backtracking along the ridge, Casso followed the cut of the box canyon to its opening. And it was not long before he was able to spot the Thompson camp. The camp boasted a smoky fire and the smell of human scat. A white man's camp. The four horses that were tied down tight for the night were the same horses that Rory had spotted when he led the Thompson gang astray.

Now that the Thompson camp was discovered, Casso made haste to steer clear of the direction of their camp. Before returning to the box canyon, and the wagon train that awaited his arrival, he would hunt up some fresh meat for the trapped Mason party. The last meal that they would enjoy in the box canyon would need to be a hearty one, as on the run, the guarantee of rations would be sporadic at best.

Counting the four corralled horses of the Thompson gang, Casso was comfortable hunting up game. He would steer Rockwell south and east, downwind from the bluster of the western winds. And he would hunt in the lower reaches of the land where the sound of his gunfire would be smothered in the foliage of the landscape and undetectable to Thompson's men.

But Rory Casso had not figured for Jack Bettle and Kipper Dunn throwing in with the party. And this dearth of information would prove to be a grave deficiency.

18

WINTERKILL

It took Rory Casso the better part of the night to mount the canyon's wall, and as he breached its rim, the crisp December dawn breathed down his neck, promising an early call to winter. Overlooking the rolling terrain, he calculated another two weeks, maybe three, until the snows would befall this vista and render the terrain impenetrable.

As Casso ambled his steed, his thoughts returned again and again to the Mason family: Isham and Eva, but especially Bronwyn. When one has never known a home, a place of sanctuary, one never becomes comfortable in one's own skin. Without a base, without the foundation that is home, a man walks the world as an apparition, never sure of his bearing, never solid with his footing. And with the discomfort of a social buttress, a man will begin to question his own merit.

At the gnawing edge of these thoughts was the great sense that he would never be worthy of a woman the likes of Bronwyn Mason.

Surveying the wilderness ahead, Casso let out a plume of warm breath into the chilled air, generating tiny droplets of ice on his mustache. This bitter cold air held the promise of a long and lonely winter. Casso had been in these hills when the glacial western winds whipped down from the Rockies and blasted vengeance on these lower foothills. And he shuddered at the thought of it catching the women in its gnashing teeth.

But for now he was to the track. Winterkill.

***

There are few things more satisfying than the hunt. Whereas some men might find their solace in good liquor and other men might find their solace in bad women, Rory Casso found his solace in the hunt. And the winterkill hunt was particularly satisfying.

In many ways, sitting astride Rockwell with the hunt for game laid out before him was the only home that Casso had known. Here, in these animal tracks, in these Western reaches, Casso found contentment. This was a home he could understand, a home with a sureness of purpose, and this was where he was his most comfortable. Rory Casso relaxed into Rockwell's saddle.

Early winter is the best time for the hunt. With winterkill, the game is choicest, fattened up over the long summer months to withstand winter's oncoming paucity. Animal pelts are their thickest and most luxuriant, offering the animal sanctuary against the worst that winter can offer. Winterkill. This was the time for the hunter to be in the field.

The dirt and the rocks were now damp where they had wrestled through the frosted sage and the sky almost crackled blue with the early winter chill. This would be a good day to hunt.

With winter peeking over the shoulder of the Rockies, game would abound. This was last call for the animals to store winter fat. The foragers were scurrying about, filling their caches with the last of summer's bounty. Too, the hibernators were topping off the fat supplies that clung to their muscles and insulated their hides. Casso's own muscles prickled with the anticipation of joining nature's primordial dance of the hunters and the hunted.

With the dirt dampened in the morning frost, tracks would be easy to spot, and Casso noted the imprints of rabbit, prairie squirrel, deer, bear, and even a solitary cougar on its meander. This was nature's trading post and the shelves were well stocked with provisions. With too little meat on the smaller game and too much fat on the bear, Casso tucked himself into the track of an elk. Judging by the spacing and

CHAPTER EIGHTEEN

the depth of its tracks, Casso estimated a good-size buck.

Turning his steed into the trace of the buck, Casso settled into a brisk saunter on the broken trail. The buck would be browsing, grinding its molars from one side of the trail to the other. Reading the steam of the elk's scat, Casso approximated a lead of half a mile, maybe less.

It was then that Casso noted tracks that brought him some grave concern. Unshorn horses. Indian ponies. The Dog Soldiers were yet afield, and this made little sense considering the proclivities of the Indian. By now these warriors would have scouted the Thompson gang and the four practiced guns that were readied for warfare. And the Indians had already experienced the display of artillery from the Conestoga contingent.

Neither of these white clusters, the Thompson gang nor the Mason train, would be easy plunder for a raid by the renegades. It was late in the season and these Indians, if convention held, should be hastening a retreat to their wintering tribes, or risk the chance of being caught on a chilled tundra. The artillery of the white man would be a splendid booty for the Indians, but it would mean going up against the business end of the artillery first. That would be suicide. It just did not make sense that these Indians would still be in mount. Not for the payroll? Not for the artillery? Then? Casso knew the motivation. It was the women.

The Dog Soldiers were looking for women to squaw for the winter. The renegade warriors would let the two warring clans of white men slug it out, and in the end, they would collect the remaining booty.

***

A mile deep into the buck's track, Rockwell snorted deep and jerked his head from the trail. A quick study of the buck's trace bespoke the cause of the steed's distress. Competition was now afoot. A cougar's wide paw was now intersecting the buck's trail. A big cat was on the hunt for this same buck that

Casso was hunting, and Casso did not shy from the company. Confident that, once the cougar scented man, it would defer to the human, Casso turned Rockwell toward the winterkill.

Most horses would not step to the track of a cougar, but Rockwell knew Casso's inclination well and, with a displeased snort, settled back into the buck's track.

Casso now eased the Winchester from its scabbard and let it rest easy on the saddletree. As he rode the tracks, Casso absentmindedly fingered the gun's chamber. This would not be the time to be without a chambered round.

The sun was rising little by December little and the dirt was drying fast, releasing a steamy mist into the ethereal air. With the loss of the ground's moisture, the buck took to a stone outcropping. On the rock of the outcropping, Rockwell would be following this trail by the scuff of stone.

Winterkill. Now the hunt was on. Focused. Time became eternally still, and sacred became the moment. All senses were now alert to the game and wisdom harkened primal. Something ancient stirred deep in Rory Casso's core as senses keened to the crusade.

The last track Casso could decipher of the cougar was tight to its body, its belly fur brushing at the dirt between its big paws. The feline had lowered its body into a stalk, and the big cat had likewise entered into the surreal hub of the primordial hunt.

Another quarter-mile into the hunt and Casso had yet to hear or see the quarry. Somehow, both animals, the buck and the puma, were lost in the boulders, and this made for an eerie quiet. Rare is the cat that will stalk for this distance. The pounce was imminent. Yet, still, Casso could detect no sight or sound of the creatures.

Pulling Rockwell to an upright stop, Casso cocked his head, side to side, listening, as he readied the rifle to his shoulder. Rockwell sniffed the air and tuned his ears first in one direction and then in the other, straining for the sound of the animals.

An attuned nose could smell the gentle whisper of the

CHAPTER EIGHTEEN

drying sage as the lifting sun evaporates the morning dew from its leaves, releasing its heady aroma. An attuned ear could hear the far-off whoosh of the turkey vultures lifting themselves into the morning sky on the rising thermals of the warming earth.

In this eternal moment the hunter and the hunted, surrender and assault spin as one, and time stands as still as an epitaph-less tombstone.

Rockwell saw the puma first and reared back on his haunches in surprise and displeasure. The big buck burst straightway through the brush, not more than four yards in front of Rockwell's rearing front hooves. With a full load of autumn's antlers, the buck was a brown blur of fur and bone and in the angst of the terror of flight. Focused on the heels of the buck charged the cougar, in full assault and swatting at the buck's haunches.

In its panic to elude the slap of the cougar's big claws, the buck drew a sharp forty-five-degree turn and plunged headlong into Rockwell's breast. The terror of the buck's flight to escape the cat had blinded it to the man and horse, and it blasted into Rockwell's torso. Like water following along the cut of a riverbank, the big cat pursued the buck's flow as it poured into Rockwell.

Rockwell, having reared to his back legs, was unbalanced when the buck and the cat slammed into his breast. With Rockwell, the buck, and the puma along for the ride, Casso and company toppled backward into the stone.

Customarily, a cougar will avoid a row with the tandem of a horse and a man. The cougar will allow man the game. But this cat had no opportunity to demur. This cougar was drafted into a dance with a man, a horse, and a big elk, and he was none too happy with the dance card.

Later, much later, Casso would recall the spinning, cavalcading tornado of jaws and claws and hooves and antlers. But mostly, Casso would remember the cougar's eyes. Flaming yellow eyes. Eyes that harkened primeval. Eyes with a singular purpose and a singular focus. These were the eyes of a predator in full assault.

It was a grand promenade of claws and hooves and fur and skin as the four mammals tumbled to the earth. Even as Rory Casso lost his rifle in the plummeting pageant, he heard a gunshot crack against the crisp winter air. Surprised that there was another gun in the field, in this hunt, Casso had little time to consider its source as the discharged slug twisted through the big cat, and, redirected, slammed into Rory Casso's leg.

As close to a ton of mammal revelry hurtled to the earth, slamming them headlong into the stone, a black calm settled over Rory Casso.

19

SCRAPE MY FACE FROM THE FLOOR

Consciousness slowly oozed over Rory Casso. It began dimly, with a vague blood-red light under his eyelids and the dull sound of stifled voices. Soon, with a rush, perception pierced awareness with an exploding pain to his skull. Keeping his eyes closed to better scrutinize his position, awareness crept in on tippy-toes.

Through the canopy of pain, Casso could discern muffled voices nearby. The voices of men. Although he could not make out the words being spoken, he could tell by the cadence of the language that they were white men. There was some difficulty when he tried to get a view, as a muddy substance had dried his eyes shut. It was blood, he reasoned. Lying on his side, Casso's hands were immobilized behind his back. This was a good sign. Whosoever had captured Casso had felt enough trepidation of his wounds that they felt the need to bind him.

And then there was the searing pain in his thigh. The pain of ravaged skin and muscle tissue. Casso remembered the dance with Rockwell, the cougar, and the elk. Slowly, memory seeped back to Casso. The memory of Juke and the Reynolds payroll. And then the women. Quickly, the entire account of the wayward wagons burst to his recollection.

Consciousness was skulking like a stalking cat as Casso studied the voices that were near. Ever so slowly he began to decipher words. And then sentences were decoded.

"Funniest thing I swear I ever did see. We got the mountain cat and our man wit' one cap. Had to chase down his horse 'ere." Jack Bettle was in full humor.

Kipper Dunn joined the merriment. "Jes' the buck got away. All these hunters on the track of the buck, and the buck is the one to vamoose."

Casso forced his eyelids open through the dried blood and laid witness to six shadows hunched over a campfire. He was in the Thompson camp.

When Casso had first scouted the Thompson camp, he had counted four riders. Four was the number of men that had been dogging his and Juke Bauque's trail. What Rory Casso had not summed was Kipper Dunn and Jack Bettle throwing in with the gang. Now the gang numbered six.

A thin wiry shadow full of elbows and joints and a low-slung gun put in, "I reckon thet leaves us wit' jes' the half-breed and the women between us an' the payroll."

"An' the women are for us, Farrot." Bettle had lost his humor now. "We've got some scores to settle with the ladies."

Farrot Pierce did not like directives put to him. "Then you two can jes' go up thet canyon and dig 'em out. We'll bury your carcasses reverent like."

"Shet up both of ya," corrected the fat shadow hunkered down at the fire. "I'm gettin' a mite tired of the noise," the shadow added, as he spit cigar phlegm into the fire and unfolded his stubby legs to stand up. Up would be a short affair for the stout man, as he was near as large horizontal as he was vertical. Rory noted that this would be Barrett Thompson.

CHAPTER NINETEEN

The fat man turned to study Casso in the outer edges of the campfire light and, gesturing with a thick thumb, "We'll let him spell the night."

In turn, Farrot Pierce studied the hard lines of Casso's shoulders and the cut of his stature. "I'm thinkin' it might be best to jes' plug him now."

Thompson worked on his cigar with fat fingers. "You may be right, there, Farrot, but I'd kinda like to see what we can get out of him first. He's been in the Mason camp. And somehow he got out 'round about us. If'n he can git out, we kin get in."

Scrutinizing Casso's bloodied head and maimed leg, Farrot answered, "'Spect we won't get much."

This was a business decision for Thompson. He held no animosity toward Rory Casso except that Casso was positioned between the Thompson brood and the Reynolds Savings and Loan payroll.

With full deliberation Thompson answered, "I 'spect yer right. We won' git much outta this boy. But if'n we do, we kill 'em. And if'n we don't, we kill 'em. But the killin' kin wait for morning."

Casso was having difficulty staving off unconsciousness. Cognition was being tumbled downstream by a raging flood, and it was hitting every boulder along the way.

Jack Bettle added, with some measure of pride, "Leastways we got this poke outta the way."

When Farrot Pierce spoke again, he spoke slowly and he spoke smoothly. He spoke with the coolness of a gunslinger with a quick hand and full cylinders. "Either way, we got the hand now and we got to figure a way to play it."

Casso noted the cool control of Farrot Pierce and noted that this would be a gun to be tallied carefully.

There was more banter amongst the outlaws, but it was lost to Casso on his rendezvous with oblivion.

20

LAST CHANCE

Is there something pushing you faster?
Is the something pressing you on?
Do you see the clock as your master?
As minutes tick like chambers in a gun.

J. Bauque

When Rory Casso failed to return to the Mason wagons for two days, supplies were dwindling and camp morale was being tested. Two hundred miles from help, backed up against a box canyon with Dog Soldiers and outlaws on the track. And now, with the first dusting of snows, December had begun in earnest.

Cricket was the first to voice it. "I suppose he's not coming back." And though nobody dared to put words to it, they all suspected the worst.

This was a sobering thought, but none was more affected than Bronwyn, and it pulled on her face. Recognizing this, Cricket sidled up to her and put her arm tight around Bronwyn's waist. "I'm supposin' he could be off to collect a posse, couldn't he?" It was a question that did not need to be answered and it lay there collecting dust.

"You got a deep pull for that boy as children, yes?" Cricket let Bronwyn have rein.

Absently, Bronwyn took the reins and rambled. "Yep. I guess you could say that our buckets were dipping the same well. We grew up together in Rawlings. He was the son of the town drunk. That boy spent his days cleaning barrooms and brothels and his nights nursing his pappy through another drunk. Home to him was a series of livery lofts and storage rooms. When Rory's pap finally drank himself to death, he lived for a spell in the back of my pap's jailhouse. As the marshal, my pap did the best he could for Rory, but the boy was scarred from those early years."

"It's a funny thing. That boy doesn't come across as a street urchin."

"That's because he's not." Bronwyn took umbrage to the idea. "Don't know where he got it from but Rory is one of the truest souls these hills ever birthed. He was true like his mother, rest her soul, and his pappy would preach that when she died delivering up Rory his mama's soul clung to Rory's in his little body. Never knowing Rory's mother myself, I couldn't argue the point."

"His mother died at birth?"

"Yep. It's what drove his pappy to the bottle and Rory to the streets. Boys like Rory were part of the inspiration for Pap and Mama bringing schooling to those hills. Rory was a good boy. He worked hard. He gave regard to people. But he never did get to know a real home."

Cricket smiled at that. "And I suspect that that's when you first sparked to Rory?" This sent Bronwyn's cheek to color-coordinate with her crimson locks.

"I'm just saying . . ."

But Cricket pursued the story. "How did he come about to be a shotgun freighter, then?"

With some sadness teasing crow's-feet to the corner of her eyes, "Don't know exactly, he was staying in Pap's jailhouse backroom until he was about sixteen or so. We tried to make it homey for him, fixing up the room comfy like and having him set with us for dinner regularly, but he never did feel settled. One day he just up and took his pappy's Bowie knife and walked off for the hills."

"At sixteen? With no horse?"

"No horse and no gun. Just the Bowie knife. Pap offered him any gun he wanted off the jailhouse rack but he turned

CHAPTER TWENTY

it down flat. Said that he'd never run out of bullets packing a knife."

"A boy, just like that, into the hills? Kind of a hard story to hear," ventured Cricket.

"Kind of a hard story to tell. He never did seem quite settled, what with no home and all. He just set out looking for Lord knows what," rejoined Bronwyn.

Redirecting the company's thoughts, Juke Bauque put in, "We'll see Rory when we see Rory. That boy's got more game in him than a dozen wildcats."

Bronwyn warmed to the idea of Rory Casso yet amongst the living. Nodding in agreement and following Juke's thoughts, "Yep. And right here and now we have our own situation. Have you got any ideas on how we play this?"

For the past day, Juke Bauque had spent much time scrutinizing the trail that Rory had cut on his ascension up the rock face of the box canyon. "Well, food's shy and we got winter beckonin'. I 'spect we're gonna have to follow Rory up thet wall."

There was steaming coffee on the fire, and Juke now moved to the pot and poured himself a cup. Drawing deep on the hot coffee, "Sooner the better is my reckoning. There's a delegation of outlaws out there somewhere, and maybe a party of Injuns as well."

Now it was Cricket's turn to shudder, because, though she was wise in the wiles of the flesh, these untamed reaches were foreign to her. With some irony she said, "At least the Indians won't kill us." But this stab at humor sent a shudder through both her and Bronwyn.

To steady herself, Bronwyn blew the red curls from across her eyes and shoved cartridges into her Winchester. "When do we go?"

Setting their chins to the wind, Juke had begun spending more time studying the rock face that blocked their flight. Somewhere up that wall was a route out and escape.

As Juke studied the rock face there was something deep, something ancient, stirring in him. He was born to wealth on a Florida ranch, raised on butter and honey and educated in the finest fashion that money could offer. Never had this half-breed of Indian and Black slave ever known want. And yet here was something arousing deep within his DNA. These rocks were Juke's link to his ancestral birthright. This wall of stone held a primeval vortex for the half-breed. They beckoned Juke Bauque with an antediluvian murmur. He could feel in the rock's slope a tracker's path that would lead the Mason party over the rim of the canyon's lip. And the path would lead Juke to his legacy.

Hickory Dixon was another matter. His liquor had run dry, and he was now in the later stages of alcohol withdrawal. He was cold and he was scared and he was not a strong man. His deteriorating condition was noted by all.

Cricket was the first to put voice to Dixon's dilemma. "He's getting the shakes now. I've seen men in Independence saloons with that look, and it will not be long before he starts seeing banshees and talking crazy."

This was one more concern that the party did not need. But Bronwyn was committed. "We'll keep him warm and fed, it's the best we can do now."

Bronwyn was becoming distracted by her own withdrawal, and though her head continually turned from the ravine's mouth to the ravine's back wall, her thoughts were on Rory Casso and his untimely disappearance. Deep within the breast of this woman was brewing a kettle of disquiet.

"We'll have to take a crack at that ridge," Juke finally offered. "I 'spect Casso made it out of this hole somehow."

Bronwyn was studied. "I reckon that he did, but he didn't have a four-party contingent to pull up that edge."

"Never the less, it 'pears to be the only play we got."

"And what are we gonna do with Dixon?" Cricket had many reservations about the wagon pilot.

"Thet's certainly something to consider."

Cricket was insistent. "I somehow just don't trust the man."

"That being said," offered Bronwyn, "we just don't leave a

CHAPTER TWENTY

man to freeze to death out here."

"But . . ." Cricket began, but choked it in when Bronwyn turned on her heel and walked away, putting an end to the conversation.

***

They had begun dismantling one of the Conestogas for firewood and kept a good spit flaming for warmth against the cold of the shadowed canyon. As prospects were slim against the outlaws taking the chance of charging up this canyon with Juke's Buffalo gun and the women's Winchesters ready for battle, the weather was the more immediate threat to the party.

Juke glanced at the trembling blanket that held Hickory Dixon by the campfire. The alcohol withdrawal cramps had begun to seize Hickory and twisted his body with pain. Bronwyn voiced the obvious. "Guess we'll pack him up with us. Can't rightly leave him here to shudder to death," and then she turned her attention to Juke and the wall. "How do you consider tackling that mountain?"

Once again Juke turned his study to the barrier. "Well, if Casso climbed that mountain, I suspect he cut a trail so's he could find his way back easy like, if'n nothing happened to him. Our business will serve us well to find thet trail that he cut and follow it over the ridge."

Cricket expressed a thought that had been thus far left unspoken. "Could be the Thompson gang is waiting for us up there."

Juke was reflective. "Could be."

"Or that band of Dog Soldiers."

"Thet, too, could be up there. We only know that there is only slow death by starvation and cold down 'ere. Choices seem a mite limited."

Bronwyn took the bull by the horns. "And so it is settled. We climb." And then to Juke, "When do you think we best tackle that mountain?"

"Well, I'm figurin' that Casso cut a pretty clean path so's he could find his way back down that ridge. And I feel pretty good about following that path up once I spot it. The rub is that we will have to scramble that wall in daylight. Casso's mark won't be much at night."

And so it was decided. The Mason contingent would pack horses with provisions and munitions for a quick flight to Cheyenne, and they would scale the ravine's wall at first light.

The final night in this box canyon was solemn around the big flame. Much was to be done to prepare the escape. Horses would be packed light, with only necessary chuck, victuals, and munitions. And Bauque would pack the Reynolds Savings and Loan payroll. The climb would be slow and careful but once the party hit the ridge, the three-week dash to Cheyenne would be rapid.

"What do we do with the extra wagon ponies?"

"Turn 'em loose to drift. Maybe the Indians will count them booty enough."

Bronwyn considered. "But they sure won't placate the Thompson gang."

Juke Bauque let that assertion rest on its own laurels.

Before light broke they had packed the horses with the essentials. "Jes' the food and artillery," calculated Juke. "I'll take the lead rein an' Bronwyn, you bring up the rear. Cricket, I'm gonna have to ask you to pull the rein of the mount that we throw Dixon on." And he turned to the blankets lying at the fire pit. Hickory Dixon's blankets had quit of their quivering. And they were empty.

Some time during the night, Hickory Dixon had slipped out of camp.

***

The escaping trio of Juke Bauque, Bronwyn Mason, and Cricket Wynot was blessed with just the lightest of snow to chart the rough track up the back wall of the box canyon. It was not enough snowfall to obscure the marking that Casso

CHAPTER TWENTY

had cut, and from a distance, the flurries would impede the view of any observer, be it the Thompson gang or the Indians.

For the most part, Rory Casso had cut clean sign up the wall. Where time or the elements had obscured sign, Juke was able to decipher track by the study of the land. There were limited options for footholds when scaling a cliff like this, and where Casso's track fainted, Juke would fill in the puzzle with terrestrial scrutiny.

It was a tough climb. Juke and the women had to walk their horses the entire way up the escarpment. These were wagon horses and not practiced in the ways of climbing mountains. Juke Bauque gave this to the man: Hickory Dixon had chosen good stock, and these ponies were steady of hoof on the gradient. But where the hell had Hickory Dixon disappeared to?

21

KNEE DEEP IN THE BLUES

Jack Bettle and Kipper Dunn were gunsmiths, not mountain men, and when they came upon Rory Casso's trail, it was by happenstance.

For his part, having discovered the Thompson camp with its four riders hunkering around their spit, Rory Casso felt comfortable in being free for the hunt of the winterkill. Casso had tracked these four men before and had been able to give them the slip. He would steer clear of the gang, avoiding any chance encounters. But Casso had not been privy to the data that Jack Bettle and Kipper Dunn had now joined their faction, and so he was not expecting company in the field. It was gunfire from Jack Bettle's rifle that had killed the cougar and, on redirection, ripped at Casso's leg.

In the camp of the outlaws, Rory Casso lay battered and woozy on the cold dirt.

It might have been the light dusting of December snow on Casso's cheek that brought him to full vigilance on that frozen earth. Or it might have been the throbbing sting of the damage to his body.

Slowly collecting his consciousness, Casso lay there silently. The first thing he had felt was the bitter cold of the frozen earth. Then it was the searing pain of his wounds that clawed at his cognizance. As consciousness crept in, Casso kept his eyes closed in study of this quandary.

Pinpointing the pain in his leg: this would have been the gunshot that Casso heard as he and Rockwell tumbled with the buck, and the cougar. The searing pain at the back of his skull would be the encounter that his cranium had had with the earth in the tumble.

It was night now. Around the fire slumbered six men in deep sleep, sharing with the night their creature cacophony of snoring. Six men? Two more men had joined this Thompson gang. But there was another sound, too, a soft whooshing sound of something softly sliding across dirt.

Risking a look, Casso forced his blood-muddied eyelids open while he collected thoughts.

Sitting upright, across the campfire, a singular shadow. This would be the outlaws' night sentry and he was deep in slumber. And then the whooshing noise again. The noise of something being dragged, slowly and incrementally, through the brush.

Lying still and studying the camp, Casso noted how the six sleeping men held close their guns. There would be no play by Casso at a weapon. Listening, he could identify where the horses were reined by the occasional snort and the shuffle of hooves. And then he saw his father's Bowie stuck like a beacon in a fire-log pile no more than six feet from where he lay. That was a comfort in itself, but there would be no play with a Bowie against six guns.

And again the whooshing sound. But this time Casso thought he recognized it. It was the full weight of a human body being pulled, or dragged, across the earth. First the sliding whoosh. Then silence. Then another sliding whoosh. Then, again, silence.

Casso took measure of his body with incremental muscle-flexing. He identified the searing pain in his thigh where the bullet had torn through. But he could flex that leg muscle, and he knew that he would have at least limited mobility. How much mobility he would not know until he tested it.

And again the slithering sound of body on earth. This time Casso was able to determine the direction of the noise. It was somewhere across camp, behind the slumbering sentry, and, with each whoosh, it was drawing nearer.

Now there was another whoosh, another slithering body, but this time the crawling sound of body on dirt was

CHAPTER TWENTY-ONE

directly behind Casso. As Casso's eyesight cleared, he risked the slightest turn of his head. Even with this slightest of movements, Casso's head exploded with fireworks. Forcing the issue, he moved through the pain. Dried blood broke free from the ground when he raised his head. If not for the winter cold and the dusting of snow coagulating the blood, Casso quite probably would have bled to death.

Now Casso was determined to identify the origins of the whooshing, dragging sound that was coming from more than one direction. Focusing hard on the sound beyond the slumping sentry across the campfire, Casso scrutinized the brush. And there it was.

A dark, rounder shadow was easing its way against the jagged backdrop of the buttonbushes. And the shadow was moving slowly. Ever so slowly. And with each slow and subtle movement of the shadow came the whooshing of a man's body weight compressing the new snow against the frozen earth. There was a man slinking ever so quietly behind the sentry.

And that same slithering sound was now slowly compressing the snow to the earth behind Casso. Two shadows were moving surreptitiously against the night. Rory Casso marveled at the stealth of the shadows.

Who could they be? They could not be any from Mason's party, for they would not command the stealth of these shadows. Indians.

This thought sent Casso's mind reeling. Never would an Indian play the game this way. First, with this many ready Winchesters, renegade Indians would have long left the arena. Second, if they had stayed in the arena, it would have been for the women. And there were no women in this camp of combatants.

Watching as the Indian, deft as a cat, moved to the lashed stallions, Rory Casso wondered at the Indian's game. With a blade that caught the sparkle of the campfire, Casso watched as the Indian slashed at the tethers of the horses. Quick as a cat, and with a smack and a whoop, the Indian bawled a war cry that sent the horses into panic. With a rush, the warrior's war cry was joined by the pounding panic of the startled horses.

With the crash of the horses, hell broke loose in the camp. The Indian who had cut loose the horses' binds now leaped to his feet and, with another whoop and flapping arms, sent the horses stampeding directly through the outlaws' camp, spilling fire and tumbling the men in their blankets. The camp burst with the racket of shouting men and the clacking of cold metal as shooters were cocked. Explosions of gunfire broke the stillness that had been the night.

When the chaos began, Casso used the opportunity to roll to the sound of the Indian that was whooshing the earth directly behind him. As he turned, Casso caught sight of a knife flashing down toward him. The whooshing Indian that had slithered up behind Rory was now swinging a knife down at Casso. Defending himself by holding his tied hands up against the blow, the Indian's knife caught the rope that bound his wrists. This did not go unnoticed or unchallenged. Two rifles barked at the Indian, and a hundred and seventy pounds of dead warrior now fell onto Casso. But the Indian's slashing blade had severed Casso's binds, and his hands were now liberated.

Instinctively, Casso rolled with the weight of the dead body and, in so doing, a bullet grazed Casso's shoulder. There was a dull thud as the bullet skimmed off Casso's now-frozen buckskin shirt and ricocheted off to the bush.

The night became a riotous spectacle of white men screaming and Indians yipping and guns cracking, and still Casso lay pinned under a dead Dog Soldier.

This was not an unwelcome development for Casso. If the Thompson gang and the Indians fell to warfare, then flight would be possible. It would just be a matter of guile. But, first, there was the matter of being trapped under this cadaver.

While Thompson was barking orders, shots were ringing out around the camp. Bullets could be heard pinging off of stone and frozen wood and the dead thudding sound like bullets spitting mud. The kind of a deadening thud that

CHAPTER TWENTY-ONE

bullets make when they strike the thick part of a man's body.

"I got one cornered in the pine." This was the notcher, Farrot Pierce.

Thompson called to the night, "Keep his head down with lead," and then to Jimmy Patterson, "You and Bank circle around and dig him out."

Casso lay quiet, attempting to discern the whereabouts of each outlaw. This would be his chance for a break, if he played it right.

Besides the unattended wounds to Casso's head and leg, his body had stiffened to the cold earth. Muscles and joints would not be fond of movement, but the muscles would need to comply. Repositioning under the Indian that had fallen dead on top of him, Casso launched his escape.

Without changing the position of the dead Indian, Rory Casso slithered from underneath. Slowly he pushed his shoulders off of the frozen dirt and surveyed the camp. He could see where four gunners had an Indian pinned-down in the cusp of a fallen tree. Thompson and Pierce were pouring slugs into the tree while Patterson and Bank were circling behind. On shouted orders from Thompson, Jack Bettle and Kipper Dunn scurried off to the bush to corral the panicked horses.

Somehow, as is the Indian way, the warrior that was trapped in the cusp of the tree disappeared like a magician's trick. The warrior was held fast to the pocket of the tree with gunfire sharding the tree's wood, and then he was gone. And, just like that, the camp was quiet again, save for the blasphemous mutterings of the confused outlaws.

The veiled shadows of the Indians had disappeared as quickly as darkness can settle.

"Get the goddamn horses," Thompson screamed to Bettle and Dunn, "and the rest can best find those Indians an' scalp 'em."

In thunderous parade, the men scrambled to their tasks.

In that frantic moment of confusion, Casso, with his Bowie, had rolled off of the encampment and into the night.

***

Rory Casso had pushed himself back to the brush, opposite the pageant being played out with the Indian in the cusp of the tree. Every chilled muscle and frozen joint in his body rebelled at this movement, but he willed his way on. Once he made the brush, he found the track that the dead Indian, the Indian that had inadvertently cut his binds, had used to steal into camp. Now Casso got lucky. He lit upon the very moccasin tracks that the Indian had left on his stalk into the camp. He would use this Indian track to obfuscate his own trace.

Lifting to his haunches, Casso swung his body to face the camp and, by so doing, fit his own moccasins into the dead Indian's prints. As the muscles in Casso's body protested, he aligned his body to a backward stride in the tread left by the Indian in the fresh snow. It was an uncomfortable and awkward stalk, but, even through the pain that wracked his body, it felt good to move. He'd backpedaled like this for a good quarter-mile when he hit rock.

Standing upright now, Casso surveyed the situation. First, his body: his leg had two big holes, front and back, but they were clean holes and the scab was holding fast. This meant that the bullet that had torn through his leg had exited without hitting bone. Next, he gingerly probed at the lesion to his skull. This was a more serious matter. He had already felt the symptoms of the concussion: nausea, murky deliberation, and the need to vomit. He would need to find asylum quickly or risk collapsing in his tracks, as unconsciousness was already bidding for his attention.

It was still dark and he could see the light from the now-splattered remains of the outlaws' fire. And he could hear the pop and see the occasional flash of guns discharging. He had studied the terrain's layout before, when he first scouted the Thompson camp, and he knew the lay of the land.

The camp's horses had been driven by the Indians through the camp at an angle that would push them just up the ridge from where he now crouched. Rockwell had been tethered to these horses, and if he could find the horses he would find Rockwell.

Knowing Jack Bettle and Kipper Dunn were hunting the horses did not concern Casso. In the dark, they would be following the general direction of the horses' breakout. But that would lead the outlaws on a false track. Rory Casso understood that the horses would be running from the noise, not the men, and that the steeds would find a path that would take them most quickly to a place of quiet. The quiet that the horses sought would not be on the ridge, where Bettle and Dunn were blindly following, but, rather, in the nearest notch of earth that the horses could bargain, for in the lower reaches would be the places that the gunshots would be best muted. This would lead the stampeded horses to veer left and down, to a small furrow of dirt to Casso's left. To intercept the steeds, Casso set his sights to that cut of the earth.

The loss of blood and the cold were now taking their toll on Casso and, even as he staggered forward, coherency oscillated. Gunshots in the distance were becoming sporadic now, and he knew that it would only be a matter of time before his escape was discovered.

On the ridge to his right he could hear Bettle and Dunn cooing a callout to the horses. And, now to his left, in the lower reaches of the land, he could hear the snort and whinny of a nervous horse. Jack Bettle and Kipper Dunn had turned to the false track.

Rory Casso did not know how he closed that final gap between himself and the horses. He could never remember locating Rockwell or pulling himself up on the steed. He had a vague recollection of steering Rockwell back toward the east: back in the direction of the gully where Casso had first scouted the Thompson gang traversing the ridge in their hunt for the Reynolds Savings and Loan payroll. There, he remembered, was a place to hide. A hollow of stick and stone that was jumbled by the wash of flooding rains into an enclosed cavity. There he would find water and he would find food. Rory would find a cup of shelter against the blast of the winter and the stalk of the hunter. Sanctuary: if he could reach it.

But now, oblivion stuck picket to its claim on Rory Casso.

***

When Hickory Dixon made the Thompson camp he was a mere shadow of a human. The cold of the ravine had taken a toll, but the liquor shakes had reduced him to a shuddering piece of flesh.

Jack Bettle introduced Dixon to Barrett Thompson. "This 'ere illustrious captain is the leader of thet Mason pack," Bettle scoffed.

Barrett Thompson studied Dixon like he was buying a horse. "You say thet they will be trying to jump thet cliff?"

A deep cough rumbled its way through Dixon's throat. "Thet is what they been talkin'."

Thompson turned his back to Dixon to study the ravine's deep cut. Although it was just the lightest of snow flurries, coupled with the distance, visibility was limited, and Thompson squinted his eyes to the canyon. "It don't seem rightly possible to mount thet wall." And, turning back to Dixon, "'N you say thet Casso went up thet wall an' didn't come back?"

"Thet's what I'm sayin'."

Thompson scratched at his stubbled cheek. "Wahl, thet explains how that Casso boy got past our sentry. But it don't seem likely thet the whole kit 'n caboodle of them women kin shinny thet wall. But I don' want to leave no stones unturned. Bettle, you 'n Dunn take a jump over thet ridge and scout about."

"You ain't figurin' thet they can scale thet brink, does ya?"

Again Barrett Thompson turned to study the wall. "Nope, don't seem likely, but I don't want no risk in them slippin' from us. Now, vamoose."

When Jack Bettle and Kipper Dunn scurried from camp

CHAPTER TWENTY-ONE

in the direction of the back ridge of the box canyon, Barrett Thompson turned to appraise the worth, now, of Hickory Dixon. Before Thompson quivered a man beaten and broken by too many tumbles over the lip of the bottle. And Barrett Thompson did not see very much industry left in the business of this man.

Farrot Pierce pressed, "An' then what do we do about him?"

Barrett Thompson rolled his cigar in study of Hickory Dixon, who was now in the pitch of a full alcoholic seizure. He studied the man like bacteria in a petri dish.

But Thompson was not without some measure of sympathy for the old man. "Give him a measure of whiskey," and, turning his back to Hickory Dixon, he added, "and then shoot 'im."

22

VICTIMLESS CRIME OF LOVE

She understood the rules,
And it didn't come as a shock of something new.
And she knew the men would leave,
But as they got what they wanted,
She was getting what she need.
And she did victimless time
For a victimless crime
Of love.

J. Bauque

 Stealing up the face of the box canyon with a paled moonlight was no easy task, and it took a toll on Juke and the women. Feet and hooves and nerves were sternly tested on the stone. Although Rory Casso had marked a clear enough track up the hillside, the terrain, coupled as it was with the early morning darkness, left little room for error. More than once a hoof would slide or a foot would fail to catch, and a shudder would run through the escaping collective. But onward they climbed, straining against the rocks and the wind and the terror.

 Slowly progressing up the rock face, Juke Bauque led the contingent, closely examining the ground as he climbed for Casso's marker and solid footing. Cricket, terrified and unsure of traction, held tight to Bauque's lead, and Bronwyn brought up the rear, cooing encouragement to Cricket.

 Up the crag they climbed in the soft light of the wispy snow flurries, testing their nerves against the strain of the incline.

Staggering on an outcropping of loose shale, Cricket was the first to lose her footing. When the shale skated out from under her, the sliding stone carried her feet down the embankment. As she grasped tight to the reins of her pony, the shale slid from under the horse, and it began to slide along with Cricket, its legs flailing madly in the attempt to grip at the moving earth.

A front hoof of the horse caught, offering small hope, and then gave way to skimming stone. Then, again, a back hoof found grip, but that catch, too, disappeared with the skating stone into the darkness below.

The steed fought valiantly against the sliding stone, thrashing its legs faster and faster, but even as the horse floundered, the slithering rock increased its slide. As the steed toppled into the black canyon below, Cricket let go of the reins and threw herself flat against the sliding shale. In this position, lying flat against the slithering rock, Cricket managed to ride the wave of rock down the hillside, coming to a rest a hundred feet below the track that she and Juke and Bronwyn had been traversing.

With her arms and legs splayed out to slow her slide, Cricket listened as her horse continued on its tumble down the shale and on over the lip of a cliff. Seconds into its fall, she heard a loud thump, and then a shrieking whinny pierced the morn. Another tumble, another dull thump, and the horse was forever silenced. Judging by the sound of the horseflesh thumping on stone, she estimated at least a hundred feet once the body cleared the cliff to the time it hit solid rock below. Only the raspy rattle of the occasional sliding shale now shared the hillside with Cricket.

In this precarious position Cricket breathed shallowly, as movement might start the shale sliding again, sending Cricket tumbling into the abyss.

When death is impending, life may or may not flash in front of one's eyes. Cricket could not take an oath either way but, certainly, reminiscence was provoked in the woman.

***

CHAPTER TWENTY-TWO

As a woman/child of barely eighteen, Cricket's life was short on biology but long on misery. Her experiences were that which would make Satan blush. Men's faces flashed across her memory like bolting lightning.

There were the men who had whimpered their loneliness and isolation to the young prostitute and there were the men that took her savagely, bruising her thighs and her psyche. Tall men and small men. Men that smelled of stale liquor and carrion and men that wore ugly like a badge. Men with severed limbs and men with severed values. All of these men were looking for her to fill a need, mostly a physical need, but not always that.

But even as these men ravished the young girl, they were helping Cricket to fulfill her own need to survive another day. To carry on for another hour. Through the worst of the men, Cricket held firm to answer to the call of life.

It was hard for Cricket to think of herself as a victim. These men, even the roughest of these men, allowed for Cricket to outlast another day of horror. Her strength came in knowing that, as these men ravaged her body, it was allowing her to sally forth into the future. A future of hope. Life is always a half-full glass of water, never half empty. If not always half full, what would be the point of life? Even as these brutes were getting what they wanted, Cricket was getting what she needed. Onward to the future.

And what of love? Isn't that the way of love? All love, Cricket wondered? Even in the healthiest of relationships, doesn't one party simply fulfill the needs of another party? Isn't all love victimless? Don't we all somehow, someway, get what we need?

Prepare yourself,
Then dare yourself
To take a fall.
It's better to have loved and lost
Than never have paid the cost
At all.

J. Bauque

***

In the shadows above her, Juke and Bronwyn reined in their mounts.

"Hallo," Juke called into the darkness, but Cricket was afraid to even suck wind for fear the movement of her expanding lungs might set the stone to slide again.

Above, Bronwyn carefully led the horses over the shale and reined them tight further up the trail.

"Hallo, are you with us?" Again, Juke called with some anxiousness in his vibrato. This time, an answer. Cricket called back up the hillside and into the darkness.

In guarded whisper, "Yes, I'm here. I'm layin' flat 'gainst the stone."

"Can you manage a grip?"

Cricket could hear the continual drip-drip-dripping of the shale going over the edge of the precipice and bouncing to the rock below. "No, no grip. I'm flat to the stone and I'm uneasy about speaking for want of this mountain to start sliding again."

Bronwyn retorted fast and firmly, "You just hang on there, honey, we're coming for you," and then she turned to Juke. "How can we get down to that girl?"

Not being a true mountain man, Juke had never dealt with the temperament of avalanching shale, and he took a few moments to appreciate the situation.

Thinking out loud, Juke reasoned, "If we rope up and clamor down there we might well set this mountain sliding again. Then I'm afraid we'd lose the girl over the edge."

Bronwyn was impatient. "I don't need you to tell me what we can't do, I need to know what we can do." This impatience was out of character for Bronwyn and belied her anxiousness.

Ignoring Bronwyn, Juke studied the trail to either side of the shale slide. There was plenty of dogwood scrub growing along the side of this canyon's edge. And Juke knew that, to reach for water in dry times, this scrub would bury its roots deep. And these deep roots would provide a steadfast grip to tether a rescue line. The problem would be in getting that line to Cricket. Lowering a body down that shale would begin a landslide that would send Cricket over the edge. Even the tossing of the rope down to Cricket would risk disturbing the shale and starting an avalanche. And an avalanche would carry Cricket over the lip of the cliff and into the void below.

Bronwyn's voice calmed as she called reassurance down to Cricket. "Hang in there, honey, we're coming for you."

There could be no rescue from directly above Cricket, as the ground was not trustworthy. And there could be no rescue from the abyss below.

Cricket clung to the precarious stone precipice, listening to the chink of shale trick-trick-trickling over the edge.

23

SOMETIMES THE WOLVES ARE SILENT

Bloodied and battered, with a bullet hole in his leg and an opened head gash, Rory Casso slumped against Rockwell's back. There was an Indian blanket that had been thrown on Rockwell, but no saddle, and Casso clung to Rockwell's ribs as the horse clopped to the terrain. Casso knew he would have to get out of this cold. He would need water. He would need food. But first he would need shelter.

Steering Rockwell in the direction of the only sanctuary he knew in these hills, Casso turned to the tangled-branch gully wash that he had discovered when back-tracking the Thompson gang. There would be water there. There would be bunchgrass for Rockwell, and, hopefully, there would yet be some small fish left in the pooled creek. But first and foremost, in the gully wash of tumbled debris, there would be a barrier against the winter's wrath.

Fading in and out of consciousness, Casso could only hope that the lightly falling snow would fill his tracks and obscure his escape, for he did not have the reserve to backtrack. Needing shelter as well, Rockwell seemed to understand the plan and needed little guidance in their pilgrimage to the gully wash haven.

Although the day was yet young, darkness slowly began to encompass Casso's world. The lack of sustenance and the loss of blood took its toll on him. Fighting nausea and with a disjointed thought process, Rory Casso clung fast to the steed's ribs.

When Rockwell turned into the gully wash, Casso did not know, but he recognized well the wash. The creek bed was narrow and foliage had grown tight along its banks. In the spring this wash would be a flooding torrent of snowmelt. Rockwell stepped to the rock as they made their way to the small pool that held the driftwood shelter.

The shelter was a box elder that had been felled by the current of the raging spring flood as it gouged the dirt out from under its roots. Recently dropped, the box elder had green leaves and, with the branches and stone that had washed down the creek, had collected into an enclosure large enough to accommodate himself and Rockwell. The leaves of the big tree caught the snow and made a natural snow cave against the wind. The haven extended over a permanent pool along the seasonal stream. With luck, this remaining pool would hold fast to trapped fish.

As Casso and Rockwell ducked into the natural cote of box elder, Casso slid from the steed and down into unconsciousness.

***

It was smell of smoke that had wheedled Rory Casso awake. There was a small fire in this tiny pouch of the cupped box elder. And on the fire, there was fish frying.

The concussion that Casso had suffered when he slammed his head to the rock must have been more severe than he thought, for he had no memory of sparking this fire or snaring the fish that now sizzled on the spit.

Twenty-four hours? Two days? More? Casso had no idea how long he had lain unconscious in this snow cave while the fever ravaged his body. Intermittent consciousness would seep its way into Casso's world only to be turned away again by pain and confusion. Then off again he would fall into the dark pit of the coma.

The box elder cave was warm, tempered by the bodies and breath of the two animals that had sought refuge here. But Casso's body now needed nourishment for recovery, and every attempt to claw away at the ice with his Bowie held

CHAPTER TWENTY-THREE

only another visit with unconsciousness.

Casso reasoned that it must have been a fit of delirium when he awakened to the three deep-pool trout now smoking on the spit fire. Save for Rockwell and the fish, there was no evidence of another animal entering this box elder world. It must have been in the frenzy of fever that Casso had managed to chip away at the ice and fire the fish, for he could recover no recollection of doing so.

> *I listen to the howl, all the baying at the moon,*
> *Suddenly somehow I've been singing that tune.*
> *But sometimes,*
> *Sometimes the wolves are silent.*
>
> *There's an itching in my heart that I don't know*
> *how to scratch.*
> *A torch in the darkness but I ain't got a match.*
> *But sometimes,*
> *Sometimes the wolves are silent.*
>
> *J. Bauque*

***

The fish was good, and, with the buttonbush tubers that grew along the wash, he nourished his bones. And so, gradually, managed to hold consciousness tighter with each wakening.

Slowly but steadily Casso became aware of the habitat. With consciousness returned the memory of the Thompson gang. And of the Reynolds Savings and Loan monies. And the memories of Juke and Cricket; but mostly, Rory Casso's thoughts turned to Bronwyn. And with the memory of all this returned the determination to live.

As cognizance gained a foothold, Rory Casso began to appraise the situation. He knew that there were four parties in the field, with two of the parties hell-bent on no good. Juke and Casso had left Independence shotgun-freighting the last seasonal run of the Reynolds Savings and Loan payroll. Then there was the wayward attempt by Bronwyn Mason to push a late summer train into Cheyenne. And there was the band of outlaws led by the iniquitous Barrett Thompson.

But the contingent in the field that gave Casso the most concern was the Dog Soldiers. Not so much because the Indians were any more dangerous than the outlaws, Indians could bleed and die like any man, but, rather, for the extraordinary behavior that these Indians were displaying.

Casso could well understand the desire of the young warriors to take women. It was a common practice among the raiding tribes. Indian coups in the late summer were often designed to kidnap women to warm the winter nest.

But Dog Soldiers were more of a hit-and-run cluster. And once they would identify a well-defended objective, as surely the Winchesters had proven the women to be, they were quick to move on to the next, less challenging, objective. And to attack the Thompson gang, a troop of tough men with ready artillery, was just madness to the Dog Soldier.

And the reasoning for these Dog Soldiers to be in the field at all troubled Rory Casso. This deep into the winter season, Indians are either at the government reservations or dug in at their wintering camps. It was an exceptional occasion for this war party to be afield.

These Indians were proving to be an enigma in this state of affairs.

Rory Casso spent his time sleeping, or, when awake, tooth-grinding the buttonbush tubers. With each cycle of sleep and sustenance came new clarity. The December cold had kept Casso's blood loss to a minimum and the fever at bay. And now Casso's cussedness was tweaked.

Another day to lie low and then Rory Casso would find the women. In whosoever's camp they may inhabit.

24

PULL ME FROM THE RUBBLE: Part 3

Like lame game
On the open plain,
Like babies in the jungle,
Come on,
Pull me from the rubble.

J. Bauque

Rory Casso was able to hold on to consciousness for longer spells now. Four days? Five days now in this cup of the gully's sanctuary? He could not be sure. But now he could retain coherent thoughts.

With some effort he slipped out of the warmth of this house of sticks and cut the bunchgrass for Rockwell's nourishment. Though the wounded leg yet pained, it felt good to move about again. Had he really, in his ache and delirium, managed to spark a flame and to feed Rockwell and himself? That memory was still lost to Casso.

Ruminating as he dined on the fresh fish, he took stock of the particulars of the events that brought him to this gully wash of stick and stone, to this respite against the winter elements.

Juke Bauque would still be with the women, Bronwyn and Cricket. He would not leave them to fend for themselves against the wolves of the Thompson gang. He might be coaxed to part with the Reynolds payroll, but he would not leave the women.

The women, in turn, were of hardy resolve, and they would

not surrender easy to an unjust master. Cricket had already suffered the worst of what ugly men could offer, and Bronwyn Mason, spawn of Marshal Isham Mason, would not be an easy test for one's mettle.

More worrisome to Rory Casso were the Indian tracks. A dozen Indian riders, with winter reaching out its icy fingers, and the Indians were still dogging the Mason party. This was atypical for these warriors, and Casso could only surmise that they were on the prowl for winter squaws. Women to keep the winter tepee warm.

The Dog Soldiers would have scouted the two parties of white men, the Thompson gang and the Mason contingent, and witnessed the throwdown between the two. They would bear witness to the adversarial positioning of the two contingents and how the Thompson gang had now trapped the Conestogas in the box canyon.

Now the Indians would be lying back, allowing the whites to kill off as many of each other as they would, leaving the Indians in good position to gather the leftovers. The gunmen's munitions would be much in demand for the Indians, and the white women would make warm their winter lodge.

Shuddering, Rory considered how Bronwyn and Cricket would fare if captured by the Dog Soldiers. Once before, Casso had witnessed a white woman ravaged by a band of marauding Indians. The memory of that woman was seared into his brain, blistering his recollection. Casso shuddered with the recall of that captive woman's plight.

It was the singular time that Rory Casso had killed a woman. And he felt no remorse for the mercy killing.

***

Rory Casso had smelled the smoke long before he had come upon the Indian tracks. It was early spring, and he was still wearing his winter buffalo wrap, following the northerly drift of game as the animals shook free from their winter coats. Young, and not many months removed from his Hunkpapa

CHAPTER TWENTY-FOUR

tiyospe, the company of an Indian brother would be welcome companionship for Boy With Sky In Eyes.

Treading lightly, for Casso did not know if these would be friendly Indians or no, he steered Rockwell to the direction of the Indian camp. What he came upon in the Indian camp turned his stomach.

There were four Indians in total and the camp was many days warm. It was unusual for a troop of Indian hunters to set this long in a singular location. Habit, prey, and camp hygiene kept the hunters continually on the move. But this camp that Casso had come upon reeked of the stench of the settlement's waste.

And then Rory Casso saw the reason that these renegade Indians were hunkered down.

Offset from the camp, bound fast across a cottonwood log was a white woman, naked to the wind. She had been lashed across the log, belly down and legs splayed, so as to present her womanhood for the renegades' pleasure. How many days this white woman had been displayed and abused in this fashion, Casso could not approximate, but the path between the fire and her mount was tramped with wear.

This woman was tethered down and paying the toll for the white man's transgressions on the Indian nation.

This white woman was being laid to compensate for every wrong the red man was wronged at the hands the white man. Her hide would pay for every rape propagated upon every Indian woman, her womanhood would be scorched with the memory of every Indian innocently murdered by the white invaders. And, eventually, her slow and brutal demise would be branded by the iron of every fire that torched and pillaged every Indian village by white villains.

Normally Rory Casso would identify a hostile Indian camp and quietly slip away into the brush. But this was not normal. Even for renegade Indians, this was not normal. Rory Casso drew rein and walked Rockwell into the middle of the Indians' encampment.

The Indian camp carried the stink of human excrement,

blood, and tizwin. Indian whiskey.

Three Indians crouched on their haunches at the fire pit while the fourth Indian was having his way with the woman lashed to the cottonwood. When Casso sauntered Rockwell into their midst, the Indians stood bolt upright, and the Indian on the woman withdrew from her and, coming to the camp, adjusted his breechcloth, covering his retribution.

Sliding down from the steed, Rory Casso spoke first, in the tongue of the Hunkpapa. "Who are these shamed warriors that would treat a woman so?"

Taken aback by the fluidity of Rory's Indian dialect, they exchanged glances of surprise and then guilt (?) with one another. An Indian that had been squatting at the fire came first to Casso, studying the white man's face. The Indian had cruel and black eyes that had fallen off the cliff of humanity. "Who is this white devil that speaks in the noble tongue of the Hunkpapa?"

Rory Casso ignored the man, and, walking past him, he drew his Bowie to cut loose the woman from her binds.

"You will leave her be," commanded the black-eyed renegade.

Paying no heed to the Indian's demand, Rory Casso walked to the bound woman and slashed the ties that trussed her. As the woman slid to the ground, an unintelligible gurgle issued from her foaming mouth. Casso inspected the woman's face and saw no emotion. He scrutinized her eyes and saw no awareness. She lay there still, a burbling hunk of human flesh.

When Rory Casso turned to face the Indian camp, the black-eyed Indian, the one that had warned him away from the woman, was already charging Casso. Knife drawn and swinging, the Indian came at Casso with a flourish. Metal on metal clanked as Casso deflected the Indian's hacking with his Bowie. For all of the fury in the black eyes, the warrior was not much of a knifesmith, and Rory Casso quickly dispatched the renegade with a sidestep and a keen slash to his throat.

Next came the Indian that had been exacting revenge on the woman when Casso came upon the camp. This was the

CHAPTER TWENTY-FOUR

largest of the four Indians, half again as large as Rory. But this big renegade wore his weight awkwardly, and they were cumbersome pounds. Quickly, Casso disposed of his attack as well.

One thing can be said for these renegade Indians: although they lived lives as scoundrels, they died as warriors. If they had all four rushed Rory Casso at once, Casso would have been filleted upon their knives. But they came one by one, as a warrior would come, and they were no match for Rory Casso, the Hunkpapa warrior. And they died, in kind, one by one. As a warrior would die.

This was the one time in Rory Casso's life that it felt right to kill a man. And it felt good to kill a man.

Having dispatched the Indians, Rory Casso turned his attention to the woman in a bloody heap on the ground. How long she had been tied to this log of horror Casso could not know. Days? Surely. A week? Maybe.

Cradling her gently in his arms, Rory brought water to her lips, but she could not drink. Her eyes rolled in their sockets and her tongue hung limp in her mouth. Deep in her throat a raspy gurgle bubbled incoherently. In her eyes there was nothing. No rationale, no reason, and no humanity. Only the bubbling babble of flesh lingered.

Rory Casso stroked her hair affectionately. He tried to imagine from where she had come. Was she a mother? A wife? A sister and a daughter? There was no age left in this despoiled body. There was no history to be found in these stripped remains. Casso whispered a solemn "thank you" to the woman for hanging on the crucifix of the white man's transgressions against the Indian nation.

Gently Rory Casso embraced this lost soul in his arms, this lump of flesh that had once been a woman. With the tenderness of a lover, he lightly kissed her forehead as he slid his Bowie under the woman's left rib, quickly and painlessly severing the woman's artery.

***

As the winds rattled the cote, Casso shivered to the recollection of the woman's battered image, and he set his meal of fish down. He could not eat with that vision exhumed from his memory.

Bearing the recall of that vanquished essence to his shoulders, Casso promised himself that Bronwyn and Cricket would never know that fate.

He would be ready, soon, to ride, and he would ride hard.

25

CHEEKS AND BONES

Cricket was pressed precariously against the unsteady earth. She had splayed her body out in order to slow her slide and she had compressed her weight flat against the unsteady shale. Afraid to breathe too deeply for risk of setting the stone to moving again, her voice was soft and shallow when calling to Juke and Bronwyn above her. "Don't toss a rope down, it'll start the stone to sliding."

When the horse had tumbled over the edge into the black below, Cricket had heard two body thumps as the horse bounced on its way to its final resting place. It may have been four seconds total in falling. Two hundred feet down to the floor of the canyon. Down would not be an option for Cricket's rescue.

Bronwyn was talking to Cricket while Juke considered the options. Burying the urgency in her voice, she spoke calmly and reassuringly. "You hang tight, sweetie, we're coming for you."

Deeply rooted, the dogwood scrub would be the best anchor for a rescue line, but the unsteady, sliding shale made throwing a line down to Cricket prohibitive. Unless . . .

Now with the early morning light, Juke could examine the rock face with more clarity. Along the trail that they had traversed, the shale slide was only three feet or so across. But below this trail, the slide opened up in an ever-widening V until it spilled over the ledge below at twenty feet across. And Cricket was sprawled in the middle of the V, mere feet from where the stone bled over the lip of the cliff's rim.

"Bronwyn, bring me that long rope and some leather

twine," Juke called up the trail to where Bronwyn had strung the remaining two horses. "And the saddle bags."

Juke leaped across the three feet of shale that intersected the trail so that he was now on the side opposite Bronwyn. "Tie it down to that big scrub yonder. 'N tie it down tight."

"We can't toss this rope down there; it'll start the rock sliding. . . ."

"Jest tie 'er down."

As Cricket clung to the shaky shale, Bronwyn secured her end of the rope to a dogwood scrub on her side of the slide, while Juke busied his end of the rope likewise to a big scrub on his side.

When the rope ends were secure, Juke estimated the centermost spot of the rope, and with the leather twine he fastened the saddlebags midpoint.

The shale slid slowly under Cricket, but it was moving. She was now inches from the cliff's precipice and a tumble into the abyss below. Breathing shallowly, she listened as the shale stones continued the plink-plink-plink as they dribbled over the edge of the precipice.

Calling down, Juke warned Cricket of the projectile that would soon be soaring over her head. "Hold fast and keep your head down."

Bronwyn was interested now. "What's your play?"

"I'm fixin' on tossin' these saddlebags clear of Cricket's head, over the edge of the cliff behind her. If I toss it clear of the shale, it shouldn't start a slide. Then we should be able to reel her in from the two ends by cupping Cricket into the cusp of the rope. If we can catch her in the rope, we can draw her up over the shale."

"But what if the rope hits the shale above her?"

Juke finished knotting his end of the rope tight. "Then she's lost. But that's what the weight of these saddlebags is for. I'm hopin' to use their weight as ballast to toss the rope high enough to clear Cricket and catch behind her. Then she will be caught in the rope."

"Nice in theory."

CHAPTER TWENTY-FIVE

"Yep, nice in theory." And then to Cricket, "You understand the plan, Cricket?"

"Yep, I understand, but the shale's picking up slide fast, let's get to it."

Estimating the vigor needed for the two-armed underhand toss, Juke slung the saddlebags, sailing them high over Cricket and into the void below her. Above Cricket, the crisp snap of the rope as it stretched taut against its grasp to the dogwood cracked the morning still. The ropes caught at the edge of cliff to either side of Cricket and the saddlebag ballast slammed against the wall below the overhang. As the ropes slapped tight against the shale, the stone hastened to the smacking rope and quickened its avalanche over the side of the precipice. The avalanching stone collected the screaming Cricket in its wake, sailing her off the overhang's lip and into the abyss below.

Even as Bronwyn called out in an anguished bawl, the rope ends tethered on either side of the shale slide slapped taut against the ground, and the scrub brush bent in strain against the sudden weight of the girl.

In a rush of sliding stone Cricket was carried over the edge of the rock face, only to be caught in the cusp of the saddlebags dangling from the rope. Luck was with her, as her arms had spread wide in the rush over the cliff, and the rope caught under her armpits. In a crucified position Cricket hung there, dangling high above the canyon below.

Hoisting Cricket over the lip of the rock face and across the shale was a painstaking affair, as the shale fought to keep Cricket in its teeth. Finally, against the strain, Juke and Bronwyn managed to pull Cricket across the slipping stone and into their arms.

It took time and it took care to reel in the rope that had caught under Cricket's arms. And the only thing lost to the spilling stone was the saddlebags that were used as ballast to throw the rope. These had been Juke's saddlebags. And these saddlebags were the reservoir for the Reynolds Savings and Loan payroll.

Free of the shale, Juke, Bronwyn, and Cricket continued

their trek to surmount the canyon. A slow, precarious climb, it took the full of the day for the party, led now by the half-breed Juke Bauque, to ascend to the apex of the box canyon. This box canyon that had become their prison. They were exhausted when they crested the ridge, but they were free of the canyon.

The ascent's toll was felt by none more than Cricket, and by the time they had reached the summit, she was a rope of frayed ends. The final half-mile of climb, Cricket clung fast to Juke's waist belt as the party clambered up the wall.

Cresting the summit had drained the party of verve, but, as fatigued as the company was, they knew that they could not set camp here. When the Thompson gang realized their escape, this would be the first ground that they would scour for fresh track. The horses had weathered the climb better than the people. Throwing themselves upon the wagon breeds, it would be a matter of sticking fast.

Cricket's dark curls clung to her face like vines to stone. "Can you ride?" Bronwyn encouraged.

Though the smile was weak, Cricket was determined. "I can ride if the horse can scuttle."

With the loss of Cricket's horse toppling over the canyon's precipice, they were down to two horses. Cricket joined Bronwyn in the saddle, nestling behind her and holding tight. As Bronwyn turned the horse's nose to the west, Juke backtracked to obscure their trace as best he could.

With Bronwyn now taking the lead rein, Juke and the women began a mad dash for Cheyenne. Down to just the two wagon breeds, they would need to hasten their escape. With Bronwyn and Cricket sharing a saddle and Juke bringing up the rear and blurring their tracks as best he could manage at this pace.

Juke understood that to fully shadow the tracks that they were setting, they would need to follow a slower and more circuitous route. But time and enemies would not allow the patience. And however vague a track Juke was able to leave for the Thompson gang, he knew that the Dog Soldiers would be able to read it. Expedience was now their best hope.

CHAPTER TWENTY-FIVE

These were fine mounts that Hickory Dixon had secured, but they were wagon ponies and they were bred for power, not for speed. The wagon breeds had plenty of muscle to mount the box canyon's walls, but their gait as saddle ponies was cumbersome. Even at a good clip, this would be two weeks of hard ride before they would manage Cheyenne and the deliverance it offered. Two weeks and two troops of bad news that were dogging their trail.

They strung along the lower lands, using as much cover as the watersheds could offer. The December snow flurries had subsided and allowed them easier terrain to transverse. But this also meant that the hunters would have a wider expanse of visibility. Keeping to cover as much as the topography allowed, the half-breed and women pressed on.

Juke had lost the Reynolds Savings and Loan payroll over the cliff when they had rescued Cricket. But those saddlebags could be recovered in the spring. And the bags might be safer where they lay. But this also meant that he and the women had now lost any bargaining chip that they had had with the Thompson gang.

"It will not be stealth but speed that will provide for our escape," reminded Juke.

***

A chilled wind blew crisp, crying mournfully as it was channeled through the gully wash. The air was bitter with cold, and the sky paled when Rory Casso had had enough of the ravine's stick and stone sanctuary. Five days, or was it more?, of fever and delirium in the grotto's womb had left him weak but in some state of recovery.

Slipping bareback onto Rockwell, he took one last survey of the solace of this snow shelter, of this interim home, and he heeled Rockwell out of the gully wash.

It was a good ten miles of rough terrain between the gully wash and the box canyon that Casso had last seen Juke and the women. And though his atrophied muscles felt every inch of those ten miles, it felt good to sit his steed and suck in the freshness of the December chill.

Would the women yet be in that coulee? Would they be captured? Would they be dead? And, of the two, captured or dead, which was the worse?

Rockwell snorted against the cold and blew ice crystals into the air. The horse was primed for travel. Too long its muscles had set dormant in the gully sanctuary, and now the steed was keen to cut trail. The trace leading up to the ravine was track free. Even so, Casso had Rockwell reined to caution.

Drawing above the box canyon, the same overlook of the canyon where he first witnessed Bronwyn Mason's party under attack from the Dog Soldiers, Rory studied the camp below. All was quiet. No movement of man or beast. The snow that had settled on the camp was fresh and unmarked by foot or hoof. With vigilance, Casso descended the box canyon's slope to the wagon's encampment.

The fire pit was five days cold. The wagons were tied down, abandoned, and the people and ponies were gone. There were no signs to indicate a fight had been staged here. And Juke Bauque and the women, he knew, would fight to the bone.

Turning his study to the steep wall that captured the back wall of this canyon, Casso surveyed the barrier's base. These were the very same rocks that he himself had scaled just days before. And now, three more humans and three more horses had mounted these rocks.

Casso deliberated on the tracks at the base of the ravine's wall. Although somewhat obscured by time and weather, it was apparent to Rory Casso that the track that Juke and the women had pursued had led up the rock face. Damned if they hadn't climbed the wall.

Casso tucked Rockwell into the trail with some excitement, for this, this reading of trace upon the earth, was Casso's place of comfort. This was Casso's element. Tracking at its most primitive. Its rawest.

Tracking, be it man or beast tracking, is not just the tracing of footsteps or blood or even scat but, rather, the reading of

CHAPTER TWENTY-FIVE

the earth itself. It is a connection to the ancients. The time before the white man or the red man. It was story upon story of the earth and how it had supported beasts through the millennium, and, as sacred as the Ten Commandments, tracking was written in stone.

The tracks of these ancients were written as an epic that began before the mountains were raised and the valleys gouged. They were written in narrative by rumblings deep in the earth's breast and suckled forth to feed the topography. They were written as yarns by drunken summits and fairy tales by wispy marshes. And over the millennium's history, the wind and the rain and the sun had edited this earth's narrative.

And somewhere in this story of stone, Casso would find its plot.

***

On their escape, Juke Bauque first sought to mask their ponies' tracks by tucking into the passageway of a herd of buffalo on their meandering migration to their wintering range. And although the buffalos' hooves did help to murky their own tracks, the buffalo were drifting in a more southwesterly direction and would lead them too far to the south for Cheyenne.

The contingent remained tucked into the buffalo tracks for the better part of a day, until the bison's path intersected a rocky river. The river was flowing from high in the mountains to the west on its own migration down to the Missouri. Here the troop turned their ponies from the buffalos' corridor and into the path of rivulet.

The plan was for Juke and the women to walk the horses in as much unfrozen water as allowed in these drains, letting the waters wash their tracks from the hunters. They must assume that they were being followed by both the Thompson outlaws and the renegade Indians. The water's passageway would slow their escape, but it might buy them precious time, as the obfuscation of their tracks would demand a more careful study by their pursuers.

It was a grueling ride for Juke and Bronwyn and Cricket. A constant cold wind washed through these river cuts and the dampness of the river kept the air chilled with ice. The horses, these wagon breeds, were not used to this kind of rocky and wet avenue, having served their time to the tracks of carts, and they stumbled along to the river stone.

To save the ponies, Cricket, in turn, rode double behind Bronwyn and then Juke. In this manner, they steadily made their way to the West. To Cheyenne. To salvation.

For the better part of twenty-four hours the fugitives sat their saddles and rode the stream. They slept in the saddle and they consumed the sinewy dried meat and hardtack provisions while in the saddle. When they needed to relieve themselves, they lowered themselves onto a rock in the stream and let the water rush away any sign of their passage.

It was a tough row. It was damp and it was cold and it was exhausting in this winter water's corridor.

And it was their only chance of escape.

26

ANOTHER ROUND OF COFFEE GROUNDS

Jack Bettle kicked at what was left of the fire. "No more games with them women. We go in there now and dig them out."

The Indian raid on the outlaws' camp had left little humor in the collective. It took the better part of a blustery winter day to round up their ponies, and it left them sloshing in slushy boots and soggy spirits.

When Rory Casso's escape had been discovered, the men had done a quick sweep of the area, but, failing to detect his track, they had had to let the quarry go. It was with some dismay to note, though, that Rory Casso's pony had likewise vanished to the hills. Consolation was taken in the sad condition that Casso was left in after the sound thrashing he had suffered at the hands, and the guns, of the gang. "Probably won't last the night in this cold."

"Play up thet fire agin. We could use a bit of flame to dry up the leather before we bust outta here," judged Barrett Thompson. "'Sides, there are some trained guns in thet canyon. We got 'em trapped good like but to go up thet cut is suicide against their artillery."

Jack Bettle's big frame now loomed over the squatting Thompson. "We can't be colder than we are now. I say we just go in there blastin' them out." By nature, Bettle was a bully, and, reflexively, he threw down a challenge to Thompson.

There was silence in the camp now, as all eyes turned to Thompson. Slowly Barrett Thompson uncorked his chubby frame from the squat and came up nose to nose with Bettle. "You offerin' to run this outfit, now, Bettle?" Barrett

Thompson was much the shorter of the men but he pressed his bulk of fat against Jack Bettle.

Bullies are not as quick to the scrap when they are confronted with an adversary of equal dimensions, and Bettle's eyes began to flicker left and right, looking for a way out. There were no eyes to meet for support, as Farrot Pierce's hand rested on his holstered Colt. Bettle looked for an escape as Thompson's fat cigar smoldered under Bettle's chin. Finally Bettle's eyes settled in the dirt at his feet, and he backtracked. "Naw, Barrett, it's your outfit and it's your play. I just know all about those guns in thet canyon, 'n I think we can take 'em."

Jack Bettle had recognized that he might have pushed too hard and was backpedaling as Thompson scrutinized him carefully. Barrett Thompson was not a man to kill another man if it was not a good business decision. He studied on the way that Jack Bettle might be of some use to him. A smile smeared Thompson's face and, keeping his eyes on Bettle, he spoke through his cigar at the side of his mouth to Farrot Pierce. "Ease thet gun, Pierce, I'm in a forgivin' mood and we're gonna need this boy."

As Jack Bettle backed away, Thompson followed him. Thompson stuck his cigar between two fat fingers and jabbed at Bettle's chest with them. "I'll tell you what, Bettle, you take your pard there and go up that draw. Tell them thet we want to talk peace with them ladies. Tell them to give up the Reynolds payroll and they kin have free passage."

Jack Bettle was now in full compliance. "Sure, boss. You plannin' on settlin' fer jes' the money?"

"I'm plannin' on tellin' 'im as much. Once we git the money, all bets are off. You kin have your own play on the women."

Recalling the last time Bettle and Dunn had tangled with Bronwyn Mason, Kipper Dunn rubbed at the remains of his ear and aired, "Wait a minute, cap, like you says, it's suicide fer us to go up the spout of thet canyon. 'Sides, after what transpired betwixt the Mason girl and us, they ain't in no

CHAPTER TWENTY-SIX

mind to negotiate with Bettle and me. Thet Mason girl made it a promise to cut us down on next sighting and thet girl's crazy enough to do it."

Thompson was tired of having his orders questioned and turned his bulk fully on Dunn. "I think thet it's suicide for you boys not to go."

And so it was settled, Jack Bettle and Kipper Dunn would go directly up the canyon to negotiate with the Mason troop. Thompson, Pierce, Jimmy Patterson, and Kelly Bank would hold the rims of the box canyon ready to spill lead into the negotiations.

***

It was Jimmy Patterson that discovered the scuffs high on the ridge above the box canyon. These were the tracks that the Mason party had scratched in the canyon's brim when they had made their escape.

Barrett Thompson and Farrot Pierce had taken lofty lookouts at the mouth of the coulee to keep Juke and the women trapped. Kelly Bank and Patterson set up their armories on the cliffs above the encampment and would have the best outlook for spattering lead into the camp. As Patterson was making a cozy gun turret on the chasm's ridge, he laid his saddle blanket down next to the tracks that were scuffed when the Mason party had crested the canyon's ledge.

For a book-learned man, Juke did a tolerable enough job of cloaking the trail. But the cut marks that Juke and Bronwyn and Cricket had left when they topped the summit could not be veiled. This track was cut in stone.

Once discovered, the outlaws were quick to tuck into the trail of the runaways.

Juke Bauque had employed backtracking, brush disguise, and stone traversing as was available for track concealment. These were all elements of concealment that he had read about in the newspaper articles and books that were trickling back to Boston from the Western reaches. And the Thompson gang had some occasion to pause to study sign, and it slowed their stalk. But any shroud of cover that Juke was able to employ was compromised by the Mason party's ultimate destination: west, always west, was their trajectory, and Barrett Thompson understood this.

On the occasion that Juke's track-secreting had befuddled the outlaws, it was only a matter for the gang to scout out a circle to once again pick up sign. Sometimes they would have to circle wide to find sign, but as the fundamental movement of the Mason party was west, the track was always hit upon quick enough.

27

BABY CAN DANCE

If it was an easy track for the Thompson gang to read, it was that much easier for Casso to catch the trace. First, the track decoys that Juke was employing were textbook stuff, and they warranted little study for Rory Casso. But more so, the track that the Thompson gang was laying in pursuit was written by confident and arrogant men with heavy artillery and no inkling that they might be hunted as well.

Although the preceding assemblies, the Mason party and the Thompson gang, had had a five-day head start on Casso, the breach between them would be quick to close.

Rory Casso spent little time in study of the tracks laid by the hunted parties. Of more concern to Casso was the occasional sign of the Dog Soldiers that he fated upon. These renegade Indian tracks were fresh. And they, too, had joined the parade of the troops pushing to Cheyenne.

Instead of reading the path marked by the track of preceding groups, Rory Casso was reading the lay of the land. Rather than following in the tracks of the preceding parties, Casso turned to high ground. He followed the cuts of the land, rather than the peopled tracks. Instead of any specific track, Casso studied the scratch of the earth itself that a rider would be expected to lean toward.

There are natural passages that a body will follow, and Rory Casso followed these corridors. Where a steep ridge might offer resistance to a rider, Casso followed the cut of the land below. Where the stone escarpment of a craggy-sided ravine would present a struggle, Casso galloped the ridges above. In this way, Rory Casso was able to cover in hours the same ground that the earlier travelers had spent days traversing.

When the Mason party had turned into the buffalo track, Casso had seen the move from an overlook. Setting his saddle on this mountain perch, he followed the buffalo track to where it intersected with a wide and shallow mountain stream. This was a river heading off into the Western reaches. And Rory Casso knew that this would be the path that the Mason party would turn to.

As he set his steed high on the overlook, Casso understood, too, that the Dog Soldiers would be following these parties in a like manner. And it was these Dog Soldiers that wearied Casso's deliberations. Already these Indians would be ahead of the Mason party, anticipating their every veer.

But even though these Indians were tracking like Indians, these Indians were not playing by Indian rules. To be in the field this late in the season was unusual. To trail prey for such a great distance was extraordinary. But to attack a camp of heavily fortified men was exceptional. Even for a band of Dog Soldiers that was on the hunt for squaws for the long winter nights ahead, this was remarkable.

But these Indian reflections would have to wait, as the more pressing problem at hand would be intercepting the Thompson gang on its quest for the Mason party.

Rory Casso heeled Rockwell into the chase.

28

FOR FORTY DAYS AND FOR FORTY NIGHTS

For forty days and for forty nights,
The lightning cracks with blinding fright.
Nowhere to run, you can take no flight,
For forty days and for forty nights.

J. Bauque

Due to the wear on the people and on the horses, Juke Bauque was now second-guessing himself about whether they should have tried to use this water alley as a route of disguise. The horses were exhausted, Juke, Bronwyn, and Cricket were worn raw, and both the people and the animals were bone-chilled.

Now, after almost twenty-four hours of drifting westward in this rivulet of stone and ice, the party spilled from its trenches. Though it was on everybody's mind, not a mention was made of the Thompson gang, or of the Dog Soldiers. Nor what their capture would mean in the hands of either party.

Turning from the watercourse, Juke, Bronwyn, and Cricket pointed their mounts nose-first into the winter winds of the west. The horses needed rest, and the people astride them were sleeping in the saddle. With more than a hundred miles of tough, cold terrain yet to traverse, they would need to rest and recuperate if they hoped to make the final push.

The good thing about spending the better part of a day in the mountain stream was the obfuscation of the ponies' tracks. The bad thing, for these wagon ponies, was that it would soften their hooves to the tough earth ahead. The wagon breeds would be no good to them on the hard stones of the trail ahead if they did not let the ponies' hooves harden to the task. Convalescence was now mandatory.

The evening was cold and clear, with a brilliant and panoramic spectacle of stars dripping their light onto the hills. It would be a spectacular moon to huddle beneath a buffalo robe with a lover and tally kisses beneath the infinity of the stars. But tonight, this crisp coldness of the everlasting starlight only served to mock the tired travelers.

Drawing into an outcropping of wood, the party trickled from their ponies. There was a light wind in this copse of trees as Juke, Bronwyn, and Cricket set camp in a small stand of willow and cottonwood trees and the red osier dogwood shrub.

"Good to be on the dirt again."

Cricket, with her thoughts on the pursuing throngs, queried, "Is it wise, yet, to flame a fire?"

It was Bronwyn, knowing the thoughts behind Cricket's question, who answered with resolve, "Damn the hunters. Fire is mandatory if we have any hope of drying our chill and jumping those hills."

As Juke Bauque torched the kindling, he added, "There is something to that, but rest quick and dry fast, for when the dawn breaks, we push hard to Cheyenne."

As the fire was sparked, a great horned owl sang out its mournful whoo, whoo-hoo, whoooo-hoo and Cricket wondered aloud, "Least we don't have to worry about Thompson's men now, without the payroll, I mean."

Bronwyn reminded her, "Thompson doesn't know that the payroll spilled over the cliff. And besides, that's assuming that the payroll is all that those boys are hunting."

With some small quaking in her voice, Cricket rejoined, "But we do know what the Indians are hunting."

In shallow sleep and wrapped tight in their pony blankets, Juke and the women surrendered their exhaustion to the star-swollen heavens.

29

WORLD OF WOE

Traveling alone, Rory Casso had made good time along the ridges. When he had identified the route, the watercourse, that Juke and the women had taken, he understood the design for escape that they had deployed. It was common and it was a book-learned maneuver, this using the cover of water to obscure track. And when Casso read sign that the Thompson gang had followed them into the waterway, he smiled to himself. There would be no skilled trackers in the Thompson gang and if he could jump ahead of the Thompson gang, he felt some measure of confidence that he would be able to throw the outlaws off the women's track.

Once again Casso turned Rockwell to the ridges. From on high, Casso studied the lay of the land and eyed the shallow river as its meandering path cut its way through the rock. Inexperienced trackers, such as Thompson and his gang, would follow the stream until they uncovered some evidence of their prey cutting from the water. This was a cumbersome process of elimination for the trackers, for they would have to study the river's bank carefully, rock by rock, lest they miss sign of their quarry's escape.

The Thompson gang was busying themselves with the trees and could not see the forest. On high, surveying the bigger picture, Rory Casso was following the conduit of the forest.

Besides the scrutiny of the river below, Rory Casso was keeping a scout-out on the rims across the river's cut. He knew that if the Indians were following Juke and Bronwyn and Cricket, they too would be riding the ridges and reading from the book of the ancients. At times he thought that he could recognize a Dog Soldier's trace, but, then, no. If the Indians were there, then they were aware of Casso's presence and they were keeping to the sly.

As Rory Casso sat Rockwell, studying the tracks of the women and the tracks of the outlaws and the tracks of the Indians, he thought of the tracks that he had laid in his life. Life tracks. The tracks that men leave in their hearts and on their souls. The traces of men that are written in the ridges and valleys of their beings. Like the memories of the sad and lonely beings that peopled the saloons where Casso bar-swabbed, cutting tracks through the misery and vanquish of their existence.

***

Although it never gave a full measure of comfort to the young Rory Casso, wandering the wilderness of the Western reaches offered some respite from the life he had known in Rawlings. The memories of those days as a boy bar swab were filled with a different kind of isolation than what he learned in the remoteness of the mountains. In the wild, Rory Casso was isolated by space. In Rawlings, it was an isolation of the spirit.

The wildness that Casso experienced in the bars and saloons of his youth was a much sadder wildness than the wildness offered by the mountains. The saloon wildness was a wildness filled with lonely men and angry men, men that were on the dodge from law and life and memories. But mostly these men were dodging themselves. Men that were more comfortable looking through the murky prism of alcohol than the clarity offered by sobriety. Rory watched the men and the women move like apparitions through the swinging

CHAPTER TWENTY-NINE

doors of those saloons and he wanted no part of that.

Some of these bar sojourners had visible scars that they wore like tattooed testimonials to their pain. These scars spoke of the tortures suffered to a man's body. These physical scars were obvious and implicit and told the story in the first person. But young Rory found the invisible scars the saddest. Scars that cut deep wounds into a man's psyche. Scars of loneliness and abandonment and emptiness and shallowness. Cavernous and deep scars that the alcohol could never heal but only cauterize the bleeding for a spell.

Turn the lights low, so they can't see the scars,
Then tuck your body in the darkest corner of this bar.
Well there you go,
Another world of woe.

And then there were the men that hid their scars under cover of bluster. Feigning bravado and believing in the deception of the bottle's fearlessness. But this courage was not real courage. It was an alcohol-fueled courage. It was the kind of courage a man gets when his senses have been compromised, and it was a courage that would never stand strong and true against the squalls of life's tribulations.

He's got bravado, he measures every word,
But he tilts his hat low so you cannot look into his hurt.
Well there you go,
Another world of woe.

But it was the women prowling these saloons that Rory Casso found to be the saddest of the lot. Women that had given up on love and on children and on their future. Women that had cashed in their hope for a ticket on another round of liquid comfort. Women that had, for reasons as sad and as varied as their number, stalked the edges of humanity from barstool to barstool.

> *You see the sufferin', you see the pain in her eyes,*
> *You want to help her but it's best just to let her cry.*
> *Well there you go,*
> *Another world of woe.*

J. Bauque

Rory Casso had seen a lot of sadness through the prism of a bar swab. It was a sadness for the ages and it was a sadness that he would have no part of.

These wild reaches of America's young and untamed West were little challenge compared to the wildness that raged in the hearts of the tortured souls of these barfly men and women, salooned in their misery.

***

Cresting the ridges, Casso did not bother with the track of man but, rather, he read the bend of the land and followed the story of the ancients. From on high Casso would pursue the arches in the cut of the terrain. He would surmise the curvature of the valleys and ensue the bend of the waterways. And he would know where Juke and the women would turn even before they themselves knew. By surveying the inclination of the earth, by reading the book of the ancients, Rory Casso was reading the future.

***

Juke Bauque and the women awoke to a sizzling fire and hot coffee on the spit. The smell of venison whiffed the camp and there was an extra set of buckskinned shoulders tending to the burn. Rory Casso's shoulders.

"Miss me?"

30

TOO MANY SHADOWS

The copse that Juke and the women had settled in was a thicket of buttonbush, chokecherries, and a singular peachleaf willow. The willow provided good cover, dispersing the spit fire's smoke as it filtered through its whip branches.

Although Rory Casso had ridden the ridges rather than trudging through the river course, the ride had nonetheless taken its toll on him. The bruises he had suffered at the hands of Thompson and his men were thick with blood and pain. His head was throbbing with the remnants of the concussion, and the bullet holes in his leg, front and back, had opened and were trickling blood.

As Bronwyn tended Casso's lesions with willow pitch, she mock-scolded him, "Most men would have the common sense to sit out this damage."

With a wink, "Most men wouldn't be hunting up such a pretty nurse to tend their damage."

Gnawing on a chip of venison, Juke surveyed Casso and then estimated, "I think that maybe you might have jumped from the pan into the fire this time." It was a settling calm in the quality of Juke's voice. It was a voice of warmth and quiet that began its travels somewhere deep in his diaphragm and journeyed to the Serengeti of his African ancestry.

"You speak the truth, and I do need to rest my eyes a spell. And Rockwell needs a piece of rest, as well, if we're going to push hard."

The chirping that was Cricket's voice was the perfect harmony for Juke's baritone. "Rest? Now? But what about the Thompson gang?"

"I did chance to spot them down the creek. They've got some hardy guns in thet troop but their trackin' skills are better to trackin' money and liquor. They don't represent well on the track of man."

Tying fast a lanyard of pitch and leaves to Casso's wounded leg, Bronwyn probed, "You seen 'em, then? Thompson and his men?"

"Yep. They're maybe eight hours or so to the arrears and sloggin' slow through thet creek."

Cricket had been hanging back at Juke's arm. She now seemed to always be within an arm's reach of Juke Bauque. With some trepidation she queried, "And what of the Indians? Any trace of 'em?"

"I'm not sure. Times I thought I glimpsed Indian sign but I couldn't give oath to that."

"If'n we got eight hours' lead on the Thompson gang, then you've got some small spell to recoup." Bronwyn was firm with this.

And Casso, dog-tired from the wear and tear of the drive, had to agree. "'Spect you're right. Best thing for me to do would be to grind some venison and catnap my blanket for a couple of hours."

Cricket offered, "Do you really think that we should be laying up here for a couple of hours? I mean, what with the Thompson gang gathering flank?"

"Nope. I'm meaning for you to fill up on some deer steak and hot coffee and pull out for Cheyenne."

Bronwyn was having none of that. "Now that we've found you, we ain't about to leave you here."

Casso had to laugh. "Now that you found me?"

Bronwyn caught what she'd said, blushed slightly and then threw it off. "You know what I'm sayin'. Now that you're with us again we are four guns strong. More than enough firepower to tangle with that Thompson brigade."

"Thet's a fair piece of reasoning, but if you leave now, I can catch a couple of hours shutdown that I need and then trail you out of camp. Following in your tracks I can make

CHAPTER THIRTY

your tread disappear into the stone."

But Bronwyn was resolute. "Nope. We all leave together. If they catch us, we make our stand as one battery." Bronwyn spoke with the command and the conviction of her father's voice and there would be no arguing with her now, and so it was settled.

As Juke, Bronwyn, and Cricket breakfasted on the venison, Rory Casso turned to the slumber of his blanket.

***

When Casso had scouted the Thompson gang plodding through the creek downstream, he had estimated an eight-hour gap between them and the Mason party. These eight hours would allow him to catch a couple of good hours of rest and still be six hours out front of their hunt.

Six hours was hedging on the minimal amount of time to bury track. Time was a necessity in secreting track because, no matter how good the backtracker, the earth itself needs time to recover from the passage of man. For Casso, there was no track that was secreted within a six-hour fissure that he could not follow. However, the Thompson gang was not studied in the way of the Hunkpapa trackers, and Casso was comfortable in his capabilities of track cloaking.

But there were two things that Casso was not privy to in his estimation of the Thompson gang. First thing: Casso did not figure on how badly Barrett Thompson wanted the payroll. Second: Casso had not figured into this equation just how badly Jack Bettle was hell-bent on evening the score with Bronwyn Mason. He wanted revenge on the woman that had faced him down and kicked him to the trail. And he wanted to exact that revenge on every inch of Bronwyn's body.

Hours deep into the hunt of the waterway on the trail of the Mason party, Barrett Thompson devised a way to quicken the chase. The gang now numbered six gun sharks, and Thompson ordered the men to ride the banks of the waterway, three men per side, in weighty study of the ground. This hastened the outlaws' pursuit twofold. First, with three sets of eyes at study on each bank, any withdrawal of the river by the Mason party would be detected quickly. Second, by riding the bank, the outlaws could hurry their pace, as they would not have to deal with the river's proclivities. Without having to push against the current of the river, and scrambling over the stones of the river's bed, the Mason party's covert trail was exposed in quick fashion.

***

The Thompson gang had pushed hard through the night up the watercourse trail, and Rory Casso awoke looking smack down the barrel of Barrett Thompson's Colt .45. Without a word, Thompson reached down and removed Casso's Bowie from his sheath and flung it to the fire. The Bowie stuck in the top log of the fire with a dull thump.

"You jes' lay there nice and peaceful, like. We've got a piece of transactin' to do."

31

RANSACKERS, BACKSTABBERS

Six guns now seized the camp.

While Kelly Bank and Jim Patterson busied themselves with the ransacking of the camp's saddlebags, Farrot Pierce and Kipper Dunn had their guns trained on the group.

Jack Bettle wasted no time in his mission, walking directly up to Bronwyn, grabbing a fistful of her hair, and, as he pulled her to him, slapping her hard across the face. "This time I'm the one holding the gun."

There was a cold moment as Bronwyn's eyes flared. A drop of blood oozed from the corner of her mouth as she glared into the eyes of Jack Bettle. Imposing his big frame over Bronwyn, he outweighed her by a hundred and fifty pounds. Bronwyn worked up juice in her mouth and spit blood into Jack Bettle's face.

At first surprised by the spatter, and then enraged, Bettle drew his arm back and balled his hand into a big fist to swing a roundhouse into Bronwyn's face.

With the fracas going on between Bronwyn and Bettle, no one had seen Casso move. Catlike he pounced on Bettle, and, intercepting Bettle's fist, Casso laid his own clout across Bettle's mouth and sent him sprawling to the dirt.

Momentarily stunned by the blow, Jack Bettle collected himself, rubbing the sting from his jaw. He scrutinized Casso up and down, and then he smiled. "So, the little hero rescues the fair damsel." Quickly he blustered to his feet, with both fists balled and ready for battle.

Thompson stepped between them. "Leave 'em be. We've got some negotiatin' to do with this boy."

Jack Bettle did not like the idea of being smacked to the ground without the opportunity for retaliation. "The hell I'll let 'em be. Nobody socks Jack Bettle and walks . . ."

"I said, leave 'em be. If we can't come to a reasonable transaction," and now Thompson turned to Casso, "then maybe you can have at 'im. And leave the girls be, too, for now."

Thwarted, Bettle was in full tantrum. "I owe thet girl."

"And I'm a whole lot less interested in what you owe thet girl than I am about the Reynolds payroll. I said, leave 'em be." And with that, Thompson turned his gun on Juke. "Where's the money, breed?"

Juke Bauque smiled. "You might say the money is in the bank. Well, leastways, over the bank."

"What the hell does thet mean?"

Jack Bettle, in a fighting mood anyways, came up beside Juke and drilled a big fist into his side, collapsing the Black Indian to the ground. "The hell with you, breed, they ain't no banks out 'ere."

As Juke doubled over to the ground, Cricket came up and laid a smack across Bettle's face that sounded like a gunshot. As she drew her left hand for another smack, Bettle grabbed her wrists and, with eyes glowering in rage, threw her down on top of the heap that was Bauque. Kicking out at the collection of Juke and Cricket at his feet, Bettle managed to lay a leaded foot across the two of them.

A second kick was interrupted by Thompson barking, "Let 'em be."

But Jack Bettle would not be denied. "The hell I will." And he landed another boot on Bauque and Cricket that jolted the both of them off the ground.

The blast from Barrett Thompson's gun stopped Bettle's next kick, but it did not ease his anger. Now he scowled, red-eyed, at Thompson, "I'm gettin' a mite tired of being smacked around by these girls."

"And I'm gettin' a mite tired of your mouth. Thet payroll is more important to me than your payback." Then he turned

CHAPTER THIRTY-ONE

to Juke. "What the hell do you mean that the payroll is in the bank, breed?"

Juke Bauque had taken the worst of Bettle's foot and was sucking wind. Cricket clung to Juke and did the talking. "It means that the payroll tumbled over a cliff bank back a piece. With you on the hunt, we didn't exactly have time to clamber down and get it."

Farrot Pierce, shorter than Bronwyn, had been holding his gun on her. "No games. You got the money stashed and we're gonna find out where. Now we can do this the easy way, or," and he rubbed the barrel of his gun along Bronwyn's crotch, "we can do this the hard way."

The pockmarks on Kipper Dunn's face squeezed into a salacious grin. "The hard way. I like thet, the hard way," and Dunn savored the word "hard." "Let's do it the hard way."

Thompson rolled his cigar in his mouth and challenged Juke, "Whataya say, breed? You gonna play hard to get with the payroll, or are the boys here gonna play the hard way with the women?"

Having been stymied in his attempt to knock around Juke and Cricket, Jack Bettle sidled back over to Rory Casso. Bettle wanted his ounce of flesh wherever he could find it. "Well, we don't need this mouth, and first ways, I need to even up with this boy here."

Watching Farrot Pierce's gun play along Bronwyn's crotch, Cricket implored, "I'm tellin' true. The payroll tumbled over that box canyon when we cleared the wall."

Thompson looked up and down at the Indian Black man. "I can't tell if'n yer a lying Indian or a traitor slave."

Waving his gun in Rory Casso's direction, Thompson directed Bettle, "Have at 'im, if'n ya want."

With that, Jack Bettle turned his bulk on Casso, but Casso was on his toes and ready. With the rush of adrenaline, Rory Casso took no notice of his already gashed skull or of the ravaged leg that had been shredded by the bullet holes. Bettle had half a foot and seventy pounds on Casso and, as they circled to the battle, the size disparity was plain. Jack

Bettle's bulk lumbered to the sphere of combat while Casso, the Indian fighter, circled on cat feet.

Bettle swung first. The big fist looped at Casso, and the Indian fighter easily leaned out of harm's reach. As Bettle's blow drifted past Casso's chin, he slipped a stiff right hand over Bettle's shoulder, drawing blood from his mouth. In one deft motion, Casso followed that blow by quickly digging his left fist hard into Bettle's kidney. These were not decisive blows, but Bettle felt them all right.

More surprised than hurt, Bettle straightened and, rubbing his chin where Casso had landed the blow, now took full measure of the young man.

Kipper Dunn found great humor in this. "You think maybe thet you have met the better man?" he egged Bettle on.

This served to enrage Bettle, and, bending over, he bull-rushed headlong into the boy. Nimbly sidestepping the charge, Casso used Bettle's own weight and momentum to redirect him downward, drilling Bettle's face into the earth. With his own full weight behind the plunge, Bettle's face slid headlong through the rocks. Coming up from the dirt, Bettle's face was a bloody jumble of skin and stone.

Before Bettle had a chance to collect himself, Casso was on him, pummeling him with a collection of rights and lefts to Bettle's face and body. But Jack Bettle was a mountain of a man, and Casso's blows, vigorous as they were, were not critical. Shucking the blows off, Bettle answered with a swooping backhanded fist that hit Casso like a tree trunk and sent the young man tumbling off.

Again the combatants squared to each other. With a bloodied and stone-gashed face, Bettle looked the worse for the scrape, but Rory Casso's damaged body was not weathering the skirmish well. The blow that had sent Casso off of Bettle had winded Casso, and recovery was coming slow to his lungs.

Bettle feinted with his right hand, and when Casso raised his arms to block the fake clout, Bettle drilled a great plunging left into Casso's ribs. It was a full-bodied left that Bettle swung into Casso's bones. It was a blow that began in the

CHAPTER THIRTY-ONE

outer reaches of yesteryear and pummeled deep into Casso's chest cavity. The crack of Casso's snapping ribs popped in the cold of the winter freeze.

Already winded, the blow that smashed Casso's ribs had spilled the remaining breath from his body and dropped him, doubled over, into the dirt. For Bettle, the cracking sound of Casso's ribs brought a renewed smile of confidence to his bloodied face. Gloating over the boy, Bettle admired his handiwork. "I guess I earned a piece of thet redheaded flame now, eh, boy?"

But Casso was an Indian fighter. And an Indian fighter uses every weakness, whether a foe's weakness or his own weakness, to his advantage. Casso knew that he would have to use his own battered bones to defeat the hulk that was Jack Bettle.

Doubled up as he was, Casso sucked wind against the strain of his busted ribs. Tucking his body into a ball and rolling over, he came to his feet in a crouch and ready for battle. Breathing was shallow for Casso, as every breath brought with it the expansion of lungs and the explosion of the pain to his shattered ribs.

Jack Bettle was firstly surprised by Casso's resilience. Then Bettle was angry. With rage he balled his two big mitts into knuckled anvils and advanced on the boy.

Casso would now need to use his broken ribs to his advantage. Rory Casso's broken ribs would need to be the bait. Lifting his arms high in a feigned attempt to protect his face, Casso offered his ribs to the rage of Bettle. And Bettle took the bait.

With both arms lowered to blast away at Casso's busted bones, Bettle advanced in full swing. Rory Casso steeled himself for the blow to his ribs, knowing full well the pain and damage he would suffer at the looping fists of the brute. But this torture would be necessary for Casso to draw Bettle into his trap. The blast of agony would allow Casso to position himself for the counterattack.

As Bettle's swinging fists dug into Casso's battered ribs,

Casso leaned into Bettle's body. Adrenaline now pumped Casso's system and his movement went on autopilot. The force of Bettle's fist drilled upward into Casso's body and lifted Casso to his toes, raising him up and above Bettle, and positioned Rory to look down into Bettle's eyes. This was the angle that Casso needed, as Bettle's blow elevated him above the much taller man.

Using the torque of the angle above Bettle, and the weight of gravity, Casso came down onto Bettle, drilling his elbow into Bettle's face. With the full body weight of gravity behind the blow, Casso's elbow bore into Bettle's beak, his forearm crushing Bettle's nose, spilling a gush of blood and bone across the camp. And with that gravity-laden blow, Casso's follow-through positioned him directly under Bettle's chin. Like a spring on a buckboard, Casso used his legs to drive the top of his skull through Bettle's massive chin.

Now Casso was in charge, and, grabbing the stunned man by the hair atop his scalp, he yanked at Jack Bettle. As Bettle stumbled under Casso's direction, Jack Bettle was slammed headlong into the trunk of the willow tree. The willow's branches whipped at the skull's impact. Bettle did not. Jack Bettle fell motionless at the foot of the willow.

For a moment the camp was silent, trying to comprehend the beating that Jack Bettle had suffered at the hands of Rory Casso.

But as Bettle lay stock-still in the dirt, Kipper Dunn, coming up from behind, smacked his .45 to the back of Casso's skull. If the gun slap had been more directed, Casso would be out cold, maybe dead, but as it was a glancing blow, it only served to knock Casso face-first to the earth. Lying still by the campfire, Casso feigned unconsciousness.

"Why'n the hell you do thet? We need thet boy for the payroll," Thompson demanded.

But Dunn was already turning to Bronwyn. "I'll git it out of this girl," and he grabbed her blouse and ripped the cloth away, exposing Bronwyn's breasts. Bronwyn pulled her arms across her chest as cover, but Kipper Dunn slapped her face

CHAPTER THIRTY-ONE

and grabbed her wrists, spreading her arms wide for a full examination. "'Sides, I think thet this pussycat owes me a little something for taking my ear."

When the big man sporting a red plaid shirt stepped into the camp, he cast a long shadow even in this soft, early morning light. And it was the voice of a ghost that directed Bronwyn. "Cover up, girl."

In unison, all of the necks in the camp spun to the voice of the ghost that had stepped from the shadows of the brush. Some of the faces in the camp registered joy, and some of the faces in the camp registered fear. But all of the faces chronicled wonderment.

The two big Schofields looked like cannons in the fists of Marshal Isham Mason.

32

LIKE A STONE

Marshal Mason had stepped into the camp from the east, with the morning sun at his back: shining directly into the eyes of the outlaws.

"Cover up, girl. And you boys," indicating with the barrels of his guns, "you boys can lay your iron down easy like."

Puzzled, and with his cigar dangling from his lower lip, for this was not in Barrett Thompson's business blueprint, "I thought you were dead."

The Marshal smiled at that. "The coyotes thought I was dead, too. They seemed mighty surprised when I came up smokin' lead."

It was Kelly Bank that whined, "But we shot you clean off of thet cliff. And then we filled your corpse with lead. I seen it with my own eyes."

"I reckon you know what you seen, alright. And you did manage to shoot me up a mite, but that lead you was pumping off that cliff was into my deputy, Pinto Shaw. And you sure did kill him good."

"But the plaid shirt . . ."

Mason smiled now. "Yep. It was my plaid shirt you shot up all right. Had barely enough time to slip it onto the dead boy before you wedged me. I'll put the cost of the shirt on your tab."

Barrett Thompson cut off the dialogue. "Thet's all well and good, but as it is standing now, Marshal, you've got two guns there and we've got six. I kinda like our odds."

Mason leveled one of the Schofields at Thompson's belly. "I reckon that's so, but I'm counting six of you, and that gives me two bullets for each belly." And waving a Schofield across Thompson's fat abdomen, the Marshal added, "You can play for your guns now or you can lay them down and go peaceful like to your hangin'. Either way, Barrett, you're a dead man."

Marshal Mason was calculating now. He had the drop on the Thompson gang with his Schofields clear of leather and in his fists. He knew these men. He would have to drop Farrot Pierce with his first shot, and he cursed himself for leaving Pierce on the periphery of his vision and of his guns. As big and intimidating as the Schofields were, they were single-action pistols, which meant that Mason would need to thumb-fan the triggers. He was used to that, but it did slow down the process.

Kelly Bank and Jim Patterson would have to stand in line for the Marshal's lead, for Farrot Pierce, far to his right, would need to be the first objective. This would mean that, if a gunfight broke out, Marshal Mason would need to splay his lead from the outside, killing Pierce first, and work his way in. He moved his right gun hand out to cover a wider field. That being decided, he had already promised Barrett Thompson his first slug, and he kept the Schofield in his left fist leveled on Thompson's gut.

Thompson scrutinized the Schofield's generous barrel trained on his midsection and judged his odds. "You really think that you can round us all up and deliver us to justice?"

"Nope, I figure thet I'll have to kill a few of you along the way. Here, along the trail, or at your hangin', makes no matter to me where you die."

As Mason held the Schofields steady at belly level, his eyes flitted from gunner to gunner, appraising each of the six outlaws before him. He analyzed how each man wore his gun, whether hip-high as a cowboy or slung low and tied down in the manner of a slinger; for this would give Mason a map of each man's craft. And Mason scrutinized how each man had positioned his body; for this would tell Mason how each man would draw iron. Finally, and most importantly, Marshal Mason would assess the outlaws' eyes; for this would let the

CHAPTER THIRTY-TWO

Marshal know just how prepared each man was to die.

The only man that was not under easy evaluation for Mason was the slinger, Farrot Pierce, who stood off to the side of Mason, shaded in the backlight of the campfire. And this was the one gun that the Marshal felt the most discomfort with. If gunplay were to be made, Pierce would need to be an early objective.

But negotiations would be with Barrett Thompson, for Barrett Thompson was a businessman and Marshal Isham Mason had a big gun trained on the easy target that was Barrett Thompson's fat belly.

Barrett Thompson studied the steady hand of Mason as the gun took sight at his abdomen. Thompson was a reasoned man. A rational man. But mostly, Barrett Thompson was a businessman.

Thompson scrutinized Marshal Mason's Schofield trained on his gut and he calculated his odds. It was simple arithmetic. He could call the charge and be the first to eat lead. On the other hand, to surrender now would mean that Marshal Mason would have to bind and transport six mean and desperate criminals over three hundred miles to the nearest lockup. Traversing these mountains would be tough enough, but with six outlaws itching to get free it would be impossible. There would be plenty of opportunities along the trail to bust up Mason's pilgrimage.

All of these equations were part of the calculus that the businessman summarized as he stood there with Marshal Isham Mason's gun trained on his belly. Balancing the chances of his own survival at a shootout here and now, or the potential opportunity for escape along the trail, the decision was plain.

Barrett Thompson directed his brood, "Lay down your guns, boys."

But it was too late. The notcher, Farrot Pierce, had already drawn leather.

"The hell I will," and with that, and with one smooth pull, the gun jumped into Farrot Pierce's hand. Pierce had been standing to the side of Mason, leaving the Marshal exposed to the flare of Pierce's gun. Mason swung a Schofield toward Pierce, but it would be too late. Farrot Pierce's .45 jumped and exploded. But the booming of Pierce's Colt sent the slug flying harmlessly high among the branches of the trees, punching the hard peachleaf willow with a thud.

What Marshal Mason had failed to estimate was the speed at which Pierce could pull iron from leather. What Farrot Pierce had failed to account for was Rory Casso. Positioning himself at the fire pit when he had feigned being knocked out by Kipper Dunn's blow to the back of his skull, Casso was in easy reach of his Bowie.

With the shot from his Colt gone awry, Farrot Pierce slowly eased down on one knee, genuflecting for a long moment. His face contorted into a wretched grimace, as the Bowie had lodged in his neck. There was a look of wonder on Pierce's face. He had always figured that it would be a wayward bullet that would take him out, but, now, this: a damned Bowie. Collapsing face-first into the dirt, the big Bowie bled the life sap from Farrot Pierce's aorta.

The position that Kipper Dunn had knocked Casso into when he had back-smacked Casso with his .45 had left Rory at the fire pit and within easy reach of the Bowie. And Casso had made good on the arrangement. A quick flick of Rory Casso's skilled wrist stilled the slinger Pierce and sent Pierce on to meet whatever Maker he had to answer to.

But the explosion of Farrot Pierce's report served to break the spell that Marshal Mason's buttonhole had brought on the camp. With the spell broken, five outlaws came up with guns a-blazing.

Mason's Schofields seemed to be barking in every direction at once. As promised, Barrett Thompson was the first to receive his allotment of lead, but he was not the first to reach the dirt. With his thumbs flailing across both of the Schofields' triggers, Mason unloaded twelve cartridges into the five desperados, and the shooting was over as quickly as it had begun.

Killing to an outlaw gunslinger was just another crease to

CHAPTER THIRTY-TWO

be carved into the gun grip. But killing to a good man, a good man like Marshal Mason, killing was another crease carved deep into the crow's-feet in the corner of his eye. This killing, like all of the necessary killing that came before, would brand age to the brow of Marshal Isham Mason.

A bullet had grazed Mason's temple and another round had knocked his holster from his belt, but Barrett Thompson and his men lay in heaps of flesh around the campfire.

The roaring booms of the gunfight exaggerated the silence that followed. The air was hazed with gun smoke and acrid with the smell of the powder.

With the pitching of the Bowie into the neck of the slinger, Farrot Pierce, Rory Casso was well nigh spent. The battering to his skull, the bullet-filleted leg, and the crushed ribs now overwhelmed the young man, and Casso folded to the ground. Bronwyn ran to Rory to cushion his collapse.

But even as the haze of the gunfight clung pungent to the air, a collection of Dog Soldiers sat their horses, ringing the camp. Guns drawn, the Indians had the drop on the white men.

With Rory Casso's Bowie wedged tight in Farrot Pierce's neck, Marshal Isham Mason stood there leaking blood from the bullet graze to his brow. The two spent Schofields were trailing smoke from the heated barrels as the guns dangled from his fists.

33

KEEP THE CHANGE

The Indian warriors totaled twelve. They had come into the camp on the wings of a whisper: in full war paint with their rifles to the ready as they silently sat their mustangs. Below the warriors, in various degrees of damage, were Casso, Marshal Mason, Bronwyn Mason, Cricket, the half-breed, Juke, and the full collection of the spent flesh that was the Thompson gang. The next move would be the warriors. Bronwyn pulled her torn shirt tight across her breasts as she cupped the battered Casso in her arms.

Silence engulfed the camp. The wind that had been murmuring through the trees had settled, and now only the sound of a bobolink singing his moniker, "bob-o-LINK, bob-o-LINK," stirred the stillness as the Indians surveyed the gathering.

The war paint was thick on the faces of the Dog Soldiers, obscuring detail. A single Indian, doubtless the leader, slid from his pony and walked, rifle in hand, from body to body of the dead outlaws that were splayed about the camp. Pausing above the body of Farrot Piece, the warrior bent down and examined the corpse. Plucking Casso's Bowie from Pierce's neck, he wiped Pierce's blood from the blade. Holding the Bowie up to the early morning light, the Indian slowly rotated the blade in careful study.

When the Indian turned his attention to the surviving members of the camp, it was Juke Bauque that intercepted his advance. Bronwyn was still clutching the battered Casso to her chest on the ground by the campfire, and the Marshal stood there with his empty Schofields dangling from his arms like a pendulum on a dead clock.

As Juke stepped into the Indian's path, the silence was broken by the simultaneous cocking of the rifles of the Dog Soldiers yet sitting their mustangs.

The Indian examined Juke with a deep curiosity. He studied the lines of Juke's face: the lines of bone structure of Juke's face that were donated to Juke by his Choctaw Indian father. And then the Indian studied the half-breed's black skin: The black skin that was donated from his African slave mother. Reaching out, the Indian attempted to finger Juke's kinky hair, but Juke pulled back. With a wave of the Bowie, the Indian warned Juke to not move.

Stroking Juke's kinky hair in confusion, the Indian challenged Juke, "What breed of man are you?"

There was no hesitation in his thoughts nor in his words. "I am American."

Again the Dog Soldier analyzed Juke. With a grunt that conveyed neither approval nor disapproval, the Indian turned his attention from Juke to Cricket, who was now standing directly behind Juke. "And who does this woman belong to?"

Again, without hesitation, "She is my woman."

The odd and twisted smile that had curved the Indian's mouth swelled at this answer. Weighing the thought of the progeny that would come from the union of this Black Indian and the Irish white woman, the Indian suggested, "And what breed will your litter be?"

This time it was Cricket that spoke without hesitation. "They will be *more* American."

The Indian considered this answer and turned from Juke.

With the Bowie twisting absently in the Indian's fist, the Dog Soldier turned his attention to the bloodied and battered Rory Casso, who lay crumbled on the ground and wrapped in the arms of Bronwyn. Bronwyn squared her chin, her father's chin, against the threat. If this warrior wanted a piece of Rory Casso, he would have to go through her first.

The Indian noted the resolve of the woman. "This fire-redhead woman, she belongs to you?"

CHAPTER THIRTY-THREE

Rory Casso stopped short as the Indian's face contorted into a crooked grin. Into a bear's grin.

"Boy With Sky In Eyes would want to fight me again?"

Recognition flashed quickly in Casso's eyes, and wonderment replaced threat.

Bear Grin flipped the Bowie in his hand and offered the knife's handle to Casso. "It has been a long time since this knife saved my life."

Stumbling with the words, Rory quizzed, "It was *you* trailing us?"

"We track, yes."

"And it was you that created a diversion when I was roped in the Thompson camp?"

Bear Grin turned and looked down at the carcass of Barrett Thompson. "This was bad man. Kill many Indian women and children. Yes, we free you, we fire your spit when you were in fever and we catch fish for you. But we were not sure you would live. You have died many times."

The crookedness of the grizzly's stamp on Bear Grin's face contorted into a smile. "You fight bear for me, I fight bear for you." Bear Grin held his hand, opened and palm down, and thumped Casso's chest twice. "Now we are level."

Rory Casso flashed back to his time hidden in the gully wash and wracked with delirium, when a spit fire was implausibly flamed and sustenance was procured for him and Rockwell. This would explain much.

Indicating the damage that was done by the grizzly to Bear Grin's face, Rory offered, "The scar heals well."

Over the years the scar that the grizzly had tattooed on Bear Grin's face had left a curl in the corner of his mouth, giving Bear Grin the appearance of a permanent smile.

"Scars are neither good nor bad. All men collect scars. It is our decisions as men that will decide how we wear our scars."

Rory considered this. "You speak with the wisdom of a medicine man I once knew. A wise Indian. Chief Wicasa."

The memory tugged at the smile scar at the edge of Bear Grin's mouth. "Yes. My father was very wise. He earned many scars and each scar he earned was another lesson for him," and, squatting down, Bear Grin examined Casso's wounds. "You came to our tiyospe as a boy with many scars inside," and he lightly touched Casso's chest. Then touching Casso's head wound gently, he added, "And now you collect scars on the outside as well."

Casso had to laugh at that. "Not by choice."

With the affect of a brother, Bear Grin gently tapped at Rory's chest, at Rory's heart. "Scars never by choice."

Rory felt the Indian's gentle hand on his chest. On his heart. "The years have made you wise like your father."

Rising, Bear Grin pondered the thought while he absently fingered the scar at the corner of his mouth.

Rory Casso pressed the thought. "Is it the years that make a man wise, or is it the scars that make a man wise?"

Still fingering the smiling scar, "It may be the years that will make a man wise. It may be the scars that will make a man wise. But whether with years or with scars, it must come down to the man that will determine the wise."

Turning to Bronwyn, Bear Grin probed, "You are Boy With Sky In Eyes' woman?"

"I am now his woman, yes."

"And do you understand the scars that Boy With Sky In Eyes holds long in his chest?"

Bronwyn thought of the times she had witnessed Rory Casso lugging spit buckets about the saloons of Rawlings. And she remembered the nights that Rory slept cold in the livery, nursing his liquor-sickened father through bout after bout of another drunk. But mostly Bronwyn remembered the loneliness of the boy, without a home, wandering the dirt streets of Rawlings until he could no longer take the shame, the pain, and the pity of his position and turned, in solitude, to the mountains.

"Yes. I know the scars that Rory Casso holds long in his chest."

With his coal-black eyes probing deep into the green of Bronwyn's eyes, the warrior shared his crooked scar smile with her, and then turned and mounted his pony. With a final survey of the camp, Bear Grin spoke one more time to Bronwyn. "You will help Boy With Sky In Eyes with his scars." In the monotone flatness of his Indian English one could not decipher if this was a question or a command.

In an equal monotone flatness, so you could not tell if she was answering a question or making a statement, Bronwyn replied, "I will help him with his scars."

Bear Grin nodded his approval to Bronwyn.

Turning to Rory Casso, Bear Grin offered his flat Indian monotone one last time. "I wish peace for your scars."

Reining his pony around, Bear Grin heeled the mustang to the brush. The collection of Dog Soldiers followed Bear Grin in kind and melted into the whisper from whence they came.

With the exit of the Indians, an early December hush again fell upon the encampment. Somewhere, "Bob-o-LINK, bob-o-LINK, bob-o-LINK."

It was Marshal Isham Mason that was the first to break the silence, as he moved to Rory Casso. Mason's big plaid frame hung above the battered young man as Bronwyn clung tight to the boy.

"Son, . . . let's go home."

THE END